BEWITCHED

Kaila Patterson

To history, which shaped the past,

and my late-night kitchen rants.

ENGLAND 1617

1

No More Hocus Pocus

For months, King Richard of England had searched for the downfall of the witch. She was the one who dared to disobey him, the one who grinned in spite, the apple that never fell far from the tree; she who was a witch.

She who would pay for it.

King Richard stood on the castle balcony, narrowing his eyes at the crowds grouped at the edge of town. James Willberry, The King's noble snoop, stood mesmerised by the castle.

There was plenty to admire in the majestic kingdom. The golden portraits of monarchs of the past, the glistening jewels lining the walls; everything there purely for show.

"A fine day for an execution," Richard said. A raindrop landed on his nose, sulking from the point. "Or not.".

Far to the left of the city, an execution took place. From Richard's standing, the people appeared like miniature bugs.

A plain clothed, middle-aged woman was tied against a stake, made of straw. A grisly knight stood to her left, with a blazing fire torch in his grip.

"Who is she?" Richard murmured, nodding to the woman.

"Mary Stanley, accused of witchcraft for attempting to hex another young woman, due to a long-term grudge.".

Richard nodded. The knight at the execution jeered his torch to the crowds, illuminating the threatened faces.

The King noticed the squirm in his servant's face. Willberry gestured to the crowds.

"This can't be entertaining for them, can it?".

King Richard's mouth curled into a snarl. "Why would it not be?".

Willberry averted his eyes. A roar came from the crowds below, as they screamed words of abuse to the stake-tied woman.

Mary Stanley's eyes shut, as she prayed underneath her breath. Once again, Richard's eyes back to Willberry.

"This-This isn't…".

"*Watch, Willberry.*".

The man shook his head, taking a long gulp. Richard placed a hand on Willberry's shoulder, forcing him forward.

"I never thought it would be like this, that 'ye would do this," Willberry whispered, his accent splitting through.

"This is what happens, to all witches," Richard scoffed, "Don't tell me you were not aware?".

Willberry flinched away, prepared to run. The King gripped his arm.

"I said, *watch.*".

The knight at the execution stumbled to the stake, raising his torch in the air. Lowering it to the grass, it came inches away from the woman's feet.

Her face was illuminated by the light, as her head rocketed forward. A gleam burned in her eyes.

Willberry's eyes focused on The King, with a face that described his fear. The woman let out an echoing laugh, setting the atmosphere.

"Let it be known to all, a curse shall foresee this town!" Mary Stanley yelled. Richard turned a blazing red, his knuckles gripping the balcony edge. The woman shut her eyes, making a prediction.

9

"I see two bonded by blood alone, but only one corpse shall hit the stone," She announced. Her eyes were wide, grinning at the crowds.

"Two who live on opposite sides, but soon that will be cast aside.".

The King turned his head away, scowling at the scene. Willberry's eyes stood willingly on the woman, no longer intimidated into staring.

"Be wary who you punish, who you choose to burn in daylight's fame," The woman continued, "For one prays to go down in history, but their opposite will take history's name.".

Willberry tugged on Richard's arm, and The King shot him a glare. No one dared speak during that moment. The knight with the torch gazed at The King, receiving a wordless command.

The knight lowered his torch, allowing it to light the straw. A roar of flame arose from the stake, but the woman's manic laughter never ceased.

The flames drove upwards, hiding the woman's feet. The crowds were silent, cowering away.

The fear of what could be; what was predicted to be, or what was happening alone.

As the flames grew, Richard stepped away. He walked from the balcony, with Willberry on his tail.

"Your Majesty!" Willberry yelled, gripping onto The King's crimson jacket. His eyes were wider than before, as he stuttered over words.

"Before you speak, *don't*." Richard harshly whispered, "That prediction is meaningless, an absurd fear tactic.".

Willberry shook his head, leaning up to The King's height. He held out his hands, acting out a scene.

"*Spinner--!*".

Richard glared down at him, alerted by that wretched name. A name that made his anger burn into endless flame.

"What did you say?".

"Think of the prediction!" Willberry cried. "You said that Spinner was like a curse to you, and the idea of living on opposite sides, *burning in daylight's fame*—".

"The woman spoke of two bonded people, you fool." Richard groaned, clutching a hand to his head. Willberry sunk, before his eyes perked up again. He trailed behind The King, raising an excited hand.

"Yes, that works too!" Willberry said, "Her companion...Lily? Laurie?".

"Lucie.".

"Yes! She's living on the opposite side of Spinner, and they are two bonded companions!" Willberry replied. Richard froze.

There was the chance, that Willberry was indeed right.

"You know..." Richard drawled, narrowing his eyes to the distance. "In a rare occasion, you do make yourself useful.".

Willberry gleamed with pride. "And think, after that prediction made, it gives a reason for Spinner's arrest."

The King smirked, gazing out the window. The stake had been swallowed inside a blaze of flame, exhuming smoke.

"That it does, Willberry," Richard mumbled, repeating the words, "That it does.".

For months on end, Spinner had caused more trouble than she was worth. He had spent long days and longer nights, establishing his force in the town; and she made it a mockery.

Richard moved on, strolling across the hall. He nodded to the nearest guard. It was a subtle but struck fear into the strongest of men.

He watched as Willberry's eyes widened, and The King's smirk reflected his malicious intent. He thrived off moments like that, the split-second watching the fear creep onto a victim's face.

" I believe you have served your purpose, Willberry." King Richard grinned, glaring away as the man fell to his knees.

"*No!* You said you would help me!" Willberry yelled, as two armoured knights grabbed his shoulders.

"I could do that," The King said, a sickening grin on his face, "But I'm not."

"*Nah!*" Willberry screamed, "Not the dungeon!".

Willberry's feet scraped across the carpet, as he was dragged away. His pleas sounded further and further away until they silenced. King Richard chuckled, thinking of the pathetic man that had ended like the one before.

To The King, it was amusing, how they fell for it each time, like rabbits with a carrot on a stick.

With Willberry's help, he had what he needed. All it took was a bit of bargaining and blackmailing to get it. Willberry had unknowingly given The King information that seemed useless, but was something he had looked for, a reason.

He peered out of the window, stalking the innocent pedestrians. They had returned to the town, in a saddened mob. His eyes lay on the cottage that sat in the back, cowered beneath the shadow.

That home belonged to the witch he sought, the one who would never cross the door of it again.

"Your Highness?" A guard asked, startling Richard's thoughts. He waved the guard off, showing a false smile. That way, no weakness shown.

Shaking himself awake, King Richard moved through the brick walls. The soft firelight of the castle surrounded him, as he gestured for the guards to open the doors.

Amid his daydreaming, even his crown had become slanted, and he fixed it straight with a swift move.

The doors opened, and the people gazed at him like he was a descending angel. He could sense, by their star-struck expressions, that they were clueless. The light illuminated him, as he stood above the specimen.

He moved quickly through them, and the people parted like an ocean, as his cloak left a trail.

The villagers mumbled and grumbled, pulling their relatives out of the path. Each were dressed in or plain linen, blending as a dull crowd.

"Where?" The King muttered, and a guard motioned to the cottage at the end of town. Richard nodded, barging into a greasy-looking young man.

The people's whispers grew stronger, and they all shook their heads. Witch-hunting was as common as the sun rising in their town, and no one could intervene.

Their voices grew louder, shouting names across the town. The pandemonium of people raised a tension, as the sound increased.

The King's head shot back and forth, alerted by the spinning crowds, the noise. The fearlessness, if they dared it.

"Silence! *Be silent I say*!" King Richard roared, clenching his fists.

He spotted the wooden play-sword of a young boy. In blinded rage and lack of control, he gripped it from the child, lifting his knee and snapping it in half. The boy cried out, tugging on his mother's skirt.

"Silence him," The King warned, eyeing the boy's mother. "Now.".

She shushed the boy, whispering apologies. The wooden sword's upper half lay broken on the ground, crumbling into pieces.

Mothers whisked their own children out of The King's path, and they bowed, what else could they do?

Everyone turned to the Spinner cottage, wiping their eyes. They had seen this before, and they would see it again for days to come.

The King spotted from the corner of his eye, a young girl peering over a guard's shoulder. She was dressed in a well-recognised blue gown, of which the ladies-in-waiting from the castle wore.

Leaving her with a glare, he continued through the crowd. Eerie tension brushed the town, and a shuffling came from behind. A voice sliced through the air.

"Your Highness—" The voice struggled, and he turned to see the lady from before.

Her blonde hair fell in gentle waves, her gold-blue gown hoisted to her knees. She struggled for breath, her poignant blue eyes focusing on him.

"Lucie Benson," King Richard greeted, squinting his eyes down to her small height. The girl interrupted him, raising her hand in the air.

"Y-You aren't going to..." Lucie wiped at her eyes, an estranged hurt reflecting within. "Are you going to *hurt* her?".

He stared to the cottage, examining the crooked home. The people were crowded around him and her, watching in fascination and awe.

"It is not your concern," He warned, leaving her stranded alone in the crowd. "If you know what is best, I suggest you go home, Benson."

"Tell me, please." Lucie begged.

"You dare to question me?" Richard asked, watching the fear creep onto her face.

Reaching for the door of the cottage, he banged on it, sighing, and getting impatient, before he started to kick.

The girl and a guard both jumped at the sound, hearing each pound on the wood echo throughout the village. The guard put his hands up towards The King before simply opening the door himself.

King Richard laughed shrugged, patting the smug guard on the back. He strolled into the shadowed cottage, the guard following him inside.

It was small, filled with boxes and parchment paper from different pieces of work. There were a few small windows, and small light leaked through them, making the room appear dark. There was an upstairs, but the shadows covered it well.

King Richard acknowledged this with a murmur, his focus being still on the room surrounding him. The guard at the corner began pacing, as he froze at the staircase, looking up.

"We should search upstairs, Your Highness." The knight announced.

The King eyed the room with suspicion. Nodding to the guard, he followed him up the stairs to find any incriminating evidence,

A chilling aura loomed the air, filling up their lungs and catching their eyes. That was the first sign, and The King covered his mouth, in case any poison or sorcery lurked the house.

While Richard walked, a piece of sharp wood lay on the floor, tripping him over and sending him tumbling. He screamed, grasping his foot, and clutching it in pain.

The guard rushed over, but The King pushed his fists into the man's chest. Richard regained his posture and began to limp across the wooden floor cautiously.

Cobwebs lined the ceiling, and the cottage itself gave off an unnerving demeanour.

King Richard treaded through the hallway, gripping his sword, prepared to take down any threatening opponents.

They peered into each room, all empty. The creak of the floorboards beneath them sent a chill down his spine.

The guard rummaged through the cupboards and drawers, throwing objects across the room and shattering valuables with a crack. Every item, Richard examined, but there was no evidence found.

An acidic scent filled the room, as the crooked walls ran under King Richard's hand.

There were bottles of unnamed liquids, and lifted one to his nose, swirling the strange substance within the glass.

"Medicine?" Richard whispered, speaking to himself. "No, *witchcraft.*".

A crack echoed across the room, causing the man to flinch. He shivered, clenching his fists. There was no one else in the shadowed room, and The King was cornered against a wall.

There was a ghostlike presence, one he hated. A shiver ran down his arms, and visions intruded through his eyes. Visions of fear.

Richard slammed the clinking bottles on the desk, storming out of the room. He pressed a hand over his eyes.

"Not again..." He growled, slamming a fist into the wall. "Go away, *stop haunting me!*".

Yelling to the air, he left the haunted room. The guard ducked out of the way, protecting himself from The King's fired temper. Richard skipped down the stairs, gesturing to his accomplice.

He froze as a thud sound came from the back of the home. He advanced towards it, as the shivering knight followed, raising his sword.

Looming down the dark corridor, Richard whipped around the corner with a sharp breath, raising his fist.

There was nothing, except a hidden door at the end of the path. It drew a smirk on The King's pale face, as he motioned for the guard to follow.

King Richard placed a gloved hand on the door, and slowly pushed it open. It creaked as it moved like it had not opened for years. He raised an elbow, and the guard swung the sword over his shoulder.

His shoulders sunk, with the reveal of nothing except storage boxes and dozens of bags of crops. The King sighed heavily and strutted inside the cupboard, shoving ancient Spinner belongings aside.

He skimmed over letters dated years before, all signed by the initials 'A. S'. There were books on the top shelf, unnoticeable for anyone without a good eye.

He reached up and grabbed a journal, as dozens fell with it, slamming down onto his head. The guard swung his sword, then lowered it.

"Help me, you fool!" King Richard yelled, scowling at the guard's petrified face. The knight ducked, taking hold of The King's arms, and lifting him to a stand.

"Sorry, Your Highness." The guard mumbled, rubbing the back of his neck.

Richard studied the journal in his hand, flicking through the blank pages. Scrawls, notes, and sketches filled the pages, all signed by the same signature.

"Well, there you have it." King Richard smirked, spinning out of the room.

The guard stumbled after him, over letters, vegetables, and books on the floor. Richard exited the Spinner home, shoving the journal in the air. The people's wide eyes stared back at him, as he threw the book in hand to the floor.

He stamped on it with a thud, scowling at the ruffled pages. The knight scampered out behind, his jaw hanging loose.

King Richard's footsteps echoed for miles, and he saw the people back away. The tension was thick then, and no one dared to speak a word to or against him.

Many returned to their homes and shut the door, to protect themselves from the threat that was King Richard of England.

The people formed a circle around him, squinting their eyes and pointing.

'*Cowards.*' he thought, exhaling fury.

A dark shadow loomed over his eyes; his face lined with fury. A fire-exhuming fury, like England had never seen. Stomping out to be the people, his face turned cold.

"*WHERE IS ELIZABETH SPINNER?*".

2

Elizabeth, The Witch

The night had been peaceful. The wind was howling, grass crunching, and the world was good. It was peaceful to watch the world pass.

Trees bustling, the water streaming past her feet, the dainty little flowers blowing through the air in rhythm with the wind, it was all therapeutic.

Elizabeth Spinner visited the woods each day, while her father was working in the country. It was not the best way to make a living, but it was what most did, and it was better than nothing.

'Does life get any better than this?' Eliza thought, taking in the moment.

The water rushed past her feet, swallowing them up and washing them away. She giggled as the coldness of the river sent a chill down her spine, making her lift her skirt up from the stream and tuck it inside her belt, so it did not soak.

Eliza danced around, waving her hands in the air, and laughing aloud. The birds chirping in the distance gave a small melody that she hummed along to, spinning, and twirling like a royal maiden in a ball.

A pair of wings caught her eye, and she danced around to see Dawn, her own pet raven, perching on her shoulder.

"Isn't this wonderful, Dawn?" Eliza laughed, skipping to-and-frow and breaking the river's waves.

"No one's missing me in town then?" She said, running her fingers through her hair.

Dawn let out a squawk, fluttering into flight. Eliza froze, groaning at the misfit of a bird.

"What is the matter with you?" Eliza whined, "Go find a squirrel to chase, leave me be.".

The day had been good, better than most days she had. It would be typical of Dawn to ruin it.

The raven squawked a second time, raising her concerns. Eliza folded her arms and stared back.

"Dawn? Is something wrong?" She asked in attempt to calm it down. If her bird were stressed, it would never silence.

Dawn was restless, it flew up from her finger and started flying in circles, giving signs of warning. Eliza tripped out of the lake and stared after her bird.

Wiping her feet on the dry grass, Eliza slipped into her dry shoes with wet feet. She struggled onto the grass and sprinted down the hills, chasing the raven's tail.

Eliza tugged her skirt down from her belt, darting down into the forest. The forest was notorious for being filled with dangers, but Dawn flew through it, leading her inside.

Eliza tripped as her foot latched onto a piece of glass in the dirt. She pulled it away with a grunt, catching her distorted appearance in the reflection.

Her hair was a mess, ending at her waist in brown waves. She fumbled inside her satchel for a pin, and efficiently put the hair into a messy tie.

Her raven had stopped flying, perching on a tree, and patiently waiting on her to follow again. She rolled her eyes at it, adjusting her blouse. Once it saw her ready again, Dawn continued to fly, expecting her to do the same.

The woods were dark, and it gave her a terrible feeling in her stomach. Rumour told that there were witches in the woods, ones that would hex you with their sorcery, but Eliza never really believed that.

It always seemed to her that when a woman was on trial for witchcraft, it was usually someone who The King did not like, or someone who disagreed with him.

The execution of Mary Stanley was happening that day, and she made a point of avoiding it. Eliza hated how the people found entertainment in the torturing of others.

'It's vile in every way, yet they call witches the evil ones.' Eliza thought.

As her own father had said, anyone who threatened The King's ego endangered themselves by the law, that was how it had always been.

'You can't win, can you?' Eliza wondered.

The wind howled and blew in her ear, giving her a strange chill. The woods were not that long, and soon the bustling voices of the village grew. They sounded different, panicked, and that was never a good sign.

Eliza and Dawn reached the back of the town, perching onto her cottage's wall. She sprinted over and stood with her back against it, peering out to the commotion.

The people were whispering, scarce under their breaths. She saw the lower halves of the pedestrians, standing in their blank scruffs.

Glimpsing past the wall, her hand jumped over her mouth to stop herself from making a sound. Hundreds of people, gathered around the Spinner home, stood ahead.

It could have been her father; he could have been ill. A hundred different possibilities formed in her mind, he and his quarrelsome attitude becoming the main one.

Her father was antisocial at best, but it did not take huge effort to spark his temper. Eliza spent most of her time in the hills, but she and her father were alike. Their matching, shadowed eyes were identical.

The village girls stood around her house, with their noses stuck up and their little giggles, which made you want to tear off your ears.

Dawn landed on her shoulder. It bobbed its head, motioning to something, and Eliza peered around to see a knight guarding her home, and The King standing behind him.

Her heart dropped when she saw that, and she loudly gasped that time.

She had been told as a child; her mother had been 'taken away' by the guards. It did not take her long to realise, their situations were history repeating itself.

Eliza knew that it must have been accusations of witchcraft that got her mother killed. It made sense, and it made it easier to understand why King Richard hated her.

He looked enraged, with his face twisted. The people backed away, and even the guard flinched each time he spoke.

'This has to be a mistake,' Eliza thought, *'Why me?'*.

"Twenty shillings, for the man who reveals the witch's location!" The King yelled, raising his fist.

Eliza felt her heart squirming in her chest. Richard continued; "A headless body for the man *who refuses to speak up!"*.

'Run, far away.' The thought provoked her mind.

Her feet felt glued to the ground, watching the scene take place. Young children cried, as Richard yelled at the height of his lungs.

Eliza watched on, feeling her heart sink. King Richard interrogated with his eyes, and he would cause a pandemonium, if he lingered.

The fright in children's eyes, the floating tension, the ticking clock. Witches were supposed to be the villains, the constant threat. In England, witches were harmless compared to their King.

"I'm here." Eliza announced, moving out of the shadows.

She gulped as her eyes met The King's own, his resembling a poisonous snake. The knight nudged King Richard's arm, holding a scroll in his grasp.

The knight cleared his throat. Eliza kept her eyes on his parchment, her sour face solemn.

He unrolled it and held it out with pride. The blurred words spun like a loophole. Yet, one word stood out, bold and clear. 'Witchcraft'.

"Elizabeth Spinner, by the power invested in The King by…" The knight's face furrowed, "…The King.".

"Get *on* with it." Richard warned, slamming his fist into the guard's shoulder.

"S-sorry," The knight flinched, "You are under arrest for accusations of witchcraft and conspiracy against…The King.".

'Witchcraft.' The word rang inside her mind.

She never liked The King, and she was often outspoken about disagreeing with many things he said, but she never cast a spell; that she would prove.

"*Witchcraft?* On what grounds?" Eliza answered. The King glared at her with a frown.

"Uh," The knight paused, fidgeting with his hands. "W-We cannot disclose that.".

"My crops *died* the other day, and for that to happen this time of year, had to be *witchcraft!*" One woman shouted.

"Trouble follows Spinner's daughter no matter where she is!" A man yelled. "*Witch!*".

"I am no witch." She declared, and the whole crowd gasped. No one rejected The King; it was asking to go to the dungeons.

King Richard silenced everyone, and walked over to the guard's side, dangerously annoyed. He grabbed her arm, and she could feel his breath on her face.

"No? Those *spell-cast* journals say *otherwise.*" The King growled, gesturing to her home. Eliza shook her head, scoffing aloud.

"My studies? Those are for *medicine*, for my father." She yelled. "I am innocent by all moral law.".

"You say my law is immoral?" He asked, daring her to answer.

"Yes, yes I do." Eliza claimed, her heart pounding inside her chest. "And I—".

She was cut off by King Richard slicing his hand through the air, pointing for the guard to arrest her.

The guard grabbed her wrists and tied them together, and Eliza put no effort in escaping.

King Richard marched away angrily, and the people created a path for him to walk through, as Eliza and the guard followed him.

All the people started to bless themselves and mumble prayers as she walked past, but she managed to keep a smile on her face the whole way.

She worried about her father, and how he would cope with hearing that his daughter was facing the exact same charges his wife did.

 He would not be able to bare it, suffering enough as it was. His incurable illness, haunting nightmares and rotting chest; all needed her assistance.

Her father, George Spinner, was a farmer on the edge of town. He travelled at dawn and returned at dusk, pushing his wheelbarrow in front, sulking over the lack of sales.

Eliza zoned out, being tugged along by the knight. Her father would suffer mentally and physically, with nothing left to live by. A thought stuck in her mind.

Medicine. *Her* medicine.

She had made it her life's goal to create a cure, a medicine for her father. She stored them in shelves amongst the other bits-and-bobs that lined them. They held all sorts of mixtures; salt water, fall leaves, ground nuts.

Things she collected to create a cure, a hope.

She studied the crafts of medicine and may have stolen parchment prescriptions from the local doctor before, once.

She was shaken from thought, as the guard shuffled her through the crowd. The King was far ahead, and Eliza felt tears water her eyes.

They met the entrance to the castle, and Eliza could not help but look back, thinking of her father and no one else.

Dawn had flown away from the commotion. It did not like loud noises, so it tended to leave when that happened, watching from above.

She hoped her father would take care of Dawn, because the poor bird would fret if she disappeared, flying away to find her, but it never would.

As she looked across the forest, she noticed a small figure on a hill, wheeling an empty bucket behind him. Her father was on his way home, oblivious to the fact his only daughter was under arrest.

He was at the end of the hill, and so close to where their cottage stood. Eliza pulled away from the guard, focusing her eyes.

She needed to speak to him, to let him know what was happening. If he returned home to find the house ruined and deserted, he would panic, and she was afraid that would be too much for him to bare.

Eliza tugged away from the guard's restraint, and he tugged her back, growling and pulling on the string. She threw herself achingly out forwards. She was seconds away from the castle doors, from the end.

"*Father!*" She screamed, pulling away from the guard. Eliza refused to look at him, she just kept shouting, anything to spark her father's attention.

He slugged down the hill, carrying two bags of crops in his arms. The sale had not gone well, because he had those when he had left earlier that morning.

"*Spinner! Father!*" Eliza yelled, resisting against the guard's arrest. 'Father' could be anyone, she needed to grasp his attention.

George Spinner flinched, staring around for the source of the noise, but it was too late. The knight managed to yank Eliza backwards, and the doors started to shut.

She collapsed onto her knees, pulling the knight's arm down with her. Eliza felt the ground rip into her knees, as she reached a free hand for her father. His eyes finally met hers.

He completely dropped his crops, spilling them all over the grass and letting them roll away. Eliza felt herself longing to help, but all she could do was mouth a word to him; 'sorry'.

Her father reached out towards her from afar, as he stumbled towards the castle doors, but it was too late. The last thing Eliza saw was him desperately trying to reach her, and then he was gone.

The knight lifted her up, causing her to lose her footing and stumble backwards. She felt tears prick at her eyes as she was trailed across the floor and towards the dungeons.

That was it; imprisoned for weeks, with no social contact or entertainment, and then she would be executed like many before her.

There was no choice. Anyone accused of witchcraft before her had suffered, and they were innocent like her.

Guards trailed her through the courtroom, and Eliza felt humiliated. All the eyes of The King's courtiers and knights were on her. Some staring had pity in their eyes, and others had disgust. Regardless, neither would make a difference to her situation.

The palace was illuminated with bright fires lining the walls, and the golden outline reflected onto anyone passing by. There was a delicacy, a tension in the castle, and their formality overruled her stained clothes.

They had formal waistcoats with pearl buttons, some wearing capes or hats, but all of them with a stern expression. They were all men, and she knew the maidens would be on the floors above, as servants or ladies in waiting to the queen.

Eliza snapped away from her thoughts as they reached the stairs to the dungeon. It was at the back of the kingdom and revealed through a miniature staircase that led down to the rooms and their prisoners. It had a looming darkness, and stained stone stairs.

They forced her down and entered a long corridor. There were cells with bars on one side, and dungeons with steel doors on the other.

They reached the end of the hallway and she spun around to face a door, covered by a knight. The guard opened the door for them to enter, acknowledging his fellow knight with a nod.

In such a hopeless time, all Eliza could think was to add some humour. To make it easier, when reality had not truly hit her yet.

"Not too ill-featured, it *could* be a bit livelier *without* the cobwebs." Eliza joked, as the guard started to untie her restraints. He answered her with a grunt, then a soft laugh.

If she let them see her afraid, or upset, she gained nothing. It gave them the upper hand their knighthood craved. That encouraged her to keep smiling, even while the world shattered around her.

Eliza raised her arms and stretched them out once the guards untied her and began to laugh under her breath. Giving her a shove, one of them pushed her into the room and slammed the door behind her.

The room had a barred window and echoing brick walls, but it was only small and let in pinpoint light. The dungeon had a dirty old bed, and a pot for sanitary purposes. It had nothing whatsoever for entertainment, and there was minimal room for any movement; she had nothing to do but sleep.

When she was out of the guard's view, Eliza felt her lip tremble, as her knees sunk to the floor.

She had questioned many things, and tended to be more inquisitive than most, sometimes to her own dismay.

Yet, one question she might never be able to answer; what made them call her a witch?

There was nothing she could do, he was The King, he was law, and anyone who disagreed had the same fate.

As she sat on the floor, she fumbled inside her blouse to find the most important thing she owned. A locket.

It belonged to her mother, and she had worn it her entire life.

Eliza knew she resembled her father; the people of the village lectured her on that when she was a child.

The same dark, shadowed eyes she bore were her father's own. They did have that same spiteful gleam.

Eliza thought of her mother, who had her entire life stolen, realising she would be the same. She would never get the chance to grow old, to have a life.

'It would have been nice to have the possibility, wouldn't it?' She thought.

Eliza felt her eyes brim with tears, at the thought of never getting to experience life. The anxiety of knowing she was in her last days, was more daunting than anything ever before.

Cuddling herself into a ball, she found herself hoping they were right. Hoping that she was a witch, that she could cast a spell and disappear in a cloud of smoke.

That she could be someone more than Elizabeth.

Elizabeth, The Witch.

3

Sink or Swim

The past two days had been long, too long. Eliza settled into the castle dungeons, crying every second, reminiscing on the past, and sleeping.

She had not received any food to survive, and she wondered if they decided to leave her to starve as punishment.

She craved a cup of water, or a piece of bread. Her lips chapped, and her head pounded like a thousand bells, but the worst part was the isolation.

If Eliza ever needed to speak, she would visit someone or even speak to a stranger just to hear her own voice. In the dungeon, she was hauntingly alone.

Eliza had to assume that The King was not going to trial her, instead sentencing her to death without consideration. that was the worrying part. Every moment could be her last, and she did not know it. The thought was terribly surreal.

The trials that took place for the women accused of witchcraft were not exceptionally reliable, but The King was convinced that they worked.

The woman in question would be restrained by knights and tied down to a chair hanging above a lake, and slowly the chair lowered down towards the water, until the string was cut.

Falling through the air, the woman collided with and sunk into the lake. If the woman floated on the water, she was a witch. If she sunk, she was innocent.

'It's insanity at its finest,' Eliza thought, *'There's no reasoning'*.

Eliza flinched as the clinking of the locks echoed throughout the room. She wiped down her skirt and stood with a steady smile, preparing herself for anything, even the end.

The croaky door opened, and a castle guard stepped into view. He looked different than the guard that brought her there.

This new knight was taller and gave an intimidating front. He looked older than the original, with a dark-brown beard, tanned skin, and an unreadable expression.

"Morning, please follow me." He announced, and Eliza's mouth stumbled over words.

The new guard's voice was strong, but she instantly felt safer in his presence. His voice had a foreign accent from somewhere she did not recognise, and she wondered if he was French.

'No, French people don't sound that way,' Eliza thought, *'They all speak with 'vees' and 'vats' and 'Oui, je suis française, stupid fille.'*.

He gestured for her to follow him outside, and obediently she did. A younger guard stood outside the dungeon, impatiently tapping his foot.

"Thomas, there's no need for that." The older guard warned, narrowing his eyes at the young man.

Thomas scoffed, folding his arms. The other knight took hold of her wrists, fastening the rope tying them together.

Eliza stared over the two knights, noting them both. Thomas was younger, with ruffled blonde hair and an oversized piece of armour.

A suffocating feeling raised in her throat, while her stomach felt like a bubbling pot. She wobbled on her feet, as the fear-induced nausea doubled.

"I feel faint, I feel like I will vomit." Eliza said, groaning with the ache.

To her surprise, the knight laughed lightly. He placed a firm hand on her shoulder while pushing her along, his eyes scanning her for a trace of illness.

"Unless you are dying, you will be fine." The guard replied, with a professional front. Thomas groaned at them, tapping his foot louder than before. His failed attempts at appearing intimidating were laughable.

"I am dying," Eliza scoffed, "That is why I am here, is it not?".

She received a greater laugh from that, whilst being marched down the hall. Eliza stumbled over her feet, her stomach sickening her.

"Will you two make *haste*?" Thomas said, tapping his foot. "You move slower than a snail with five left feet.".

Softly, she giggled at that. Her mind urged her to correct him, to say that snails in fact did not have feet.

Eliza did not know what age Thomas was, but he was young, not much older than her.

He and his mother lived across from where her father lived, who had been more devasted than anyone at the news of Thomas' father's at-war death.

As prideful and headstrong as a man could be, her father had lamented, but all-in-all a true man.

"We *are* behind you, Thomas." The older knight sighed, prompting her to move along.

"Who are you?" Eliza asked, turning to him. The older guard gave her a stern look, taking a breath.

"Edward, Captain Edward." He answered, smiling, and turning away.

Edward pulled her along the corridor, and Eliza found herself humming a tune from her childhood.

The song was a French lullaby, and she did not speak French, so she spent her days wondering what it meant.

Edward's eyes narrowed towards her, as he shook his head. They reached the end of the hall, as the end of Thomas' feet skipped up the steps before they could.

He trailed her up the stairs, stomping his feet against the brick. Thomas walked ahead, occasionally turning around to sneer at them or grumble. The same court men that had been there two days ago were back, and similarly to Thomas, they glared at her.

Eliza fake-smiled at them as widely as she could, which made them stare even more. As they got closer to the castle doors, she could hear commotion from the village, a sound she had never thought she would miss as much as she did.

Edward paused at the castle doors, letting out a muffled groan. He looked sick, pressing his free hand to his chest, and wheezing. In sounded inhumane, and her costly concern grew.

"That is *sickening*, and would you hurry up? You do not have the *plague*, and frankly, we do not have long before the *trial* begins." Thomas mocked, strutting through the open castle doors.

Eliza's blood boiled, as she bent down to meet the coughing guard, watching him with a flare in her eyes.

"Are you alright?" Eliza asked worriedly, all hints of laughter and remark gone, replaced by a furrowed look. Edward took a smooth breath, shakily rising to his feet.

"Excuse me?" He asked, a caution in his tone.

Eliza smiled, and stood back up.

Edward's eyes widened, as he shakily gripped onto the restraints behind her back.

"*Unless you're dying--.*" Eliza tauntingly whispered, being cut off by Edward's silencing glare. He tugged on her restraints, before straightening his own posture.

"*Very* amusing." Edward sighed; sarcasm forced in his tone.

"Thank you." Eliza giggled, as he escorted her out of the doors. Daylight dawned on her face, and that same nausea sunk into her stomach again.

She still did not know where she was walking to, and internally, she dreaded it. There was a tense uncertainty within the air, and even her knightly escort turned stiff.

The town was bustling and loud, with all the villagers standing in a crowd. They took a left, and Eliza's fear multiplied. Creating a map within her mind, she plotted out the town.

The merchant stalls, countless homes and hard-knocking barrels were ahead. Edward pushed her along, passing all three.

Groups of people stared at her from afar, and she stood up on her toes. Eliza's heart sunk, as her eyes met the distance. The lake was ahead, with a chair hanging overhead by rope, accompanied by crowds of people.

There was an arch of wood over it, and a man tugging the string, pulling the chair to surface.

The ducking-stool trial, an unreliable tool for proving witchcraft.

'That's why I'm here,' Eliza thought, *'I should have known.'.*

There was no way to win; if she sunk, she proved innocent, if she floated, she proved guilty.

The idea was that witches could save themselves from sinking due to witchcraft and sorcery, that they could not drown.

Marching on, Edward pushed her through crowds of people. Whispers surfaced overhead, and snarling faces met her. The foul taste of rotten breath hit her, which was bearable compared to the rotten faces.

"*Witch*," One man grumbled, "Get what 'ye deserve.".

Eliza was too wrapped inside her thoughts to answer, unable to give a weak smile in response. Her eyes flickered to the floor, while Edward's blurred announcements filled her ears.

"Out of the way." Edward warned, side-stepping through the crowds. "Make way, make haste.".

She wondered what it was that made The King despise her, made him want to see her in nothing but swirling flame. Eliza knew she never fit his agenda, his ideas of perfection; she was everything he sought to abolish.

He did not want young girls educated, but Eliza had a good education.

He did not want young girls to voice their opinion, but she was outspoken.

He did not want young girls to be independent, but she was independent, she had to be. For her father, at least.

That sent a sinking in her heart, the thought of him. Her own selfishness had been what had left her father deserted, she felt that she betrayed him.

The memories flashed back, of him sitting at their table in misery. He covered it well, but she knew he never truly recovered from the loss of her mother.

It haunted him, and he blamed himself. On the rare occasions he spoke of it, he lamented that he should have agreed to flee the town, even if it risked everything.

"Miss Spinner?" Edward said, narrowing his eyes at her. He must have noticed that she dazed off, lost in her own thoughts and feelings.

Eliza nodded on the brink of tears, and that said it all.

"I'm fine, or I wish I could be." Eliza mumbled. Her scarce voice, ghostly face and lanky figure was drained to the maximum, as if already dead.

Edward cleared his throat, as they reached the podium. His eyes were dull and off-scene, like he was rethinking it all.

Reaching the end of the crowds, she saw the scene ahead. A masked man stood with his hands gripping the rope, and there was a wooden stand to her far right.

Thomas was there, bantering with a fellow knight. The crowds were behind her, the ducking-chair ahead, and the stand to her left.

A glimpse of light caught her eye, from the far-right stand.

King Richard and Queen Grace sat on a wooden platform, higher than any other spectator. Richard sat with his eyes scanning the trial, his hands gripping his knees.

Grace was an awkward distance from him, twirling a stand of faint blonde hair in her finger.

"Elizabeth Spinner, this is your trial for accusation of witchcraft and threat against His Majesty." The anonymous knight spoke.

"I would *never* have guessed." Eliza groaned, and the entire crowd gave a gasp. Edward shot his elbow into her back, but a light laugh came from him.

She searched amongst the crowd behind, examining each person. The faces were familiar, but she searched only for one. Her father was nowhere in sight.

'He would not be able to come,' She reminded herself, *'He could not bear it, to see this.'*.

Then, one familiar face stuck out among the rest. She had to blink twice to make sure, but it was. The Queen's ladies-in-waiting sat on the left of the royal's platform, on three confined seats.

Lucie Benson, her childhood friend, sat on the seat closest to the end. Her blonde hair blew in the wind, tied into a bun. Formal as ever, her dress was in top-notch shape, glimmering with majestic patterns.

Eliza smiled, and the maiden met her gaze. Lucie looked alarmed, locking eyes with her. The girl mouthed a few words, but they were blowing away in the wind.

She and Lucie had met when they were young, when Lucie had moved into the far-side of town, after leaving her home in France.

The two formed a quick friendship, Lucie as the girl who was adored by all, and Eliza as the girl that trailed after her.

Lucie taught Eliza basic etiquette and how to style a gown, Eliza taught Lucie how to speak English and read it too.

Eliza helped her see the brighter side of the world, while Lucie helped her see the finer side of life.

Shaking her thoughts away, Eliza turned back to the masked man, who had been speaking nonsense.

Eliza flinched, as a man began tying up her hair. He clipped it into a small bun at the back and pulled a hair cover over, before untying her wrists and grabbing hold of her shoulders, guiding her to The King's platform.

She was expected to beg for mercy, to cry out and state her innocence. They had set their expectations too high, in that case.

Richard glared down at her, awaiting her testimony. Eliza took a long breath, watching the rustling grass at her feet.

"This trial is not reliable, none of this is," Eliza stated, whisking her head to the crowds. "Do you truly base your beliefs on what this man says? Have any of you *seen* a spell-casting with your own eyes, or a *curse* being placed upon anyone?".

Richard rose to his feet, standing at the edge of his platform. The crowds sucked in sharp breaths, and no one dared give her an answer.

"Curses have been made," King Richard declared, waving his arms to the people, "They will continue to cause our suffering unless we abolish their source.".

Eliza squinted her eyes, focusing on the lake. There was a spine-chilling tension, one she was glad to end.

"Then it appears that we are all mistaken," Eliza announced, turning to the crowd, "If it is the source of the town's curse that we need, look no further than the man you call King.".

The King's fist clenched. He sat up and cleared his throat. "I have shaped this city into a greater nation than it ever was, I am not a *curse*, but a remedy.".

"You're sickening." Eliza spat, shaking her head.

"Perhaps, but better that than a fool.".

"This *trial* is not *foolish*, to you?".

"Why would it be?" King Richard asked, strolling to the front of his high platform, "If you float despite the chair's restraints, your own *vile* sorcery has saved you, and you are therefore a *witch*. However, if you sink, you are innocent, and shall be treated as such."

The crowd began to speak again, whispering to one another about who was right or wrong. Eliza smiled over at The King, nodding, before raising her hand again to speak.

"And if I sink, just how shall I be treated, Your Majesty?" Eliza queried, spiteful challenge gleaming in her eyes. The King said nothing, shifting his gaze to his wife.

Queen Grace's face was drained, as she avoided his eyes. Her shoulders were clenched, as she refrained from any objections.

The crowd spoke again, and people began to point at The King. For once, he did not have a justified answer.

"*You will live.*" He growled back, squinting his shaded eyes. "Is that not fair?".

He was lying, and she needed a way to prove it. Averting her eyes, she turned to the trialling chair. It caught her eye.

The legs were lanky, flaking at the sides. Her arms gave an uneasy shiver.

"It is not fair if it is untrue." Eliza stated, "Mary Stanley sunk on her trial. She struggled and was close to drowning, in fact. Did she live?".

She watched his eyes go alert, widening at the pupils. The crowds echoed through the air. Mary, the woman executed days before, had been critically injured in her trial. She struck the water, then had sunk for good. Moments after, she arose again, gasping for air.

The crowd's whispers grew, as an unnerved Richard nodded to the knight clutching her shoulder. With a nod, the knight marched her along.

A striking wind brushed Eliza's face, as the river and podium ahead sent shivers down her spine. Her cheeks were flushed, and eyes off-centre towards the lake.

"May we start the trial, Your Highness?" the gruff man asked. The King hesitated for a second, giving her a final glare. He waved a response.

Eliza had no more spite left within her, all replaced by suffocating fear. Her heart was pounding, and her slight fingers gripped at her blouse, clutching the locket beneath it through the linen.

She placed a shaking foot onto the wooden platform, pushing herself into a stand. The wood croaked beneath her, as Eliza wobbled.

The crooked old chair was ahead, in the grip of a masked man. Eliza clutched her flushed arms, eyes transfixed on the chair.

Turning her back to the crowds, Eliza met his harsh gaze. He gestured to the wooden seat.

Eliza gripped its handle, sitting down on the wood. The sight ahead of her was nothing but river. Her knees trembled, like they would collapse.

Closing her eyes, she took a deep breath. It would have been a crime to let them see her cry. Reality struck as rope was wrapped three times around her forearms, before being tightened, scratching at her skin.

A grunt came from the knight, as he tugged on the rope. Eliza froze, as she was raised into the air. A rope was being tied around her waist, breathlessly attacking her ribs.

A clunk came from behind, and Eliza had been raised feet above the podium. The chair wobbled in the air, as waves of nausea hit her.

Her arm's ached as her head spun, pounding like she had been struck with a hammer.

A splash of ice-cold water struck her, harsh enough to burn. Eliza flinched, gripping the chair's handle.

Staring into the sky, the blue visions swam above. Freezing water blazed her shins, tracing her trembling knees. Her skirt turned an ebony shade, drenched in the frigid waves.

Eliza focused on the sound of her own breathing, as messed up and short as it was. She hitched a breath and shut her eyes.

Her corset protected her waist, from the shocking waves, and the pneumonia. Slowly, she was lowered down, waist-deep in the waves.

The chair froze. He did not lower her or test her. Eliza opened her eyes wide, and she wished she had not.

The rope clenched onto her waist, and her arms were trapped within the restraints.

The hold on her got tighter, and by an inch she was raised from the water's grasp. It was not over, not at all.

Her chair dipped in the air, drooping her feet into the water. They were turning blue, emphasized by the pale. Eliza shivered and longed for a blanket, as goosebumps graced her arms.

Her heart sunk in her chest each time the chair dipped, and it sunk entirely when the chair was loosened.

With a crash, the old chair struck the waves, sending a fleshy pain into Eliza's leg. The frozen water attacked her arms, like slashes of a blade.

Her whole body submerged underneath the waves, as flesh-eating bubbles bit at her ghostly face.

The drifting waves of the water blazed her skin, as her breath caught in her throat.

'Swim,' Her mind said, *'Swim away, get out.'*.

Her arms barged into the rope, fighting to get out. Eliza kicked out her legs, moving herself upwards. Air was trapped within her throat, like a ticking bomb inside her chest.

Heart hammering inside, Eliza swung her legs through swift waves, stricken with numbing pain.

She thought of her father, and how he would never survive without her help. She was all he had.

She thought of her mother, and her studies that took years of preparation.

Then, she thought of herself. She was all her family had, and at the end of the day, she was all she had.

Swirls of blood escaped her mouth, swishing away in the river. Her muscles screamed out as she mercilessly kicked out, whipping her head from side to side.

Eliza's head pounded while water ran through her nose, and her soaked frame relaxed. Faintness poured over her like shadow, and her head lolled back into the chair's wood.

'Stay, stay' Eliza's thoughts were painfully forced, *'Stay alive.'*.

Like a terror-stricken lullaby, Eliza's mind slowly drifted off. Her legs sunk against the chair's, as it carefully rose. She felt herself being elevated, as her head braced the air.

The suffocation in her chest was minutes from exploding into nothing.

Her eyes shot wide open as she reached the air, joyously launching her head backwards for a taste of the sweet air. Relief filled her, as her shoulders graced the outdoors.

A shiver ran over her with the impact, reaching the harsh air. Eliza helplessly kicked out her aching legs, rising to float.

That word hit her like a slap to the face.

'Float,' She thought, *'You're floating; witches float.'*.

Panic struck her, thundering from wall-to-wall inside her chest. A mix of tears and lake water ran down her face; she was floating.

Eliza's knees had collapsed into numbed-out pain, while her lungs refilled with sharp air. The chair beneath her floated fully to the surface, and she had no fight left.

A gasp came from behind, and the murmurs of people filled the air. She felt the rope slicing into her arms, as they prepared to resurface her. Dipping her eyes, the faulty buttons of her blouse hung loose. Her clothes were slightly transparent, revealing her corpse-like soaking skin.

"*A witch!*" King Richard yelled from afar. "*Proof at last!*".

Tilting her head back, Eliza could see him from the edge of her eye. He stood jeering a cruel finger at her in jubilant pride.

Queen Grace was gripping his arm, tugging him down from his stand. Reluctantly, he sat down at her side.

Eliza shook her head away, clenching her eyes shut. The rope pierced her skin, as her chair was drifted back to the podium. Water caressed her legs, as she was floated back to shore.

"*Elizabeth!*" An anonymous voice shouted, in a hesitant cry.

She flinched at the mention of her name. The voice was not a cruel jeer, or hurtful remark. It seemed genuine, as it trembled through the air.

Glimpsing to the surface, she had a clearer view. Richard's eyes had gone a detestable cold, narrowed to the floor. The crowd's voices overpowered the unknown voice.

The chair clunked against the podium, as the rope tugged her upwards. Eliza's head shot back and forth, searching for the voice.

Her ears, spilling out residue water, listened for the voice. The tension had been broken by countless tones and sayings.

Shutting her eyes, she focused on its muffled cries alone. Blurring voices of the crowds struck her, but her concentration was pinpointed on that voice. It grew stronger, as Eliza's mind drew comparisons.

45

Her mind landed on one, as the voice faded into a memory within her mind, aligning with the tone of a man she knew well.

"Put me down!" Eliza screamed, kicking out her tortured knees. Teeth clenched with a tight grip, she called out to the masked knight. He flinched, nodding.

Her feet slammed into the wood, and with shivering hands the knight untied the rope.

It loosened on her arms leaving flaming red stripes, then swung off her waist.

The masked man's arm swung out to grip her, as Eliza ducked and dodged it. Receiving a flabbergasted expression, she darted across the wooden platform and jumped down the steps with a bang.

Her eyes met the centre of the grass, and he stood there. George Spinner's drooping eyes met her with a flash.

His beige jacket was carelessly resting on his shoulders, clinging to his awkward frame. The man's greying hair was dripping with grease, as his ebony eyes met her own.

Diving from the knight's swinging fist, Eliza sprinted towards her father. Knights from all directions chased behind her, all except one.

Eliza ran from them, sprinting across the wet grass. Her father looked terrible, his eyes were red and swollen, with drooping bags underneath.

The knights grabbed her arms and pulled her back, as Eliza arched her chest out forward. A band of knights grabbed onto her father's arms, yanking him backwards.

"No!" Eliza screamed, shooting one hand out to her injured father, "Please, leave him be! *Stop!*".

The guard slammed his knuckles into her father's chest sending a splutter of blood out of the man's mouth. His face was looming and grey, as her fears came to life.

Eliza flung herself to her knees, elbowing a feisty guard away. Her father winced as the guard's swung their fists, and panic raised in her throat.

"Silent! *Enough!*" Richard yelled, slamming his fist to the wood.

Turning back to her father, the two locked wide eyes. 'It's ok', Eliza mouthed, shaking her head. George Spinner continued to fend off the guards, as Eliza's knees were dragged across the sharp grass by knights.

She froze as one knight grabbed her father's collar, raising their fist over their shoulder. Eliza elbowed one of her guards in the low chin, before waving her hand quickly through the air.

"*I'll go!*" Eliza screamed, "I'll go with you, I will do whatever you say, but *only* if you let my father go, *please.*".

The guard's turned to her, mouths ajar and eyes wide. King Richard squinted his eyes at her with a cautious gleam, before nodding to the knights.

The man gripping her father gave him a final foul look, before hesitantly dropping him. George Spinner fell to his knees, choking on the air.

"E- Elizabeth," Her father croaked, clutching his chest. "D-Don't.".

"Go home, father," Eliza smiled, trembling all the more, "*Please, I'll be fine.*".

The guard's pulled her away, tying the restraints around her wrists. Eliza was walked to and pressed against the brick wall, as they fastened the rope.

"I will escort Miss Spinner to the tower," A voice called, "Continue as you were."

Eliza spotted Captain Edward strolling towards them, with a mellow smile on his face. She wondered if he had seen the scene at all.

"I'll do it, Captain!" One guard said, taking her tied wrists.

"*No,* you won't." Edward warned, "You will do as *I* say.".

The younger knight shuddered, sticking out a sulking lip. Edward strolled over and pressed a hand to her shoulder, marching Eliza along.

She turned to see his head held high, avoiding any eye contact with her. Eliza marched along beside with her head low.

The castle doors were open wide, as Edward pushed her through them. He grumbled underneath his breath, nodding to the staring courtiers.

The regal décor shined over them, as the halls gradually got darker. Edward quickly walked her down a different hall, opposite from the dungeons.

"Captain, why is *she* here?" One noble man asked, staring her up and down. Edward cleared his throat, gripping Eliza's shoulder.

"I am not one to ask," Edward whispered lowly, "I am only following commands.".

"Shouldn't *she* be in the dungeons?" The man spat, squinting his eyes at her.

"Apparently not," Edward said, "As said, I am following an order.".

The man scoffed, eyeing her before pushing past. He strolled down the hall behind, slamming the door at the end.

"I'm not going to the dungeons?" Eliza asked, "Why *not*?".

Edward shifted away, clicking his tongue. He continued pushing her to the end of the hall, and around the doorframe.

"You are being transferred to the tower, until a final decision is made for execution." Edward said, "In summary, you will be under *my* watch during that time.".

"No one goes to the tower," Eliza replied, shaking her head. "There must be a mistake.".

"It was The King's order; he is not wrong." Edward warned.

Eliza stepped away; her face curled into disgust. The knight seemed confident in his words, but not prideful.

"I disagree," Eliza murmured, watching as his face changed. "I once heard that those who are never *wrong*, have never stood for what is *right*.".

Edward stopped, gazing towards her. His eyes drifted off, with a conflicted look.

"Yet, that depends on what you define as being right," Edward whispered, "Does it not?".

Eliza did not reply, turning away from the knight. She knew he had a point, but if everything came down to what individuals defined as good doing, the line would never be drawn.

Politics, her father had once said, should never interfere with a person's right to live.

They walked side-by-side through the dim-lit corridor, then towards a grand staircase, decorated in shades of crimson, and fires illuminating the walls.

The steps clicked beneath her feet, as Edward speedily dragged her through.

The castle gardens were rumoured to be astonishingly beautiful, and seeing them, Eliza could understand why.

There were flowers blooming in harmony, with vegetable patches and trees, everything glistening with the golden sunset. It had to be the most incredible sight Eliza had ever seen.

Edward smiled, eyeing a sun-kissed rose. Eliza gazed longingly at the flower, tempted to take one with her. Ahead, there was a tall, daunting tower.

The brick was coarse and wide, marked with stain and crumbling stone. A cross-hatched window was locked overhead, forced shut. Eliza shook, as the sky turned a ghastly grey.

Edward remained silent throughout the walk. He banged on the wooden door and it swung open, as he gestured his gloved hand.

"This is where you will stay, controlled by myself. Go up the stone steps and into the room, until--" Edward's voice shook, "Until your execution.".

A stone staircase was at her feet, spiralling above. Eliza shot around, clutching her slightly dried arms.

Her eyes glimpsed Edward, who gave her what looked like a pitiful look, before he was gone.

The door shut behind her, and she sat in the dark, with nothing to do but accept her fate as it was, and as it would always be.

4

The Sword in the Stone Tower

"Elizabeth?" A voice whispered, pricking their fingers into Eliza's arm. "Wake up!".

She felt like she had slept for days, as sleep and stickiness crumbled from her face. The tower room had been locked behind her, leaving only the bed, window, and mirror.

Maidens from the castle had been delivering trays of limited food to her room, tidied it, then hastily left without a second glance.

The room had a plain bed and barred-shut windows that gave her a small view of the wonderful castle gardens. There was a mirror, with white-cloth clothes draped over the edge.

For the first few days, Edward had visited, to clarify that she was alive. He would speak to her for a few minutes, and each day she had asked how her father was, if he was alive. The knight had sighed, before answering that her father was fine.

"Make haste! Are you *awake*?" The high-pitched voice whined. With half-an-ounce of effort, Eliza rolled over with the blanket tugged over her shoulders.

"No." Eliza grunted back, pulling the blanket over her head. The unknown person's hand gripped the sheets, revealing her trembling frame.

"What are you--?" Eliza sat up, glaring at the figure. Her voice cut short as her eyes drifted upwards, slowly recognising the beaming face.

The figure's blue gown was patterned with different gold flowers, and the person was slim but small, with strawberry-blonde hair flowing past their shoulders and a blue headband on their head.

"*Lucie?*" Eliza asked, rubbing at her eyes. Lucie's navy eyes gleamed, as her mouth curled into a smile. The perfect maiden was neat and postured, compared to Eliza's sulked state.

'The ever-so practical, Lucie Benson.' Eliza thought.

Eliza's hair was sticking up in every direction, fallen in strands over her eyes. Lucie tilted her head, scoffing at the sight.

"Elizabeth," Lucie said, plopping down onto the bed. "Apologies, I didn't come sooner. The town is a pandemonium, these days.".

"I don't blame them," Eliza grumbled, "Not when their King is an old—".

"Bite your tongue!" Lucie scolded, eyeing her. "It is not *just* His Majesty at the root of the chaos.".

"*Me?*" Eliza said, "I've been locked in a dungeon, for goodness' sake!".

Lucie rolled her eyes, pushing away the silver tray at her feet. Eliza sat up, dusting down her paper-thin nightgown. The coarse metal of her locket stung against her skin, as she clutched her trembling arms.

"I *know* that," Lucie replied, "But, you caused a stir at *your own* trial, and you are not the people's *most trusted* person.".

"No, I'm their scapegoat for when trouble hits." Eliza sulked, "Are people so *dim-witted*, that they cannot accept that things *do* go wrong, simply by *chance?*".

Lucie said nothing, staring outside the tower window. Flocks of birds flew in the breeze, reminding Eliza of her own lost critter.

"How *are* you feeling?" Lucie asked, gripping the edge of the bed. After a sudden life-reflecting moment, the maiden's eyes had perked up once more.

"*Fantastical.*" Eliza scoffed. Lucie's eyes glistened, as she reached out her hand, leaving it inches from Eliza's own.

"I-I'm sorry, that you have to go through all of *this*," Lucie murmured, placing her fingers atop Eliza's.

Eliza knew that her foul demeanour made Lucie uncomfortable, as the maiden shifted slightly away from her.

"It isn't your fault." Eliza murmured.

Lucie's hand drifted away, landing snugly in her lap. Inches apart, the two sat on the edge of the bed.

It was strange, Eliza thought, for them to be so awkward. The maiden had been on a trip alongside her father, to meet a far-off suitor. Lucie had only returned the day Eliza had been arrested, unluckily.

"Did your trip go well?" Eliza asked. "I had worried that, if your potential-husband was in France, you might have stayed there.".

"No, of course not," Lucie replied, her face flushed. "It turned out that the suitor had…other arrangements, as did I.".

"Other arrangements?" Eliza queried, "Then, why did you go?".

Lucie said nothing. Eliza knew the maiden had searched for a partner for a long time, but it never had a good result.

"To visit my family," Lucie answered, "The voyage to France was set, we couldn't *not* go.".

Eliza nodded. Her heart poured out to the maiden, who had to leave her whole family, only for a royal employment.

To Lucie's father, it was worth the trouble of emigrating to England, for the lady-in-waiting job his daughter was promised.

"There is still hope, and for what it is worth, I hope that you find your person." Eliza said.

"That makes two of us." Lucie sniffed, dabbing at her eyes. She froze, raising her hand over her face. "Goodness, I must sound so *selfish*, ranting on about my troubles to *you*.".

Eliza agreed with that but held her tongue. Instead of accepting what was going to happen, she had denied it. During those imprisoned days, she slept and occupied her mind, to avoid facing the sad fact; she would die.

"You don't sound selfish," Eliza lied, searching for words. "Anyhow, worrying myself sick over what *might* happen will not change what *will*.".

Lucie wiped down her eyes, a shaking smile on her face. The two shared a moment, with mutual understanding.

"It will be fine, all of it." Eliza whispered, trying to lighten the mood. "They won't get rid of me that easy, I promise.".

"*He* will, Elizabeth," Lucie cried, chewing on her nails. "You don't *know* what he's capable of, not like *I* do.".

Eliza understood. Working for The King had been both a curse and a blessing for Lucie. One time, the girl had spoken of a night when a man was being interrogated in the dungeons. The screams echoed from the cell right to her bedroom in the servant's quarters.

"I have seen what he has done, and it boils more hatred than it does fear." Eliza shrugged.

The two sat in silence, as Eliza's gaze drifted to her bony feet. Lucie gripped the bedsheet, edging closer to her until they were side-by-side.

"E-Elizabeth?" Lucie cried, taking hold of her arm. "Is that—".

Eliza gazed to the window, spotting a black orb in the sky. It appeared frozen still, with pointed triangles at either side of it. To her horror, it got closer at the speed of light.

"Down!" Eliza yelled, clasping Lucie's hand. She flung herself awkwardly to the floor, tugging a shrieking Lucie down with her. The two landed on their sides, half-lying on the floor.

A crack and a bang came from the window, as the glass doors rocketed apart. The black orb had collided with the windowpane and sped right into the room, as it soared through the sky.

Dawn's pointed head targeted Eliza, as the raven flew to her side. A squawk came from the bird, as it nuzzled against her.

Eliza felt relieved, stroking the birds head. Lucie screamed, pulling the sheets over her head; the sheets that had been tugged off the bed along with her.

"It's only Dawn," Eliza laughed, as the raven perched on her finger.

The maiden's eyes peeked out from beneath the sheet, as she glared at the bird. Lucie had landed in a strange position, face-first on the ground with her hips upwards.

"It's a foul creature, it's *ugly*." Lucie spat out, with her cheeks as red as a spring strawberry.

Eliza scanned the open window, looking from it to Dawn. The raven must have spotted her from far off, sending it spiralling towards the tower.

Dawn wobbled on its stick-like legs, its neck curling around in circles. Eliza giggled, stroking its head.

"That is what you deserve, for flying head-first into a window." Eliza said, "You *are* a *daft* bird.".

Peering at the mirror, Eliza's eyes widened. Her hair was frizzled and thick, landing in a heap. Her used nightgown was sweat-drenched and loosely hanging from her shoulders.

"I look like I'm already *dead*." Eliza groaned.

"Do not say that, you look fine." Lucie scolded.

Eliza opened her mouth to reply, as a thud came from beneath them. The two froze. Footsteps came from the staircase, echoing throughout.

Lucie stumbled over words, skipping to her feet. The noise grew louder.

Taking hold of Lucie, Eliza threw the maiden behind her, pulling the wardrobe door open, and pushing the girl inside.

Lucie squealed; her eyes wide as she collided with the dense wood.

Eliza slammed the wardrobe doors shut before Lucie could protest, locking her inside. Stumbling across the tower room, she searched for a hiding place.

The tower door swung open, revealing two distressed knights. Thomas and Edward stood in the stone entrance; swords aimed.

"*Surrender!*" Thomas yelled, sprinting toward Eliza. He grabbed hold of her and swung her into the wall, pressing her against it.

Colliding with the wall, her head started pounding. Turning around through gritted teeth, she saw his sword inches from her neck.

"*Stop!*" Edward yelled, marching to them. "I told you, do not jump to conclusions.".

Thomas' armour clinked and clanked as he moved, embarrassingly sunken from his frame.

"It was her, I told you she'd pull a trick on us!" Thomas shouted. "I knew you would hurt her, you witch!".

"What are you talking about?" Eliza winced. Thomas scowled, as his eyes searched the room. He let go of her arms.

Edward sighed, briefly nodding toward her. Thomas had reached the open window, leaning on the edge, and peering down to the ground.

'*I'd push him, if I had the energy.*' Eliza thought, before shaking the violent thoughts away.

"Before he throws a tantrum, where is the lady?" Edward whispered to her, shaking his head at the young knight.

"She's hexed her, I know she has!" Thomas yelled, "If I had it my way, she would *never* associate with a *witch* like you!".

"Jealous?" Eliza scoffed, with a sour look. "You drooled over her for four *years*, and she never gave you a second *glance*.".

Eliza remembered the first time Thomas McGlynn had met Lucie Benson, and how he set his heart on marrying her. His infamous attempts became the talk of the town, as he became fascinated with every move she made.

Lucie, despite needing to marry a nobleman, never once considered him as a suitor.

"No, I've *changed* from my old ways, now I—" Thomas froze, as a bang echoed throughout.

A shriek came from across the room. Lucie came tumbling out of the wardrobe, landing flat on her stomach with a grunt. Her gown flowed out across the floor, as her hair covered her eyes.

"I-I'm here…" Lucie croaked, raising a hand with her face on the floor.

Thomas sucked in a breath, rushing over to Lucie's side. He flung his sword across the floor, as he gripped her arms, lifting Lucie to her knees.

Lucie's wobbled in a daze, as she tried to stand onto her feet.

"Stay down, you're faint." Thomas whispered, in a comforting tone Eliza had never heard.

 Lifting her like a glass doll, Thomas lay a light-headed Lucie onto the floor. He knelt beside her, with a proud smirk on his face.

Edward coughed, averting his eyes. Thomas said nothing, unmoving from his place beside the maiden.

Eliza marched across the room, stifling a humourless laugh. Reaching the tray beside her bed, she gripped the goblet of water in her hand.

Thomas glared at her, as she marched over to Lucie. The maiden, even while half-fainted, remained perfect. Her face was pale and lips a soft pink, like a fairy-tale princess awaiting true love's kiss.

"Get up!" Eliza exclaimed, splashing the full cup of water over Lucie's face. The maiden immediately sat up, water dripping from her and mouth open wide.

"Don't do that to her!" Thomas growled.

"She's awake, is she not?" Eliza replied, "Lucie faints all the time, especially after falling face-first out of a wardrobe.".

Lucie, struggling for breaths, half-nodded. She wiped away the water from her soaking face, as droplets fell from her flustered cheeks.

"That's true, I'm used to it..." Lucie drawled, her eyes floating off-centre.

Thomas sulked, still crouching at the maiden's side. It was clear he hoped to be the knight in shining armour, and the one to save the girl.

"Ah-hem," Edward coughed, gesturing to Thomas. "I believe our business here is done.".

"I believe it is not," Thomas replied, "I will stay with the lady until she has recovered.",

"No, you won't!" Eliza and Edward said, simultaneously.

Thomas shot her a nasty look, firmly knelt in place. Eliza's eyes darted over to Thomas' abandoned sword, inches away from her.

Her hand reached out, gripping the swords' hold. Slowly, focusing her eyes, Eliza pointed it at the kneeling knight.

"Out." Eliza warned, as Thomas' eyes sparked his fear.

"Don't you *dare* touch me, w-witch!" He gulped, fumbling in his back pockets. He scampered to his trembling feet, whilst Eliza stepped over Lucie.

'He's a coward, at heart,' Eliza thought, *'Use that.'*.

Edward remained silent; his feet glued to the floor. His eyes skimmed between the two, as he clutched his own sword.

Thomas backed away from her. His eyes flickered over to Edward, as he nodded towards her.

"S-She's using my own sword against me, that's not fair!" Thomas cried, narrowing his eyes at her. He stopped pacing backwards and took one step toward her.

"I'll give you your sword," Eliza murmured, shaded eyes focused on the boy. "*If* you leave.".

Edward glared at her, pushing past them both. He took hold of Thomas' shoulder blade and pulled the boy to the door.

"N-No!" Thomas whined, "I can fend *her* off, I don't fear *her*!".

"That's *not* what I am worried about," Edward grumbled, swinging the tower door open and pushing the knight out. Thomas' pleading face was the final sight, before he was covered by mahogany wood.

"Put the sword down," Edward warned her, and Eliza dropped it at her feet. The sword hit the floor with a bang.

Dawn began to chirp from the back of the room, as all three eyes turned to the new sound. Edward gasped, reaching for Thomas' sword.

"No!" Eliza yelled, taking hold of his arm. The knight froze, with the sword in mid-air. Edward squinted his eyes at her, then Dawn. His face mellowed from its irritated state, as the sword lowered to his feet.

"It's yours?" Edward asked, gesturing to Dawn. Eliza nodded.

"It's my company," Eliza said, "There's no crime in that.".

Lucie pushed herself to her feet, stumbling over to the two. She placed a hand on Eliza's shoulder, balancing her shaken self. Edward's eyes shot between them.

"You two are friends?".

"No." said Eliza.

"Yes." said Lucie.

The two girls turned to one another, like they were talking in telekinesis. With a wordless nod, they both returned to Edward.

"Yes." said Eliza.

"No." said Lucie.

The knight's brow raised, as he stifled a laugh. Eliza and Lucie shot each other another confused look, whispering under their breaths.

"I'll take that as a yes," Edward said, "Or not.".

He turned back to Lucie, with an unreadable face.

"You must remember your professional duties, Lady Benson." Edward warned. "Provide Miss Spinner with necessities, no more.".

Lucie hesitated, before lowering her eyes. The maiden spun around and began pacing the room, balancing recklessly tossed sheets on her arms.

Edward directed his gaze at Eliza, scanning her with his eyes. Standing in her paper-thin nightgown, she knew she looked a state compared to Lucie.

"And you," Edward began, eyeing Eliza. "You're a wildcard; unpredictable.".

"Aren't you a charmer." Eliza scoffed. His hand braced her shoulder.

"It is not an insult," Edward said, "If you play your cards right.".

Edward smirked, turning to leave the room. He noticed Eliza's furrowed eyes, as she thought over his words. With that, he left the room, leaving the two girls stunned. Lucie nudged Eliza's arm.

"That was…wise," Lucie said, "What did it mean?".

"Who knows?" Eliza smirked, "He's a bit strange too, they ought to lock him in a tower.".

Lucie giggled, nudging her elbow into Eliza's again. The smirk on her face was contagious, as her hand clutched her mouth. Eliza stared, with a lost look. The girl continued to laugh, as her giggles filled the void room. Lucie's cheeks had flushed boiling red.

"Two strange people who use a lot of long words I cannot understand," Lucie giggled, "*C'est l'amour.*".

"Oh, *hush*," Eliza scoffed, giggling under her breath. "He's guarding the tower that I am imprisoned in, that is certainly not love.".

"Well, it was a mere suggestion," Lucie shrugged, "The look he gave you, there was admiration in it.".

"I am the last person to be admired, Lucie," Eliza said, "He's nicer to me than the other knights have been, yes, but being *nice* is the bare *minimum*. If you swoon over every man who is *nice*, where do you draw the line?".

Lucie folded her arms, shaking her head. Eliza knew all-too-well that the maiden was a hopeless romantic, but unfortunately, Lucie tended to fall for the ones that would not give her a second glance.

Then, the maiden perked up. Her eyes met Eliza's own, as she leant in. Eliza prayed that it was not another love suggestion.

"The plan, I forgot!" Lucie whispered, gripping onto Eliza's hand. The two shared a glance, before Eliza stepped away.

"Plan? What plan?".

Lucie hesitated, with her eyes floating adrift. Whatever the 'plan' was, Eliza knew Lucie was hesitant, that she was doubtful.

"Lucie, tell me.".

"I have an idea, listen;" Lucie said, "We both know that Elizabeth cannot make it out of here alive, but…what if someone else can?".

5

Watch Your Back

Eliza sat on the edge of the windowpane, patiently awaiting the arrival of her maiden-friend. Dawn's eyes squinted toward her, as it fluttered over her head.

"I could care less that you are angry, Dawn," Eliza said, "Eat the stale bread, if you are *that* hungry. I am not allowing you to eat a *shoe*.".

Her pet's boundless appetite had worsened overnight. Dawn nipped on her arms and sat on her head, desperate for a bite of food. To Eliza's disgust, it had tried eating her worn shoe.

Dawn bit her forearm between its teeth, pecking at her skin. Eliza flicked it away with her hand, earning a cry from the bird.

"Shoo!" Eliza said, waving Dawn away.

She had managed to dress, after one of the maidens had popped in with clothes while she slept. Her navy-blue skirt ran down past her ankles, and a white linen shirt gave her warmth.

It was prisoner clothing at best, but more complimenting than her worn-out nightgown.

The room had gotten uglier, she was sure. The dusty-old wardrobe seemed to stare into her soul, and the stained antique mirror had fingerprint marks. The walls were smeared in a strange substance, while the tower itself was cold, suiting for a prisoner in every aspect.

After spending her tower days in misery, while forcing a brave smile for Lucie, her emotions were quick-changing.

It was easier to pretend she was fine, that she was paving her way through with a smile. The late nights shadows knew that was not true.

The wind brushed her face, while Dawn perched on her shoulder. The world passed by, as it always did.

Still, Lucie's masterplan brought her more hope than anything. The risk it took could cost her head, but she knew, she had nothing left to lose. Her head was the least of her concerns.

Eliza straightened out her skirt and turned towards the mirror. For the first time in forever, she smiled. Her face felt strange doing so, and her cheeks melted. A bittersweet feeling struck her heart.

Lucie would sneak past the guards soon and arrive to the tower room for their plan to be set in action. There would be limited time, and if they were a minute overdue, the knights would get suspicious.

A squawk came, as Dawn came flying head-first towards her. Eliza screamed, ducking away.

"*Stop that!*" She yelled, pushing the bird off. She was fully convinced that the bird was a human soul in an animal's body; it was far too eerie how self-aware it was.

Dawn began circling the room, squawking, and chirping in its flight. That was never a good sign. When Dawn got exceedingly restless, it was usually a sign of trouble.

"You are either creepily possessive or creepily possessed, stupid bird." Eliza grumbled, sighing at the window. Her own reflection could be seen in the glass, covered by the drooling rainfall.

'If Dawn acts this possessed with Lucie, she'll throw a tantrum.'
Eliza thought.

"Did I raise you like this? No." Eliza smirked, playfully scowling at the bird. "Poor Lucie, you'll scare her to death.".

She had listened all morning, her ears perking up each time the door creaked open. To her dismay, it had been Thomas entering the tower, listening for anything to use against her.

Gazing out the window once more, she saw King Richard and his men, as the soldiers marched back and forth. Eliza smiled.

"Why do they move their arms like that?" She laughed, turning to Dawn. "When they march, they swing their arms forward and back, did you notice?".

Dawn ignored her, and she expected no reply. Eliza turned back to the marching men, resting her face on her hand.

She never understood why The King could not march with them on the training grounds, where they trained for war.

Their bulging boots squashed the small flower petals, ruining the sweetness of the castle gardens.

Eliza realised that if the guards were at their training, Lucie could sneak past them. She scanned the outside world, and her gaze landed on a hooded figure, crouched beside the evergreen hedges.

Her eyes squinted, focused on the strange person. Their face was covered by the charcoal hood, along with their clothes.

'Lucie would wear her maiden clothes, would she not?' Eliza thought. *'Perhaps she is taking incognito to heart.'.*

Then, with a closer look, she realised the figure was far too tall. They moved cautiously, taking side steps along the hedge, keeping a firm hold on their hood.

A pit of suspicion grew in Eliza's stomach, and a feeling that something was wrong, very wrong.

Lurking around the castle grounds in such an antisocial manner was highly forbidden.

The figure reached into their cloak. They pulled out a sword, sharp and shimmering, edging closer to The King.

"Is that…" Eliza's voice wandered off, as she anxiously watched.

'I have to do something, anything.' Eliza thought, gripping the windowpane.

For once, Eliza watched in awe as the roles reversed in front of her very eyes. The King likened to prey, and the anonymous figure the hunter.

Like a blood-hungry animal, the hunter's moves were slow and deliberate. The sword swung around a few times on the figure's arm, and he creeped up behind His Highness' back.

Eliza had to admit, this hooded person had a logical approach. They chose to strike The King at a rare point in time.

The guards were pre-occupied with their training, and some would be on break. It was a dangerously intelligent plan, and a fair one.

Shaking her head, Eliza shook herself back to reality. The matter at hand was someone would die today, if she did not act. Eliza's heart thumped in her chest.

'Think Elizabeth, if you kill him, he cannot kill you.' One eager voice of her mind said. The other, more sensible voice disagreed; *'You'd regret not saving him, it's blood on your hands.'*.

Eliza pulled on her hair, debating over what to do. If she let him live, it meant even more innocent lives would disappear, including her own.

If she let the strange assassin kill The King, she would be the one to see it, and cold-blood or not, it was still blood on her hands.

She turned to her reasonable mindset. She would never outlive the fact she had let someone die, no matter who.

Reluctantly, she ran over to her room door, grabbing the handle and twisting it. If she got the guards' attention, she could stop it all from happening before it was too late.

The King had been nothing but cruel, and he was the one who had her sentenced to death. However, deep down, she knew that she would be the one to get the blame for it.

"Someone, *listen!*" Eliza yelled, facing the door.

She kicked the wood, slamming her fists into the surface. There was no reaction, no sound from beneath.

"Will you two horse-faced *imbeciles* do something?!" She screamed, pounding on the door.

Voices rose from below. There were footsteps marching up the stairs, and taking a breath, she backed away from the door.

There was a mumbled commotion sound from the other side of the door, a series of arguing and insulting, before the two guards finally unscrewed the lock.

Edward and Thomas barged through the door. The two guard's mouths sprawled open like two deprived dogs, and they both gasped for breath. Edward immediately caught her distressed face, while Thomas was doubled over, clutching his side.

Her finger shot to the window, and Edward nodded. He grabbed Thomas by the collar, and the boy let out a yell. The two sprinted over, steadying at the window.

"An assassin!" Thomas yelled, banging his fist on the crooked window. All the in-training knights had their backs turned to The King, and no one saw the figure raise his weapon; no one would see him kill The King.

Both Thomas and Edward sprinted towards the door, and hesitantly, Eliza ran after them. She spun around the doorframe and to the staircase, behind the two knights back.

Thomas kicked open the tower front door and ran out in front of the other two. Edward turned, catching a glimpse of Eliza. She stood froze, but he did not speak, he had no time to stop her.

"*Stop!*" Thomas yelled, swinging his sword overhead. He missed the intruder, as they dodged his force.

The assassin thought on their feet, stumbling across the grass, and sprinting away.

Their hood flew out behind them, as they clumsily ran away. Both hands clutched their cloak, and no one got a sight of who bore it.

The training guards, startled by the scene, ran towards the disappearing hood. A crowd of them, dressed in silver, disappeared with the assassin. The King was pushed aside by the frenzy, as he stepped into clear view.

His face was a flaming red, as he raised a trembling fist. The frigid winter grass crunched under his boots, as he marched toward Edward.

"What is this!?" King Richard roared, throwing Thomas away.

The King, widely shaking his fist, turned to Thomas. His eye had caught Eliza, as his pupils widened in alarm.

His jaw turned sharp, and his cheeks flushed scarlet. He turned to the nearest knight, Thomas, and gripped him by the collar.

"Why is *she* out of the tower on *your watch!?*" He yelled, his knuckles sticking out like thorns on a bush.

Eliza noticed the countless scars that lined Richard's hand, and his face. They were faint, but one mark made a thin white line, right under his chin.

'It looks like someone tried to kill him.' She thought, before wincing at the ugly thought.

She wished her gift of noticing minor details was not so prominent.

Thomas stuttered, muttering an apology. His eyes were wide and afraid, while his face had gone grey.

"Your Highness, as I hate to admit it, she was the one that warned us of the vigilant." Edward said, gesturing to Eliza. "I take full responsibility.".

Edward rushed over, taking a grip of her wrists. There was silence.

Richard dropped Thomas to the floor, and the boy fell to the grass. The King's expression fell, and his eyes rested on her.

'It's like he's looking right through me.'.

Her eyes shifted away, instead turning to Edward. He gave her a sharp side-glance, silent.

"Captain; a piece of advice," Richard began, focused on the knight. "Lying for the wicked gets you no salvation.".

"I speak only the truth, Your Highness.".

"Indeed, but do remember what I said," Richard said, "We never lie for the wicked, *truth* or *not*.".

In ways, she understood what he said, in others, she was lost entirely. To lie or not to lie, was the question; but how can you be sure who is wicked, when both sides claim to be good?

Richard gazed upwards, as a short smirk met his face. He turned to her with a glint in his eyes.

"A friend of yours, Spinner?".

Eliza shot him a look, before following his eye to the tower window. The wind attacked her before she could see, but when her vision cleared, she saw what The King meant.

Lucie peered out of the window, watching the scene.

King Richard laughed, as Eliza turned away. From the corner of her eye, she saw him smirking at the maiden. Lucie's face turned red, as she ducked down and disappeared.

'I should have left him to be attacked, I should have.'.

Richard nodded at Edward. His smile was not the comforting, or the compassionate kind. It was the wicked kind of smirk that made her blood boil.

"There you have it, Captain" The King announced. "It must have been the lady, to warn you of the assassin.".

Thomas stood to trembling feet, gazing up to the tower in disbelief. He limped toward The King, shaking his head.

"The maiden *wasn't*---" Thomas was cut off by Richard, who shot him a silencing glare.

'His desperate ego wouldn't allow him to believe it, that I saved him.'.

She could see Edward staring down at her, his firm face now one of pity.

With a final look, King Richard spun on his heel and marched away, his cape flying wide behind him. All three waited until he was merely a speck in the far grass, before Edward spoke.

"It was you to save him, wasn't it?" He asked, eyeing her.

"You know that answer," Eliza said, "Now, I'm beginning to think I should never have done it.".

"You did the right thing.".

"For people like *you*, not for people like me.".

She turned and walked away, the wind brushing her collar. The bittersweet air met her tongue, as a storm started to brew overhead.

A hand gripped her shoulder. Edward spun her around, and his dark eyes stared into her own.

"Thank you, truly," He nodded, coming close to a smile. "That could have cost me my head.".

"You're welcome." Eliza shrugged. "It's not like I have anything left to lose, is it?".

Watching him, she could not understand why he would choose to work for such a twisted man, royalty or not.

"Right." He whispered, but nothing more. Eliza's heart sank in a way she had never felt, watching his face fall. Turning herself away, she walked faster than before.

She reached the door and tried to kick it open, earning a harsh pain in her foot. Edward reached behind her, pushing the door open with ease. Flushing pink at her own stupidity, Eliza idly turned to the garden.

It emptied entirely, with the knights chasing and Thomas behind Edward, slouching like a half-dead slug. The flowers were slowly dying due to the frozen winter, and the evergreen hedge contrasted the flaking brown.

Everything, even nature, had gotten much darker.

Eliza walked in, and the door locked behind her. Edward turned his back and stayed that way, avoiding her look.

Stepping forward, Eliza trudged up the stone steps, each foot making an echoing sound throughout the silence. She heard Edward clear his throat once or twice, but the tension was deadly.

She heaved herself to the top of the staircase and opened the door, closing it shut. It made a loud creak as it closed, and all she wanted to do was fling herself onto the bed.

A hand gripped her shoulder and flung her, sending her spinning through the air.

"What did you *do!?*" Lucie yelled, yanking her arm. Eliza felt like the room was spinning, as the maiden tugged her back and forth.

"That must be the hundredth time you have asked me that," Eliza scoffed, "I never did recover from the time you threw me into the bush.".

"You were supposed to be here!" Lucie wailed, shaking Eliza back and forth.

"Sorry," Eliza grumbled, "It was an assassination attempt, that's all.".

"That's all?".

"Mm-hm.".

The maiden rolled her eyes, gesturing to her clothes. Eliza realised then; Lucie was not wearing her maiden dress.

She wore a simple blouse and skirt, with a little blue bow on the back. Her hair up neatly in a bun, and she had a satchel with who-knows-what inside.

"Do you still want to do this, the plan?" Lucie asked.

Eliza nodded.

"Right," Lucie mumbled, averting her eyes. "I'll admit, I was up all night plotting out scenarios, worrying myself.".

"I was too," Eliza said. "I came to realise that it is better to focus on what will happen, rather than what could. If we are put in a bad scenario, think on your feet.".

Lucie's face went slightly pale. She gripped the satchel and dropped it into Eliza's open arms. The top of the bag was open and had a hole, revealing a pile of clothes, glistening in blue and gold.

"Let's do it.".

6

The Plan Without A Plan

"This might be your worst idea." Eliza said, brushing out the fake-blonde wig on her head. "Or your most brilliant.".

Their plan was in action, and it was more absurd than anything she had ever heard. Lucie would become Eliza, the lonesome tower prisoner; Eliza would become Lucie, the fairest-of-the-fair lady.

Her new outfit made her wonder how the queen's ladies put up with wearing the too-tight-for-comfort gowns and complicated hairstyles.

It was all strange, like seeing a version of her that was not her, but Lucie. Her hair was covered by the blonde wig, and she wore Lucie's own blue-gold maiden gown.

"Worst idea, by far," Lucie replied, "I'm petrified.".

This was not what she had ever wanted to be like. The suffocating frocks, the tight pull her hair, the wobbling shoes that made her ankles swell, everything.

Lucie had told her that the hair was tight to stretch out her forehead, to meet the royal 'beauty standard'.

"I will be fine, Lucie," Eliza laughed, "You seem afraid that I'll ruin your royal reputation.".

"Exactly.".

Eliza turned to see the maiden, who was not herself at all.

Lucie wore Eliza's own prisoner clothes, and a deep brown wig.

Even her face had been smeared in moistures and tints, covering all the things that made her Lucie.

Even while uncomfortable, Eliza's jittery nerves turned to excitement. She swore to Lucie that, while outside the tower, she would not try to escape.

If she did, Lucie would be the one to inevitably face execution. In Eliza's place, or as the one who helped the witch escape.

Everything was surreal, and nothing like their plan had ever happened before. It was her one chance, and one chance alone.

Thinking of the past and present, it made her pity the prisoners before her. The innocent women that stood inside that very tower, left with nothing but acceptance for what would come.

As the woe washed away, Eliza felt more determined. She wished she could somehow avenge them all, but it would ruin everything, and her feeling of selfishness came flooding back.

"Lucie, do you think we should do this?" She asked.

"No," Lucie announced, spinning in her new skirt. "However, I want you to see your father, to see the world again. After all you've done for me.".

Dawn flew over, resting on her shoulder. Its eyes were squinted at her face, unsure of the difference between her and Lucie.

The common village garments she once wore now abandoned and replaced with a shimmering royal gown, with a light blue tone and golden patterning, a matching headband resting on her head.

Even she had to blink twice when she saw herself. Lucie had been caking her face with powder all morning, emphasizing certain features. Her cheeks were rosier, face appeared fuller, and lips pink.

"When you go out there, remember to keep your head low," Lucie said. "Lower your eyes, keep your back straight.".

"Mm-hm.".

It would be a struggle, to maintain the Lucie-persona. The three golden rules remained firm in her mind: Eyes low, head low, back straight.

Lucie bent over, patting a powdery blush on her face. The powdered makeup made her wheeze, and her lips and cheeks were dramatically scarlet.

'Beauty standard, Lucie says,' Eliza thought, *'Royals have strange ideals of beauty.'*.

Eliza looked down at her chest, to see her mother's locket tucked safely beneath the gown. She had been adamant about wearing it, and reluctantly, Lucie had given in.

Eliza believed it brought her protection, which was something she needed more than ever.

"I look flushed, is having such red cheeks normal?" Eliza asked, turning to Lucie. The maiden shrugged, patting down her own face with white powders.

"It is for me, and other women in the palace," Lucie said. "It makes you look healthier, more poised.".

"Healthier?".

"My mother told me, having red face makes suitors more inclined to approach. With the flush, it makes you look livelier.".

"I have no plans for a suitor, Lucie.".

"Not you, *me.*" Lucie sighed, "I am making *you* look like *me,* and I wear the powder because it makes *me* look livelier.".

Eliza laughed, shaking her head. Never had she found that having exaggeratedly flushed cheeks made you look livelier. When she saw the royal ladies with their red tints, she thought it looked strange.

"I think I'm ready." Eliza announced, curling a strand of fake-blonde wig in her finger. The more she stared at her reflection, the more she was convinced that she looked more like Lucie than Lucie did.

She could remember when she was young, and how nothing and everything had changed between them.

Little Lucie loved dressing up in fancy frocks and tying ribbons in her hair, and she would spin in circles, pretending she were dancing with a prince.

Eliza was the opposite; in their youth, Lucie would dance around a tree, imagining she was in a royal ball.

Eliza would be up the tree, hanging upside down from a branch. One time, she slipped from the tree branch and landed on Lucie: crushing her, and her dreams.

"Elizabeth?".

She spun around, taken from her thoughts. Lucie stood next to her, shaking on her shoulder.

"Do you remember when we used to play in the tree, when we were young?" Eliza asked, taking the girl by surprise.

"I do," Lucie replied. "Especially the day you fell from that tree, crushing me and my dreams.".

Eliza laughed, thinking of the day. She had seen her whole life flashing before her eyes, when she came tumbling down from that old tree. It was easy to imagine how horrified Lucie was, to see her falling atop of her head.

Lucie reached over, taking hold of Eliza's old shoes. Her face curled up into a look of disgust, as she held the shoe out at arms' length.

"How can you *wear* these?" Lucie said, awkwardly pulling the on her own feet. She sat on a stool with one foot in the air, nearly toppling herself to the ground.

"Growing up, I was taught to make use of what I had," Eliza smirked, "My father would not let you throw away a shoe unless your foot cut a hole in it.".

Lucie cringed in disgust, wincing as put half of her foot into the shoe. Eliza, wobbling in Lucie's heels, knelt ahead of her. Gently, she lifted the maiden's ankle and pushed her foot into the shoe.

"It's only a shoe, Lucie.".

"It's a *dirty* shoe.".

Lucie stood up and walked towards the mirror. Eliza stared after her, still perplexed and how strange they both looked.

Lucie's usually bouncing-blonde hair was now a deep brown, and her glimmering dress was abandoned for common villager cloth.

She wore Eliza's skirt and blouse, and her face had changed. It was ghostly pale, and her usual rosy cheeks were white and hollow.

"This is new." Lucie mumbled, raising her hand to her face. Her eyes fell to the floor, in a disheartening way.

"You look fine.".

Eliza reached out her hand and placed it on Lucie's shoulder. She hoped the maiden would not change her mind, that she was not having second thoughts.

"No, it isn't that." Lucie said, barely above a whisper. In that moment, Eliza wondered if it were the powder making Lucie turn grey, or the fear.

Lucie grasped Eliza's hand on her shoulder, clutching it between her fingers. The two stared into the mirror ahead, as the new versions of each other.

"Elizabeth, what if they come for you?" Lucie asked. Eliza had feared that question. "If they come for your execution and take me?".

"If you feel it is coming close to that, tell me. I know a way.".

Eliza, having a bright stroke of inspiration, ran over to the closet. Lucie peered over her shoulder.

Pulling out a black sheet, Eliza held it against the barred window. She measured it across and vertically, turning to Lucie.

"If emergencies happen, tie that sheet to the tower window," She explained. "I'll come to the tower, and we can swap back.".

"Yes, but what if they can see that we look different?" Lucie asked, rubbing at her arms.

Eliza could see that she was nervous, it was never hard to see. She glanced over at her reflection in the mirror. There was a chance someone would notice, but there was a greater chance that they would not.

"Then it will all be over, and I will hand myself in." Eliza said.

'I'm putting her in danger,' Eliza thought, *'Why are we doing this?'*.

80

She was endangering her friend's life for her own sake. Lucie still had a life to live, a person to be. Yet, she was the one risking that.

"Lucie, I'm starting to realise how terrible this idea is," Eliza sighed. "It will never work, and it's risking your life—".

"Stop it, Elizabeth." Lucie warned, gripping a tight hold on her arm.

Eliza showed a fake smile, acting like the air sparked her interest to avoid Lucie's glare. The reality was hitting her in sudden thoughts, and her gut said to go back, to forget the idea ever surfaced.

She had forever been the mischievous one of the two, the one who took risks and produced the plans.

Lucie was the one who begged her not to, who ran away at the smallest of challenges. She would never understand what had changed.

"I'm serious." Eliza said, watching as Lucie walked away. The maiden crossed the room and reached an arm into her satchel.

Eliza's fight mode froze as a hard object collided with the back of her head. A striking pain flooded through her, as she spun around in a rage.

"Lucie!" She yelled, watching the maiden's face show a tinge of regret. Eliza clasped her head and turned to the floor.

A book lay at her feet, as her blurring eyes focused on the title. 'The Maiden's Handbook'.

Bending down, she gripped the handbook and held it in the air. Lucie folded her arms, nodding to the novel.

"The Maiden's Handbook?" Eliza laughed. "It looks useful.".

"It will be," Lucie replied, "It was given to me when I first joined the royal court, as a rulebook.".

"You didn't need to hit me with it.".

"You were being foolish." Lucie said, "We both think we should not be doing this, which is precisely why we are.".

Eliza opened the handbook, glancing at the words inside. Chapter titles and formal fonts met her eye, hand-written by an unknown author. Smirking up at Lucie, she handed it back.

"I don't follow rules.".

"You do now; you're in my shoes," Lucie paused, "And I'm in your dirty ones.".

Lucie took the novel from Eliza's hand, dropping it into the satchel on her arm. Taking the hint, Eliza took the bag from her.

"This is it?" Eliza said, brushing the wig-hairs behind her ear. Lucie pulled her brown hairs over her face and fixed the collar on her shirt. Their plan was set, and there was no going back, without getting hit with a book.

Lucie's maiden outfit was slightly painful, but bearable. Eliza had never worn an outfit so elegant before, with its countless layers and glistening crystals, Lucie's dress made her look like a first-class courtier.

"This is it." Lucie smiled, reaching out her hand for Eliza's. She held it in her own, and gripped tighter realising that both hands were trembling like snow-struck leaves.

Eliza had been reckless, but this would be the wildest thing she had ever done. A strong will surged within her, masking the feelings of fear. Whatever it was, something forced her to push on.

"Remember; keep your head low, don't interact with guards, and don't be near The King." Lucie warned.

"What if he recognises me?".

Lucie had pulled out a metal tray, placing it atop of the satchel in Eliza's hand. It covered it well, until Lucie began placing a silver cup and plate on the wobbling tray.

"That is what I would fear; he's been hunting you down for months." Lucie said. "Thankfully, he never acknowledges the ladies-in-waiting.".

The satchel tucked beneath the tray, and her disguise perfected, Eliza prepared to set off. Lucie was right, she was not herself.

For what little time they had, she was a well-respected maiden who plastered on a smile.

"Remind me again, where is your room?" Eliza asked, as they walked over to the tower door.

She knew Lucie's room was in the depths of the castle but had never thought on exactly where. The kingdom itself was gigantic, like a single dungeon cell could be the size of her house.

"You go through the back, up the staircases, and there you find The King and Queen's quarters. My room is downstairs from there." Lucie sighed, opening the tower door.

With a final glance, she walked out towards the staircase. The stone echoed beneath her heels, and the tray trembled in her hands.

Dawn fluttered out to join her, stopped by Lucie slamming the door half-shut, leaving enough space to peek out.

"Goodbye." Eliza whispered, "I will return, I promise.".

"You swear?".

"Solemnly.".

Eliza started walking down the spinning stairs, the gown flouncing at her feet. Lucie's shaking smile was the last of what she saw, before the tower door shut, and she was alone.

'You're Lucie now, you must be.'.

Even if it were not hers, she felt proud in the ladylike uniform. She thought of where she was to go, and what she had to do.

Working underneath Richard's wife, she did not know what to expect.

Rumours told her The Queen was sweet, and that she and The King admired one another greatly.

The people romanticised her like a summer rose, and her marriage to King Richard had lasted over fifteen years.

Eliza felt a chill down her spine, rushing down the stone steps. Faintness fell over her, and the spiralled staircase made matters worse.

The leather satchel trembled beneath her tray, making the cups on top shake. She prayed internally for them to balance, to silence.

Wobbling her way down the stairs, her foot stuck on a crack in the stone, tripping her over.

Eliza felt herself toppling forward, her hands loosening from the satchel and tray.

A flash of the silver cups flew past her eyes, before she only saw stone. She fell forward and struck the coarse stone, laying face-first on the stairs.

The solid surface pressed into her ribs, sending a sharp strike of pain. The cups and tray collided with the stairs, making a deafening bang.

Eliza instinctively clutched her ears. Her eyes were shut, and nose pressed against the stone.

"Ma'am?" A voice called out. Eliza groggily raised her head, to see two boots standing ahead of her. Two hands clutched hold of her forearms, slowly lifting her to her feet.

Standing onto shaking legs, she dusted down her gown. Her heart skipped a beat, as she reached for the wig on her head. It still sat firmly over her hair.

"Lucie?" The voice asked, "Are you hurt?".

Thomas McGlynn stood ahead of her, smiling in pride. His face looked softer than before, as he stood like a literal knight in shining armour.

Eliza scoffed, watching as his face fell. The sudden courtesy was strange, like he was a new man entirely.

'Lucie, you're Lucie now,'.

Thomas reached for her hand, taking it in his own. He looked up at her in bright assurance.

"Come with me, I can take you to a doctor," Thomas said, "You'll be safe with me."

'Dramatic,' Eliza thought, wincing with second-hand embarrassment. *'Even Lucie never knew why he cared about her, he just did, didn't he?'.*

"Forgive me," Eliza replied, in Lucie's dainty tone. "I lost my footing, but I am fine.".

That was a lie. The pain in her lungs made her head shake, while Thomas' face became a long-sighted blur.

"No! Forgive me!" Thomas mumbled, giving a half-hearted smile. "I mean to say, sorry.".

'Fool.' Eliza thought.

Nodding, she walked around him and continued down the steps, lifting the tray and cups.

When Thomas had his back turned, she scooped up the satchel and hid it again.

Thomas moved to her side and walked downstairs alongside her. His jolly attitude returned, as he opened his mouth to speak.

"I can walk myself down, thank you." Eliza said. It was agonizingly annoying to be nice to him, and she could understand why Lucie believed that the guards were good. They would have been nice to Lucie.

Thomas froze on a step, and she could sense him gazing after her. Eliza continued walking, while he did not.

"Oh, I see." Thomas answered, disheartened. He followed down the stairs five steps behind her, mumbling to himself.

Turning back, she gave Thomas one last look. His face was fallen to the ground, as he mumbled and scolded himself. Opening the tower door with her free hand, she left the tower.

"He's still an arrogant *toad*," Eliza whispered, as a reminder to herself.

Reaching the outdoors, the cold breeze hit her face, and the wind blew her blonde-hairs through the air. The winter had indefinitely reached the town, as the days got darker than before.

"Good morning, madam." A familiar voice greeted. Captain Edward stood behind her, with a proud smile. "Did I permit you to enter?".

"P-Permit?".

"I never noticed you enter the tower," Edward said, "It was to deliver essentials, presumably?".

"Yes.".

Eliza was at a loss of what to say. There was an intelligent tone in his words, and she prayed that he did not see through her, that he knew.

"I see," Edward murmured, "I mean no harm to you, but there was some trouble this morning.".

Eliza kept her head low, nodding into the satchel. The echoing steps of Thomas could be heard from the tower, as he backtracked to lock her tower room door.

"Indeed, I heard the commotion." Eliza said.

Her heart worried that she had made a mess of things, that she had ruined the plan before it begun. There was no denying that Edward was a strange one, for she could not sense if he were oblivious, or extremely self-aware.

"I suggest you return to the castle with haste, and be careful," Edward warned, "You never know who could be wearing a disguise.".

She felt her chest sink. He truly was the most confusing man she had met, the most unreadable of characters.

"Sorry?".

"The assassin, they wore a hood; a disguise." Edward said, "I advise you be cautious, until we arrest the vigilant.".

"Yes," Eliza muttered, "Yes, of course.".

In an awkward spin, she stepped away from the knight. Her feet sped along the grass, and she never gave a final glance.

'I've broken a rule already,' Eliza thought, *'Don't talk to knights.'.*

In the first few moments of their plan, she had fallen down the steps, spoken to two knights and almost shattered the silver tray.

She entered through the gardens, proud and tall like she knew where she was headed.

Once again, she was mesmerised by the majestic flowers that existed there, each holding its individual colours, marks, and stories.

Eliza made a mental map of the castle, using what she knew and what she had learned from Lucie. She made a note to not let herself become revealed, and simply act like Lucie would.

'Only if it were that easy.' She thought.

The large doors of the castle were ahead, with two knights on stand-by. Lowering her head, she skipped through the back entrance.

Entering through the doors, she kept her head low and back tall. The tray trembled in her shaking hands, clinking with the silver.

Her muscles strained as she held on tight to them, careful not to repeat her mistakes. The corridors felt longer as she skipped through them, thinking of the last time she had passed the walls.

The memory of that day gave her a daunting chill down her spine.

"To your right, up the stairs," Eliza whispered, repeating it under her breath. No sooner than she said it, the staircase appeared in front of her, glistening in gold and royal décor.

Her feet moved efficiently down the halls, as her gown flounced out ahead. The corridors were deserted, the only sound her own breathing.

The two doors of The King and Queen's quarters appeared, and she knew where she was headed in a heartbeat.

She met the Queen's quarter's door before she could find herself any unwanted acquaintances.

Taking a huge breath in, Eliza tried to knock the door, knocking with her right hand, and holding the tray in her left.

Her knock made such a faint sound with her shaking hands, and she knocked again, a little too loud.

A shuffling came from inside the room, and a few inaudible whispers to match. A click came from the lock.

The tall door pulled open, revealing a sour-looking woman.

"It is about time *you* appeared, Lady Benson.".

7

Royalty and Roses

Elizabeth stood motionless, keeping her head low. The sour-faced woman had let her in, eyeing her with beady eyes.

"Were you supposed to be on duty today, Miss Benson?"

"I was..." Eliza paused, "...Ma'am.".

"*Lady Theresa*, to you." The sour woman objected. "Goodness, you have lost your manners and your posture.".

Lady Theresa marched toward her, raising a wrinkling hand to her chin. She forced her head upwards, and her shoulders back.

Eliza already loathed the woman. Her sour face, her long wrinkles, her entitled manners. She was horrid, no doubt.

'No surprise she works for The King.' Eliza thought.

There was a keen sense that the woman hated her, or Lucie, too. Lady Theresa scowled at her like she was a stubborn child.

'She's old enough to be my ancestor.' Eliza thought.

Eliza remembered the satchel in her hands, and carefully raised the handle of the bag with her hidden index finger, covering it with the tray.

"A word of advice for you all," Lady Theresa announced, turning her back to Eliza and looking to the other two maidens.

"This town is facing threat, from witches to assassins." The woman began, "Furthermore, rumours are surfacing the castle, regarding our King and Queen. You must not speak of this to any outsiders, to maintain the royal reputation. Are we clear?".

All three maidens nodded, and silence filled the room. Giving a final nod, Lady Theresa swept out of the room, the door slamming behind her.

"Dear me, that was quite a show." A sweet voice spoke. "Lucie?".

Eliza's eyes perked up, meeting that of the two maidens. One had crossed the room to her, with crystal-blonde hair bouncing in her stride.

The girl took hold of the tray and placed it down on a chair. Eliza gently placed the satchel on top, clutching her hands behind her back.

"Hello." Eliza said, forcing a smile.

"You look like a ghost!" The maiden squealed, "Don't worry, we all know Lady Theresa's a wicked--".

"Cynthia! Enough from you!" A second maiden interrupted, gesturing toward Eliza. "Come here, we need to warm you up.".

The other maiden took hold of her shoulders, guiding her toward a steaming fireplace. Eliza felt safer in the arms of this other woman, than she ever could have with Lady Theresa.

"She's ice-cold, Mariah!" Cynthia called.

The Queen's chamber surrounded her, filled with grandeur. There was a wide bed with satin sheets, and cross-hatched windows with gold lining.

A large dome was overhead, and the walls were grey brick and wood. There were plush chairs, portraits, and exquisite flowers. The room felt too rich for Eliza to look at.

"Thank you." Eliza said, imitating Lucie's well-spoken tone. Mariah rested down beside her, crossing her legs. Eliza imitated her posture.

"We wondered where you disappeared to," Mariah said, "We feared the assassin had gotten to you.".

"No, I was only caught in the trouble." Eliza replied,

"I see," Mariah nodded. "Is that why you are trembling?".

With that, she stared down at her arms. Mariah was right, she was shaking. She gripped hold of her arms, and Mariah placed a gentle arm around her shoulder.

When the lady did that, she felt a strange comfort. Mariah and Cynthia seemed sweet, sweeter than she expected.

"Don't smother her! Lucie hates being smothered." Cynthia said from across the room, giggling to herself.

"I'm warming her up, Cynthia!" Mariah replied, "You two dress with little to nothing over your undergarments, you'll catch a cold!".

"Or the plague." Cynthia chimed in.

Eliza could not help herself from laughing. In the town, it was deemed as crude to even mention your own underwear.

The two maidens stared at her, then one another. Her laughter slowly died. She made a mental note not to laugh about undergarments.

She made sure to mentally note down who they both were and where she was, in case she did manage to get lost.

Turning around, she only then got a real look at both maidens. Mariah had waves of black hair and deep brown skin. She wore a welcoming smile and a tight grip on Eliza's shoulder. She looked in her late-thirties and wore the same gown Eliza and Cynthia did.

Cynthia was small and ditzy, like a music-box ballerina. She had waist-length, cream hair with a pale complexion and petite figure.

The maiden was standing at the window, gazing out in a dream. Mariah clutched a hand to her head, rolling her eyes.

"Cynthia! Your priorities might lay in your dreams, but we have work to do!" Mariah bellowed, causing Cynthia to flinch.

Eliza pretended to be cleaning the table beside her, dusting it down with her hand. *'What am I to do? What duties does Lucie have?'*.

"Sorry, that tower-witch has been plaguing my mind for days," Cynthia stated, "Why did they insist on using the tower for *her?*".

Eliza froze on the spot, and Cynthia clearly noticed her discomfort. 'Tower-girl' was the phrase that made her heart skip a beat.

Cynthia rushed over and threw her arms around her, pulling her into a sudden tight hug. Awkwardly, Eliza patted the girl on the back.

"Oh, Lucie, you must be distraught." Cynthia said, nodding like she knew completely understood. She did not, of course, but it was the thought that counted.

"Ah, yes." Eliza stuttered, edging away from the maiden, "Yes, I am".

Mariah had moved over to the window, staring out to the tower. She kept her gaze firmly on the sight, like solving a puzzle.

"You two were close, weren't you?" Mariah murmured, turning to her. "You and the witch.".

Eliza gulped, staying silent. Cynthia's hand still rubbed against her shoulder, with reassurance.

"She was a friend of mine, yes." Eliza nodded.

Mariah had scolded Cynthia for becoming distracted by the view, but her own eyes never left it. Eliza felt it worth saying this but bit her tongue.

Cynthia pulled her over to a plush seat, sitting her down beside her. Mariah followed, sitting on Eliza's right. She squished between the two, and she felt a sense of claustrophobia.

"The King's been restless, unstopping in his plans against the witch," Mariah said.

"Why? Spinner's been arrested, he could have her dead by dawn," Cynthia interrupted, "What is stopping him?".

"No one knows," Mariah shrugged, "Rumour tells that he's plotting against Spinner, that he's brewing something *worse* than execution.".

Eliza remained silent; her heart had stopped beating entirely. Her mind was restless, overwhelmed by their words.

"What could be worse than death itself?" Cynthia asked, waving her arms in the air. Mariah paused, leaning in with a whisper.

"Well, I heard that the reason she's still alive is the prophecy," Mariah whispered, "The prediction Mary Stanley made, before she was killed.".

"Oh, stop it!" Cynthia cried, covering her ears. "That prophecy gave me nightmares, dreadful ones.".

"It feels like this town is trapped in a nightmare," Mariah shook her head, "Yesterday, the tower-witch's father had his home ransacked by knights, and the old man was dragged out of his own home.".

With that, her eyes shot up. She turned to Mariah, with her eyes wide in alarm. Cynthia shrugged.

"It isn't without reason," The maiden replied, clutching her arms. "He was father to a witch, and you cannot say he was not suspicious-looking.".

With all the talk of her home ransacked, her father, her arrest; Eliza felt increasingly uncomfortable. Yet, she knew she needed to know more, needed to ask more. She jumped to face Mariah.

"What happened to him, George Spinner?" Eliza asked, trying to sound natural. Internally, her heart raced.

The thought of her sickly father, being dragged out of his own home. It sickened her to her stomach. Her father had done no wrong, to anyone.

"The guards dragged him out, holding him back while they searched," Mariah explained. "We could hear the old man's yelling from here, and it was not very…polite.".

"No, it was not *polite*," Cynthia laughed, "He warned the guards that if they hurt his daughter, he would beat them so badly they'd be hearing colours!".

'That's accurate,' Eliza thought, *'Still, he would stand no chance against ten armed guards, but he'd try.'.*

Eliza tended to focus on the fact that they were after her. The King's unruly victim was her. The criminal here was her. To go after her father was something separate entirely.

It was easier to know she was the one being mistreated, than knowing it was someone she loved, who was only guilty by association.

Cynthia started giggling once again, dancing around in circles. Mariah folded her arms.

"It's a grave mistake, to start her giggling," Mariah sighed, "She never stops.".

"Spinner's an old fool, isn't he?" Cynthia said, "He gets more crops thrown at him than he sells!".

Eliza's posture turned cold; she gave the girl a confused glare. Cynthia did not notice, giggling at her own remark, and Mariah chuckled along.

'Fool? Her father?' Eliza thought, prepared to unleash rage on the clueless girl. The entitled girl, who was oblivious to how hard her father worked just to put food on their table; oblivious to how much he cared.

Then, a reasonable side of her intervened the revenge-ridden thoughts. *'Remember; you are Lucie.'.*

When the laughter died down, there was a tension amongst the maidens. Eliza turned to them, eager to change the subject.

"Where is The Queen?" Cynthia asked, resting her head on her fist.

"Dealing with business, presumably.".

"And we still need to be here?" Cynthia whined, "We cannot be ladies-in-waiting, when there is no one to await commands from.".

Mariah opened her mouth to speak, as the doors to the Queen's chamber opened.

A young man strode in, well-dressed and well-postured. He bore curled brown hair a tanned face, with a dazzling smile.

"Darling!" The man called, strutting over to the maidens. Eliza shifted cautiously out of his way.

He walked over to Cynthia, who faked a short smile.

Mariah shook her head, not bothering to disguise her disgust. The man spoke with a strange accent, leaning down to Cynthia.

He scooped her into his arms, lifting her into the air. She faked a laugh, glancing over wide-eyed to Eliza.

"Gabriel, why are you here?" Cynthia spoke, through gritted teeth. There was a suspicion surrounding the pair, an underlying tension that Eliza could notice first-hand.

Sensing the maiden's discomfort, she opened her mouth to speak. Mariah elbowed her in the ribs, causing a sharp pain.

Gabriel's face fell, as he hesitantly dropped Cynthia to her feet. The girl wobbled, shooting her eyes from the ladies to him.

"I thought you would be *pleased*," Gabriel grumbled, strutting his way across the room.

He walked over to the nearest chair and sat down, resting his feet on a nearby stool. Eliza had never experienced socialising with royalty, but even she knew common courtesy. This man was clearly unbothered.

Cynthia skipped over to him, standing at the side of the chair. His hands supported the back of his head, as he casually relaxed.

The maiden's eyes were desperate, as her cheeks flushed a flaming red. She pulled on his arm.

97

"Please, you cannot be *here*!".

Gabriel chuckled to himself, ignoring her complains. He glanced over at Eliza, giving her a wink. Her face furrowed in obvious disgust, at his attitude and his vanity.

"Get out, you fool!" Mariah shouted, marching toward him. "What would The King say?".

"You are not permitted to speak to me like that," Gabriel growled, his snarl turning to a smirk. "*What would The King say?*".

Mariah shook her head, squinting her eyes at his irritable face. Eliza stood behind her, prepared to jump to defence, even if she barely knew either of them.

"I'll speak to you how I wish," Mariah spat, "How do you plan to explain to The King *why* you were intruding his wife's *private* room?".

The man froze, as he stood to his feet. He strolled toward Cynthia, muttering a few words under his breath.

Eliza could not hear what he said, but she picked up on one word. Mariah's jaw dropped, her face flushing in anger.

"What did you call me!?" She yelled, clenching her fists.

The man gave a cold smirk. Mariah started to march toward him, until she froze. Cynthia stood behind Gabriel, pleading with her eyes.

'Does she not want help?' Eliza asked herself, confused.

The three maidens stood staring at one another. Mariah nodded in a moment of mutual peace, before retreating. Gabriel scoffed.

He grabbed Cynthia's hand and looked up at her, direct into her eyes.

'There's something not right here, I know it.' Eliza thought, narrowing her eyes towards the man.

He gave her a sick feeling in her stomach, and a wicked aura followed his every step.

"Prepare yourself to leave, the marriage was arranged this morning." Gabriel whispered. "You will come with me, and the wedding will be at the proper time.".

Mariah gasped, placing her hand to her chin. She stared over to Eliza, who pretended to look equally as horrified.

"Arranged?" Cynthia asked, her face in disbelief. She whipped her hand from his like it was hot coal. "No, it is too soon!".

Then, Eliza's distrust in the man came to life. Before she could react, he grabbed Cynthia by the front of her gown. Eliza jumped up to intervene, but Mariah threw out her hand.

"*No?*" Gabriel laughed, sarcasm lining his tone. "You don't want to *marry* me, is that it?".

Cynthia shook her head, grabbing onto the front of his coat.

"I do! Listen I—".

"I have heard *enough* from *you*.".

Cynthia's face was sticky and scarlet as she cried. His face was scarlet with fury.

"Look at yourself," Gabriel scowled at her, "You look *disgusting*, for goodness' sakes.".

The maiden's short breaths hitched, as she gave a trembling nod. Tears swirled down her face, like a flowing river. Eliza had no experience with love, but her heart broke for the mistreated girl.

"I-I'm sorry," Cynthia whispered, "I'll do better, I will.".

"I *hope* so," Gabriel spat, "All the beautiful women I could be courting, and yet I stay with *you*. Do you realise that?".

"D-Don't say that, *please*.".

"It's *true*, you *owe* me for staying with you," Gabriel said, leaning in so his nose touched Cynthia's. "Look at Genevieve; an auburn-haired, ocean-eyed, small-figured…".

"Stop it, Gabriel." Cynthia cried, tears running freely down her face.

"Why, because you know I'm right?" Gabriel laughed, "What do you compare to her?".

Cynthia's eyes were puffed and red, buried inside her hand. She sniffled and cried out, trembling in his gaze.

Eliza turned to Mariah, who still held her arm out. The other maiden stood with tears in her own eyes, avoiding Eliza's staring.

"I-I care about you.".

"That's all?" Gabriel scoffed, "I care that my future wife won't be a teary-eyed mess, but we can't pick and choose, can we?".

Cynthia shook her head, plastering on a fake smile. Her face was blotched and red, and tears ran like a waterfall; but she smiled.

He smirked, slowly stepping away from her. Eliza could not understand it, why Cynthia allowed him to manipulate her, to play with her feelings.

Gabriel dug his hand into his coat, fumbling inside. At last, he pulled out a red rose, twirling the stem in his fingers.

The flower had lost petals buried inside Gabriel's coat, and was dying at the ends.

"Thank you." Cynthia smiled back, her voice breaking in the sentence.

With a proud nod, the man turned to leave. He gave one final look to Eliza and Mariah, before turning back to Cynthia.

"Prepare your belongings for our departure, I'm sure the ladies could assist you with that." Gabriel taunted.

'If this is romance, I would rather live without it.' Eliza thought.

Cynthia nodded to him, glancing towards Mariah. The man stared with a bright gleam in his eyes.

"I will, yes." Cynthia replied, clutching her hands to stop the shaking.

"Delightful." Gabriel said, with a dull tone. Cynthia shakily waved him goodbye, as he slammed the doors behind him.

"S-See? He's—" She took a long sigh, breath hitching and eyes watering, "Nice.".

Mariah's eyes had turned pitiful, and Eliza felt both the maiden's pain. She had assumed the ladies-in-waiting lived pristine-perfect lives, that love came naturally to them.

She then saw how wrong she was, very wrong. Cynthia braved a smile, but Eliza knew better.

'Her smile looks more believable than a genuine one.'.

Eliza knew that she had only known these maidens for an hour, or several, but she could feel their pain as clear as they felt it.

It was obvious the turmoil they suffered. She saw the panic in Cynthia's eyes, and the pain in Mariah's.

The only sound was Cynthia's sniffling. The maiden covered her mouth, while tears streamed down her face. She wiped them away faster than they came.

"He hates me, doesn't he?" Cynthia sobbed, "It is my fault, I cannot live up to his standard, his wants.".

'She blames herself for this?' Eliza thought.

Mariah sighed. She led the young girl over to the nearest chair, sitting her down. Eliza sat beside them, unsure of what to say.

"It is not your fault; he was the one that grabbed you." Mariah whispered, but Cynthia shook her head.

Cynthia took her head from her hands and stared at the floor. Her gaze looked as though it was set upon the rose, dead and broken on the floor. That made her wail even louder.

"Yes, it is my fault; I defied him." Cynthia cried, "But I can't leave this castle, it's all I have ever known.".

Eliza then understood. Cynthia was in an arranged marriage with Gabriel, but he was from a foreign place. That meant she would have to leave to live with him, against her will.

Mariah continued rubbing on Cynthia's back and combing her hair while Eliza sat thinking.

Her father never believed in a woman's subservience to a man, and never believed in any person being superior to their neighbour. With that, she was taught that no being was better than the other.

Now, looking at Cynthia's state, she was grateful for her father's unpopular views on society.

'That's reality.' She thought.

Cynthia's cries began to echo across the room, while her mumbling spoke of how she will never make a good wife. Mariah looked at Eliza, that same pity in her eyes for the young girl.

'Yes,' Eliza agreed to herself, *'Reality.'*.

8

Her Mother's Daughter

Eliza sat perched on the side of the bed, rubbing the sleep from her burning eyes. She felt miserable, enduring a burning fever all morning.

'Father needs you, Elizabeth,' That reasonable voice told her, *'For his own sake, and yours'.*

With gentle motivation, she pushed herself to stand, only to fall back onto the bed again.

"This will be *fun*." She scoffed; her voice gone low.

Her muscles ached, her head throbbed, her eyes were burning, and her face had gone a pale white. She had considered a fever, the plague and everything in between.

Lucie's maiden room was small and comfortable. It did not compare to Queen Grace's grand chambers, but it was fancier than Eliza's own dingy cottage.

The bed was short and plump, edged up against the brick wall. There was a miniature table with a rose lying upon it, and Eliza's locket.

'What is the fascination with roses?'.

There was a wooden wardrobe holding Lucie's gowns, and a barred window above the bed.

The room was simple, but undoubtedly Lucie's.

The night before, she had stumbled into the room and almost collapsed onto the bed. She pulled on one of Lucie's old nightgowns and fell asleep in seconds.

"Time to get out of bed, or else you never will again." Eliza pep-talked herself, pushing sore muscles into doing some good. Once again, she stood to her wobbling feet.

Her limbs struck pain with each move, as she marched toward the wardrobe.

'The Queen's out on business.' She thought, remembering the night before. A message had been sent that The Queen was dealing with urgent matters abroad that day and would not need their assistance.

Eliza knew exactly how she would spend the free time; with the one person she needed to see, even if it were for the last time.

"Lucie, your pristine taste is not helping me right now." Eliza moaned, swinging the wardrobe open. All the gowns were in shades of rosemary, lilac, honey, or turquoise.

At random, she pulled out one dress. It was an elegant blue, patterned in pink. The sleeves were puffed, and the waist fitted.

Eliza rubbed the silk texture between her fingers, holding it against herself. It made her look like a top-class 1617 woman.

'Perfect.' Eliza thought.

Lifting Lucie's comb, she brushed and clipped her hair into place. The wig sat across from her. Tugging it onto her head, it refused to comply.

"I hate *everything*." Eliza groaned, stretching out the wig with a loud snip. A crack echoed throughout the room, and the wig sat firmly on her head.

Then, she dabbed the red tint onto her lips, and rubbed the powder onto her face. The metal lids had been flung across the room, as she winced applying the sticky contents.

Looking back, it was concerning how long she and Lucie had spent nose-to-nose, analysing each other's features.

Eliza pushed out her lips and sucked in her cheeks, imitating Lucie with a slight laugh. She pulled the nightgown over her head and stepped into the gown. Raising it up, the front of the dress got stuck at her thighs.

"Give me *strength*." Eliza grunted, sighing to the air.

The gown made a crack, as she forced it upwards. In a quick tug, it found her waist.

The dress' tightness was suffocating. Gritting her teeth, she pinched the satin ribbon, gently pulling the fabric into a tie.

Eliza grabbed the locket from the table and clicked it around her neck, hiding it inside the dress.

She slipped on the same pair of heels from before and swung the door open wide. The firelit corridor was ahead of her, empty in the early hours.

She tip-toed outside, cautious for danger. The brick walls surrounded her, like they watched her every move.

Moving quietly, she made her way up the stairs to her right. Dust blew into her face, and distant voices spoke overhead.

The top of the staircase gave her two options, on her far left and right. One led up to the central castle, and the other led out to the village. She decided in a heartbeat.

No voices surfaced from the town, for the first time in forever. Eliza skipped up a stone staircase, leading to town.

There were no sounds of children playing games, or adults fussing over food. No people debating over the usual royal dramas; there was nothing but silence. All except for some.

Two giddy voices came from behind her, as a hearty laugh echoed from a hidden man's throat.

"Stop there, darling!" A voice called. Eliza froze, half-turning to see two strange-looking men stumbling towards her. One tall, with a face speckled in pimples and hair drenched in grease. The other small, with a crumb-filled red beard.

"What's a lady like yourself doing 'round here?".

The red-haired man's breath stank strongly of alcohol and bad taste, brewing a sick feeling in her stomach.

Eliza remained silent, turning, and walking away. Her quick breath blew out vividly with the wind, likened to the winter air. A grimy hand gripped her wrist, and she froze a second time.

The taller man gave her a grin, lined with rotting teeth. His fellow man laughed along. They nodded to one another, before the dark-haired man tightened his grip on her hand.

"The lady's lost her way, huh?" He laughed, leaning toward her. Eliza realised, it was not pimples on his face, but gory scars. "*Dear, oh dear.*".

Eliza shook her head. Fools in their town never once targeted her growing up, they only targeted well-off maidens. Unfortunately, they chose the wrong day, and the wrong lady.

"Take your hand *off* me".

"Or what?".

Eliza stared the man in the eyes, unmoving and direct. He scoffed to the red-haired man, laughing mockingly.

"Why don't you come with *us?*" The man smirked, snaking his hand out toward her.

"No.".

"It wasn't a *request*.".

Eliza focused her eyes on the man's own. She pretended not to see his arm, slithering toward her like a snake with its prey.

She bided her time, waiting on him to make the worst mistake of his life, as she knew he would.

His hand slithered around her waist, and landed on her mid-back, as he pressed his fingers against her.

"Do you know that the name, Lucie, means light?" Eliza asked, perfecting the sweetest tone she could master. The grease-haired man stared in confusion.

"And?".

Eliza gave him one, final look in his eyes.

"If you don't take your hand *off* me," She leant in, taking full advantage. "I can guarantee *you'll* be seeing it.".

His eyes went wide, as he shifted away. His friend tugged on his free arm, clearly uncomfortable with the situation.

"Trying to scare me, are you?" The man warned, pinching her skin with his hand, still on her back.

"I'm not trying to scare you," Eliza murmured, gazing down at his stomach. "But *this* will.".

In a swift kick, Eliza swung her leg into the man's ribs. Pressing the sharpest part of her knee into his lungs.

The man's entire frame rocketed forwards, and his hand left her waist faster than light itself.

He choked on air and spluttered widely, clutching his ribs. The other man grabbed onto him for support, ducking away from Eliza in horror.

"Oh, I'm sorry!" Eliza fake-gasped, covering her obvious laugh. "How foolish of me.".

The man's bloodshot eyes stared up at her, and his lip trembled on the edge of tears.

She reached out a soft hand to him, and he grasped it. To her surprise, that same smirk settled on his face.

"You've got a strong kick, for a *lady*," He drawled out. "Did no one ever tell you not to start *trouble?*".

Eliza pretended to giggle. She was most surprised at how his idiocy still trusted her, how he still attempted to test her.

"Yes, they did." Eliza paused, "They never said not to *punch* it.".

Eliza swung her fist out, aiming for the man's nose. A sensation of pain ran through her knuckles, as they collided with his face.

A small crack echoed, followed by the man's scream of agony. He grasped his grimy fingernails up to his face, as a fountain of blood ran from his nose.

"*You—*" The man cried out, shoving his greased finger toward her. "*You witch!*".

Eliza, by now, was unfazed by this insult and would have remarked on it, but she knew she had to remain incognito, for Lucie.

'You've made an excellent job of staying out of trouble.' Eliza laughed to herself.

The man lugged out breaths, scampering around like a horse on wheels. His red-haired friend had thrown his arm around the man's shoulder, carrying him away.

"*Move, Joe!*" The man whispered, into the injured man's ear. Broke-nosed Joe shook his head, trying to stand up, only to fall again.

"I'll get'cha for 'es, ya' dimwit!" Broke-nosed Joe slurred out, his speech drawled and mumbled.

"I am sure you will." Eliza smirked, leaning down to greet Joe's face.

Broke-nosed Joe's mouth crawled into a dirty snarl, and she heard him whisper about, 'beating her', and 'getting revenge'.

"Joe, she'll kill you!" The red-haired man whispered, "The lady's insane!".

'He's right,' Eliza giggled to herself, *'Unless Joe wants a broken foot to match.'.*

Broke-nosed Joe had a firm clench on his nose, blood running down past his sleeve and dripping onto the ground. Cursing insults and whining, they both started to hop away.

The two men scrambled to their feet, with Joe pressing his hand to his bloody nose. In an instant, they had disappeared around a brick wall.

Eliza laughed in the distance, the sound of her laughter no longer Lucie's, but instead her own deep tone.

Shrugging, Eliza walked along. She peered down to see that Lucie's dress now had a small tear from her kicking so far out.

The skirt had a nasty rip, revealing a white layer from underneath.

She knelt, folding the torn silk together. If anyone looked, they would know something was not right. If she had truly been Lucie, she would have had a tantrum over it.

Her eyes glazed the abandoned town. The Spinner cottage sat behind a wall, dusty and old. There was no sign of any residents, and the windows were all bolted shuts.

It was never particularly clean, but they tried. Now, it was ransacked.

Eliza had a sickly feeling, walking closer towards what was once her home. The empty village, her deserted home and the unnerving silence all sparked red flags.

Her shoes crunched against the winter leaves that lay flattened on the cobbled streets, and the wind blew the blonde wig clean out of her face.

'Back. Go Back.' Her mind warned her, *'It's not right here.'*.

Eliza got such chills, her fingers rushed to brace her forearm.

'It's not long after dawn, everyone could be avoiding the iced weather.'.

Eliza passed each house on her way, all of them had wooden barriers guarding their front doors. The sky was dark and cloudless, and the woods in the distance emphasised it, mystic and shadowed over.

Finally, she met the wall blocking her home. There were symbols, phrases and runes scribbled onto it, all in the messiest and unreadable handwriting, but a few words stood out.

'WITCHES'.

'HEARTLESS'.

'MONSTERS'.

Eliza's heart dropped inside her chest. That last word struck an impact within her, until she read the next piece of sprawled writing.

'LONG LIVE OUR KING.'

That sentence alone was enough to get her blood boiling. She felt a sensation spark within her chest, this time not of hurt, but of rage. Her face flushed crimson, as she spun and marched away.

The people despised her, yet they worshipped him. The brick wall felt sharp against her arm, as she passed with a fiery expression.

'Enough, Elizabeth,' She scolded herself, *'Bite your tongue.'.*

Dusting down her dress and straightening herself out, Eliza turned down the corner and journeyed on.

Her feet moved quick, that way she had to focus on walking, to make sure she did not walk into anything. That was one way to distract her mind.

Eliza stood in front of her cottage, scanning the pitiful scene. A window had shattered, by force.

Glass pieces scattered across the stone, falling onto the wooden frame of the house. She took a breath, walking up to the door.

Her hand hesitated before knocking. She wondered if she should be knocking at her own home.

Still, her hand froze in mid-air, with a bitter flood of nostalgia.

The door in front of her was the same one she saw every day for the past sixteen years of her life; why couldn't she knock on it?

Shaking herself straight, she gently pushed the door open. The door croaked and swung wide.

Her home's inside was like an endless void, dark and gloomy. The first smell that breached her nose was smoke; fire-induced smoke.

The house was empty from what she could see, like no one had lived there for a lifetime.

Smoke loomed the air, as she clutched her hand over her mouth. Once her vision cleared, she got a proper look inside her home.

There had been pieces of parchment, journals, clothing, and belongings discarded on the floor. Empty wood drawers had been yanked out of place, and the chairs were overturned.

Her eyes turned to the floor, noticing the mucky footprints and spill-stains from days-old soup.

'If father is living here,' Eliza thought, *'It must be unbearable for him.'*.

The door blew shut behind her, and darkness overshadowed her slowly like a bad dream.

Eliza felt it should be her first action to lift it up, to make things a bit tidier. Her knees cracked as she knelt, reaching out and grabbing hold. Satisfied, she was half-stood, when she froze.

Creak. The floor made a sound, and she knew before it happened.

Eliza turned around, her heart thundering like sonorous metal. A shadow of a person stood behind her, in that cold, desperate darkness.

A sword sliced through the air. Eliza screamed, stumbling backwards. Her heel stuck in a crack in the wood, and she tumbled backwards with a thud. With a bang, Eliza slammed against the floor, landing on her backside.

"*Wait!*" Eliza screamed, curling up into a ball. She froze on the frozen floor, preparing for the sword to strike, for the striking pain.

Nothing.

She trembled on the spot, and Eliza could feel the heat of her forearm against her face. Another moment passed; nothing had happened.

No intense pain, no tragic death; nothing.

Her hands shaking, she pushed herself up onto her elbows, shakily gazing upwards. The attacker was a blur, but their presence was strong.

To her shock, the blade was inches from her face. They held it in mid-air, frozen at the final moment. One wrong move, and that was it.

"Lucie Benson? No…" The voice croaked out, dry and pained. It was a voice she recognised, but not one she expected.

The shadowed attacker swung their sword away, and it made a metallic clunk as it hit the floor.

Eliza's breath cut short as she felt a warm, large hand connect with the side of her face.

The hand lifted her head up, and her dizzy eyes now met those of the stranger, who might not have been one at all.

"F-Father?" Eliza whispered, her voice breaking. Her throat burned, but to say that name again; she would have suffered the pain a hundred times over.

Father and daughter were seconds away from one another, seconds away from him making the worst mistake he ever could.

He stood, stepping over her and reaching towards the table. She saw him scratch two pieces of shining metal together, his hands fumbling in the air.

A flame sparked, and he raised it to the fireplace. It blazed and lit up, creating a new light in the room.

George Spinner trembled above her, but he did not look the same.

He bent over her, offering out his hand. Hesitantly, she grabbed it. Father and daughter's hands conjoined, hers light and soft, his rough and scarred.

Either way, both reunited, after thinking they had saw the last of one another.

He pulled her up from her knees to her feet, and she gripped his shoulder for support.

There was a strong pain in her ankle after twisting it from falling, but none of it mattered anymore, no pain in the world could have.

"Lucie, I-I'm sorry," George Spinner stammered, grasping her hand.

His hair had dark streaks of grey, and his face lined with dead scars. He bore puffed eyes and a drained pale face.

Even his nose was covered in dirt and soot. It made her think of a part of her life she wished she could forget.

Not saving her mother had been his biggest regret, and annually on her death date, he fell into a pit of suffering.

He denied food, took long walks in the graveyard, and slept no longer than an hour each night.

Yet, even while the man's heart was breaking, his smile did not once.

"Father, it's me." Eliza whispered. She clutched his hand tighter, firmer. His jaw fell, and all the lines on his face straightened.

"Elizabeth." George murmured. He shook his head, like what he saw was not real at all. "*H-How?* I—".

He paused, wasting no time to throw his arms around her. Eliza held tightly onto him, and the two shared an embrace neither wanted to let go of.

He squished her inside his arms. Eliza's heart sent a bittersweet feeling through her, a mixed of sadness and joy, hope and regret.

Eliza pulled her arms away, smiling uncontrollably. Her father hesitantly let go of her, instead holding her hands in his.

"Lucie and I swapped places, she's in the tower and I'm acting as a maiden. I came here the moment I could." She stumbled over words, trying to create a quick summary.

George Spinner seemed at a loss for words, shaking his head with a smile. He opened his mouth once or twice to speak, but no words had come out.

Her father led her over to the standing chair and gestured for her to sit. He bent down beside her and reached for his sword, which lay on the floor. His hands shook as he carried it over to a hold.

"You—" He paused, "You never should have sacrificed yourself for me, at the trial. You should have let them beat me; you should have run.".

"I couldn't have run," Eliza said, "And if I did, they would have killed you.".

"I'm an old man, Elizabeth," George replied, with warning. "You have a life ahead of you, I've had one behind me. You must escape while you can, flee this town and never return.".

Averting her eyes, she stared around the small room. Even after the damage, it still felt familiar.

It felt the same way it did ten years ago when she sat at that same table, mixing herbs and leaves together in a mix-pot, whispering short-sighted promises that she would find a cure.

A cure for her father's life.

"I cannot flee, father," Eliza whispered back, "I swore to Lucie that I would return, in exchange for her kindness. If I do not, they will kill her for helping me.".

"Yet, *you* would live.".

Eliza stopped. She knew he was right.

"No, I can't do that to her.".

"You can't make the same mistake I did!" George yelled, quick tears welling in his eyes. "She, she wanted to leave this town, but I was naïve, I said they would never come for her. *And--*".

"She?" Eliza asked, shocked at the sudden outburst. "My mother?".

George winced, with his eyes bloodshot. Tears ran down his face, and he clenched his fists.

"I-I'm sorry, I *just—*" His voice broke. "I can't fail you both, *I can't.*".

"You never could, father.".

"Yes, I *can*, and I *have.*" He took a hitching breath. "I failed as a husband, but I am not failing as a father; I can't let you die knowing I could have stopped it.".

Eliza turned to the floor. Deep down, she wanted to agree, she wanted to run, she wanted to live.

Still, if she lived, Eliza knew she would never outlive the fact that the one friend she had, the one person who cared had died in her place.

"I'm sorry, father," Eliza said. "Lucie risked herself for me, to help me. I won't turn my back on someone like that, even if it kills me.".

Her father's face fell, as though the hope he had been clinging to was stolen.

A tinge of regret flooded inside her heart, but her decision stood firm, even when she was not.

"You are your mother's daughter, through and through." He said, barely above a whisper. "If she saw you now, proud would be an understatement.".

Eliza smiled, through equally teary eyes. A silence filled the room, louder than noise could have been. George Spinner rested on the opposite chair, staring into the distance.

"How have you been, father?" Eliza prompted, eager to change the subject.

He wiped his tears away, shrugging. It hurt her to see him so lost, going from raging tears one moment, to a void silence the next.

"Fine, fine." Her father mumbled. Scratching the back of his head.

'That's a lie,' Eliza thought to herself, *'He's been anything but fine.'.*

The casual, slow conversation felt wrong. Eliza tried to distract him, to take his mind from the thought of her mother. It was simply too late for that.

"You look strange as Lucie," Her father commented, "You don't look like Elizabeth at all.".

"That is the idea," Eliza smirked, "It's incognito.".

"Why?" Her father croaked, rubbing forcefully at his eyes. "What is the use in disguising yourself as Lucie, escaping the tower, if not for escape?".

Eliza froze, maintaining a poker-face. She had to repeat the question a few times in her head, struggling for an answer.

"To see you, the world, everything once more." Eliza sighed, "You don't realise what you have, how much it's worth, until it is gone.".

"That's true." Her father froze, shutting his eyes. "I'm sorry.".

"For what?".

The wind blew outside the cottage, and winter rain pounded against their weak windows.

"I don't know what to say to you, what is there to say?" George whimpered, "Is there anything to speak of?".

"Yes, there is. Speak of anything, I'll listen to anything." Eliza prompted. "I want to make the most of what time we have, what time I have. I cannot waste that time being sad, I won't allow myself to.".

Even with the light, dark shadows roamed over them both.

"Yes, I—" Her father paused, reaching a hand to his mouth.

Her father coughed up into his grimy hand, his throat aching dry. His breaths were screechy and strained, like an injured animal screeching for rescue.

Eliza knew how bad his fits could get all too well. She pushed herself back from the table, as the chair screeched against the floor, falling behind her with a thud.

He was losing his breath, slamming his fists into the table, and croaking her name with every breath.

"E-Elizabeth...".

Her footsteps slammed against the floor as she threw up her dress and ran over to the medicine cupboard. Eliza threw her knee onto the ledge, and gripping the wood of the cupboard, climbed upwards.

Her father's wheezing increased, as he were doubled over on his chair, gasping for breath. He spluttered out phlegm and blood, as it foamed from his cracked lips.

She knocked over glass bottles with a clank. Each were labelled in parchment, as clinking bottles hit off one another, swirling faint-coloured liquid inside.

"Aha!" Eliza exclaimed, grasping a bottle at the back.

It was a green-tinted makeshift cure, which had strangely been cast aside to the back.

She knocked one bottle to the floor, and it shattered into small glass pieces with a bang. Stepping over it, she sprinted across the room.

Eliza unscrewed the cork from the bottle and grabbing his face in her hands, forced it down his throat.

He gagged as the medicine ran its course, his mouth wide and eyes strained shut.

The bottle was soon empty, leaving only the stained remains of the formula. Eliza squeezed her father's mouth shut, tilting his head back.

Truth be told, she was never sure if the self-attempted cure did actual good, but it washed down his sickness.

His coughing fits only got that bad if he had not taken her medicine, which somehow worked.

Her father swallowed the medicine with a loud gulp, Phlegm and blood still hung from his bottom lip, and he wiped it away onto his dirtied sleeve.

"T-Thank you.".

"You haven't been taking my medicine, have you?" Eliza confronted; her face gone stern. Her father shrugged, mumbling wordlessly to himself.

'It's never been that bad,' Her mind said, *'Why would he not simply take the medicine? Why be so frustrating?'*.

George Spinner remained silent, meddling with his hands. She knew that he knew there were no more excuses, that he had made no effort to cure himself at all.

"Why not take the medicine, why allow yourself to suffer?" Eliza pleaded, desperation creeping in her voice. "How can I help someone who doesn't help themselves?".

His eyes had darkened. George Spinner stared endlessly to the floor, unable to work up a response. Eliza knew, he couldn't give an excuse.

"Listen, Elizabeth—" He took a deep breath, with a dreaded cry in his voice. "What good would it have done?".

Eliza's face creased, as she stumbled backwards. *'What good?'* She thought, *'Has he gone positively mad?'*.

"What *good?* The good of keeping you *healthy, alive!*" Eliza spat, fighting back tears.

Eliza would admit, the medicine did taste revolting, but it was a chance he should have been willing to take.

She was no expert pharmacist, but she studied, and even if the medicine did not cure him, it held off the blood and excess.

"Do you not *understand,* my girl? I lose your mother, I thought I lost my only daughter; I had no one in this town! Those folks threaten me, they think of me as a fool." George Spinner pleaded.

Her father, the man she idolised, had succumbed to carelessness for life.

She knew how he felt equally, but for a different reason. Her father sighed, hitting his palm against his head.

He was never a violent person, he tried to please everyone. All and any frustration he had he directed at himself.

"I do understand, but--" Eliza paused, "I *can't* let you do this to yourself.".

Her father shook his head, wiping his running nose against his sleeve. He continued to cough and splutter, clearing his throat.

"And I you," George said, "I cannot let you give up your life, when you had the chance to save it.".

Those words struck her, in a surge of realisation. He was right.

She wanted him to care for his life, he wanted her to do the same. In the end, neither would have their way. She nodded, sniffling in the dark.

Eliza reached and grabbed his hand, squeezing it tight. The aura had changed so suddenly, from frustration to a strange, uncertain comfort.

"Father, promise me you will take that medicine." Eliza begged, smiling despite her sticky, scarlet face.

He turned to her, sighing heavily against her hand, before nodding.

The two remained silent for a moment, smiling with stained faces. Eliza noticed how, minus her wig and Lucie's attire, they looked so similar yet so unsimilar.

"I know I cannot convince you, but perhaps this might," Her father said, running over to the fireplace.

He grumbled as he knocked things over, fussing with his hands until he spotted something. Reaching across with a grunt, he grabbed hold of it.

She watched as he dusted the object down, handing it to her with a soft grin.

It was an old, dusty journal. Two initials were carved into the cover, as she carefully traced her fingers over the dips. 'A.S'.

"Anne Spinner." Eliza whispered. "How did you hide this from the knights?".

"It was well hidden," George murmured, "Your mother hid it, years ago.".

Her father nodded to her, encouraging her to open it. She flicked to the first page, finding a small introduction handwritten in ink.

'This is the diary of Anne Spinner, yours truly.'.

"She told me to give this to you, when the time was right." Her father mumbled, nodding to her. "I don't know what is written in there, but you deserve to know.".

Eliza turned a page, opening to an outdated entry from her mother's own words. Her mother had the prettiest handwriting, she noticed, and the first letter was brief.

"Have you read it?" She asked. Her father shook his head.

"No, she made me swear that I wouldn't.".

Eliza laughed, as she traced each word. With one final breath, she started to read her mother's words.

Dear, Elizabeth

Welcome to the journal of me. I am writing this journal in the hopes that, with whatever the future holds, you can look back on it. Right now, you are no larger than a shoebox, and only a few days old. In your time, I hope you are well, wherever you are.

Sorry for that brief introduction, I am not great with them nor writing itself. However, I will try, and pray that it does not sound ridiculous.

Sincerely, despite the awkwardness,

A. S

Eliza's heart swelled with the same pride and love she knew her mother must have felt.

Her mother's entry, awkward as it was, had given her a strange wave of nostalgia; for something she never had.

"Thank you." Eliza whispered, looking up to her father. She shut the journal closed, clutching it closely to her chest.

In that moment, Eliza knew that if she were her mother's daughter, proud would be an understatement.

9

Silent Night

Eliza had cried to sleep that night. She had lost all track of the days, and would never have knew what the day meant, if her father had not said.

'What a celebration, it is.'.

In a few minutes, she would be officially seventeen. If it had been a usual year, she would be lying in her own bed, her father making his yearly jokes; both together again.

It was not a normal year, it had to be the worst of them all, and the last.

Reluctantly, she had slugged back to the castle and snuck in past the maidens, into Lucie's room as the sun started to set.

She did not bother going to find dinner, or eat at all, besides the bread her father had provided.

Eliza waited patiently, watching for hours as the sun set, becoming replaced with swallowing darkness.

She knelt on the top of Lucie's bed, resting her arms on the windowpane, and staring at the moon.

"Seventeen years," She whispered to herself, a tear falling from her eye. "And it went by in the blink of an eye.".

Her heart ached in the strongest way, hoping that the force of time would swoop her away to a simpler stage.

A time in which she had not realised how fortunate she was.

126

Eliza's eyes glimmered in the moonlight, emulating the stars above. When she was gone, she knew the world would not change.

That each night, the moon would still fall, and the sun would still rise. The difference was that she would not see it.

"The world will still turn," Eliza murmured, tears spilling from her eyes. "And it'll miss me, dancing in the rivers like gravity couldn't stop me.".

She shook herself to reality, rubbing her face red. Her eyes still wandered out the window.

The city covered and surrounded by a deep, evergreen forest. Then, the trees of the left caught her eye. Through the bronze gate, there was a graveyard.

It started at the bottom of the hill and as the trees separated, leading into the woods, continued by high mountains, where only the richest deceased were buried.

'That's where mother is.', She thought, her eyes wandering to the satchel. It held the diary, her mother's.

She bent down and picked the journal up, tracing her fingers delicately along the spine. The cover was harsh and ripped, but other than that the accounts, the important parts, protected.

Anyone watching her would be disgusted, seeing a girl cuddling an old, ruined book. To her, it was much more than that.

This was her mother's identity. It was the only source that would allow her to uncover who she was.

Eliza knew any reasonable person would have read every diary entry in one night, if they were genuinely curious, but she wanted to savour it.

She wanted to preserve the anticipation, the knowledge, for as long as humanly possible.

She turned back to the graveyard, breaching the window open to see it clearly. She knew what she wanted to do, but this time, she was doing it as herself, as Elizabeth.

The blonde wig, she had scrapped hours ago; due to the unbearable itch it caused her head, and it would not be worn again that night.

Tip-toing in the frigid night, she reached for a silver goblet of water, pouring it out onto her bare hand.

The cold liquid spilled through her fingers and onto the floor. Hesitantly, Eliza splashed the water over her face.

Beige-tinted droplets ran from her face, washing off the powder and tints.

Eliza rubbed the excess makeup off with her sleeve, revealing her own greying face.

Looking up into the mirror, she saw herself. Her own azure eyes, thin face, slight mouth. Not Lucie, not anymore. Instead, Eliza.

She ran her fingers through her ivory hair in the mirror, pulling it up into a tie. She knew she was taking a risk, with no disguise or self-defence, but it was the closure she needed, for her sake.

Whether it was an identity crisis or a birthday celebration, it felt necessary. She reached for a white blouse, sat at the edge of the bed.

The abandoned tight gown and wig lay on the floor, curled together in a ball. Finding a light-blue skirt in the wardrobe, she pulled it out.

Eliza quickly ran it up her waist, buttoning it on the side. It fit like a glove; unlike the restrained, awful gown she wore.

She pulled the white shirt over her freezing back and shoulders, buttoning it at the front and tucking it into the skirt.

It was long-sleeved, and the skirt ran past her ankles, beating the December weather.

'This is one way to celebrate becoming seventeen,' A voice said, *'Visiting an abandoned grave, studying your deceased mother's diary...'.*

"Shush." Eliza mumbled, shivering in realisation of the emptiness she spoke to. She turned to assure there were no hidden forces, or ghosts, watching from another dimension.

'Obviously not'.

Swiftly, she grabbed her satchel by the string. A detailed hood was inside Lucie's wardrobe, and she wasted no time pulling it over her head. The hood covered her head-to-toe, as a noteworthy disguise.

Pulling the room door open, she slipped into the corridor. The hall was deserted, without a soul in sight.

A pig-like snore came from down the corridor, echoing through the brick walls.

Eliza shut the door, tip-toing onto the solid stone. In a dash, she sprinted over to the stairs.

The silence sent a shiver down her spine. Her hand reached down, clutching the satchel, and feeling for the book inside.

Her feet travelled speedily up the staircase and she slowly, silently unscrewed the lock at the door.

It made a cracking sound, making her freeze and seize up. She could hear no one, and no one should have heard.

Once again, Eliza crawled through the door, her stomach pressing up against the wood.

The chances she was taking were riskier than anything she had ever done before, except the plan.

Her feet treaded against the hard floor, striking the freezing of a muscle and pain in her foot.

Eliza had learned to ignore pain a long time ago, but that was raw and aching, making her yelp out in agony.

'You best hope no one here sleepwalks.', Her mind said.

Taking a breath, she skipped up the steps leading to the outdoor village. The first thing that struck her was the icy-cold air, breezing against her face.

'Better than the calls of a dirty, stumbling man.'.

The village was coarse, empty. The moonlight highlighted the squat little homes, and stars pepped the sky once more.

Eliza stared up in awe, captured by the sight.

Her eyes wandered to the creaking gate to her left, shadowed by vine. The gate sat behind layers of brick houses and cobbled streets.

Taking a sharp breath, Eliza stuck out her foot and began to tread quietly across the abandoned town.

She pulled on the strings of her hood, clutching it over her face.

A chill went down her spine, and she felt strangely paranoid of her surroundings. The sky was pitch black, and she could only see the outline of where she headed.

'Quiet, quiet, quiet,' Her mind repeated, *'Silent, silent, silent.'*.

Eliza brushed past each home, walking direct towards the graveyard. The castle was on one side of her, the village on the other. Her body seized up, as Eliza peered upwards to see if there were knights on standby.

'If they look once, you're dead,' Her mind said, *'Dead-er'*.

Immediately, she quickened her pace, shuffling past each home. The cape of her hood waved behind her, rising in the frigid air.

She felt a freezing sensation in her nose, like it had turned into an icicle with the weather.

Her eyes rested on the rusted gate in front of her, and she breezed past the barrels and boxes at the edge of the town.

Hesitantly, she rested her hand on the metal. Eliza shrieked as the faulty gate swung her forward with a creak.

She turned her head to the side, squinting her eyes in the dark. Not a person was in sight.

Shivering, she took a step into the graveyard grass. It crunched beneath her, and she closed the creaking gate behind her.

Stone graves could be seen in front, stretching across for miles, but straight north there was a large grass hill.

The muck in the grass stuck groggily to her shoe, making Eliza's scowl more vivid. Wiping it on the grass, she continued through the muck, walking to the right.

She knew where her mother's grave was situated, after visiting hundreds of times before. Towards the back, on the nearest right.

She strolled across, reading some names on each of the graves. She recognised a few recent ones, recalling certain deaths from within the village.

Eliza stopped as one name caught her eye. It was a neat grave, and a few sinking lilies sat on it. The surname was familiar, and she bent to read.

'HERE LIES HENRY MCGLYNN.

BELOVED FATHER OF THOMAS AND CLARA MCGLYNN.

HUSBAND OF MARGARET MCGLYNN.'.

Thomas McGlynn. His father's grave. From what Eliza knew, his father had died out in the war.

She recalled how, when they were young, Thomas would forever claim that he would be as brave and glorified as his father one day. He said that they would regret picking on him.

Ten-year-old Eliza laughed aloud, taunting that he was afraid of his own shadow. That remark got her a deserved whack in the face.

Shaking the memories away, Eliza carried on with her journey. There were other recognisable names, one of which was that of an old man that owned the library.

Eliza smiled, seeing her mother's grave in the distance. She walked over with her eyes on the satchel, unbuckling it and pulling out the journal inside.

If any time were best to read a chapter, this was it.

Eliza loomed over the grave, shining in the tree-divided moonlight. The words carved onto the grave were like that of the other deceased.

'HERE LIES, ANNE SPINNER.

BELOVED MOTHER OF ELIZABETH SPINNER.

WIFE OF GEORGE SPINNER.'.

Kneeling, she clasped her hands together, closing her eyes. When she did that, she could swear it was her mother's face she saw, in the void dark of her closed eyes.

The nurturing face, blazing blue eyes. It could have been imagination, but still comforting, real or not.

"Mother, I *wish* you could hear me." Eliza whispered. A gust of wind blew across her face, like a hand clutching her cheek. "Perhaps you can.".

She opened her eyes, looking down at the grass beneath her. Her father told her years ago, her mother had not lay buried inside that grave, it was instead a sign of remembrance and respect.

That was another source of evidence to Eliza's young self that her mother faced execution.

It felt strange to speak to the dead, and she had forever been sceptical of it, but the comfort that they could be listening was enough.

Eliza stared around her, in the pitch-black dark. From what she could see, all the other graves had been abandoned for weeks, years even.

No one seemed to care for their lost loved ones, until their own time came.

She stared at the journal in her lap, flickering through the pages. To her surprise, there were few accounts in the entire book. It ended a quarter of the way through the pages.

Eliza found herself on the second diary entry, and running her finger over the letters, began to read.

Dear Elizabeth,

Congratulations! You have made it to the second page. Yes, the duties of motherhood have kept me on my toes for a while, but now I am back updating you, and yes, you are most welcome. As an infant, you seem too sweet, too cute, but I see your father's mischievous glint in your eyes, and I will be the damsel chasing after you both!

I do hope you get his intellectual mind, and not my clumsiness instead. For now, you are utterly your father's daughter.

I fear I shall become forgotten, for you have no interest in me! Alas, I love you dearly, despite the fact your father is much preferred.

The journal's paper pages blew in the wind, and she closed it tightly shut to preserve it. With a gentle hand, Eliza sat the diary back into the satchel on her hip.

"For what it is worth, I love you, mother." Eliza mumbled.

Eliza smiled to herself, tracing over the words, 'love you dearly,'. From her mother's account, it shows that she had always adored her father.

Still, she was sure that she would have loved her mother as much, had things been different.

The wind blew over her once more, her hood sitting firmly on her head.

She shut her eyes closed, clutching her hands together and bowing her head in the frozen darkness.

"Mother, please keep father safe, guide him," Eliza whispered, nodding to the grave. "While and when I cannot.".

Eliza paused, she knew there was more to say, but no ways to summarise it. She sighed.

"Please, guide me too. I know I cannot change the inevitable but help me to embrace it." Eliza mumbled, "And, when I reach what the other side holds, I suppose we will finally meet.".

She pressed her hand onto her knee, standing up. It was peaceful, standing there. She felt comforted, and even surrounded by darkness and death, she felt at home.

Her eye caught an empty spot of grass beside her mother's grave.

'That's where my headstone should be, next to my mother,' She thought, *'I'd like that.'*.

It was strange for her to think, a seventeen-year-old planning her death. Still, she knew well that she had no choice, no changing the inevitable.

A whimpering noise echoed throughout the graveyard. Eliza stopped dead, spinning around to her left.

It came from behind the hill, the sound of movement.

'The gate was open,' Her mind said, *'I should have known, someone was here before me.'.*

The noise lowered, giving her time to breathe. The crunching sound was still there, but no noise.

Then, the inaudible voice raised a second time. It was a human voice. The person was mumbling to themselves, speaking aloud.

Eliza sucked in a breath, her feet dragging her towards the sound. She knew if caught, it was over for her.

Yet, curiosity pulled her closer. The grass scrunched beneath her feet, and she left her mother's grave.

'Who would be in a graveyard this time of night?' Eliza thought.

She wandered in the cemetery, like what your worst nightmares would envision of a witch. The hood loomed over her eyes, her face drained and grey, bone-like fingers, sharp fingernails. A scary sight.

She reached a tree, and pressed her palms against the bark wood, edging her head closer. A man was knelt at a grave, murmuring under his breath.

His palms clutched together, while he spoke to the grave. She could make out his figure, but not his face.

He wore a black cape, and she poked her nose in to read the grave's headstone.

'HERE LIES, HIS AND HER ROYAL MAJESTY, KING RUPERT AND QUEEN KATHERYN OF ENGLAND.'

'The last King and Queen of England.', Eliza thought.

Carved underneath their names were paragraphs about their reign and successes, far more important to royals than acknowledgement of their family.

Careful to not tip herself, Eliza curved around the tree slightly, to see the face of who was speaking to the former King and Queen.

Then, she clasped her hand over her mouth faster than she could think.

King Richard knelt at the grave, murmuring to himself and speaking to his parents. There was a glimmer in his eye, but he was not crying.

He seemed more depressed, grasping his hands, bowing his head into the ground. He could not see her, and he was foolishly unguarded; alone and vulnerable.

Eliza, for a split-second, felt the slightest sympathy for the man. He had lost not one, but both his parents in a shipwreck years before, when he was around her own age.

She shook her thoughts away, watching for a final moment. He was deep within thought and prayer, on that freezing winter night. His buried face was stern; unreadable.

'Speaking to a lost parent,' Eliza thought, *'Two of them.'.*

She knew in that moment; she had her chance.

A chance to kill The King.

To make it all right.

To save her own life.

Yet, as Eliza stared after the man, on his knees, talking to a lost loved one as she had done; she decided to do nothing.

She knew she would regret ever sympathising him, ever offering her pity or letting him live.

However, a stronger piece of mind stopped her. Whatever it was, something stopped her that night. She had an opportunity that she should have taken, but a greater force intervened.

Eliza left the graveyard without killing him, or laughing at him, or even saying a word. She left in silence, and it was a silent night.

10

The Maiden-Witch and The Witch-Maiden

Eliza laughed harder than she had in a while, wiping at her eyes. The tray on her knee wobbled, almost toppling to the floor.

"*Dawn* attacked you?" She laughed.

Lucie sucked on her bottom lip. She sat sulking like a five-year-old child, even if she were eighteen.

"Yes, it flew at me and toppled me over!" Lucie whined, her cheeks flushing a bright red. "Laugh all you wish, but it was not *that* funny.".

"It truly was."

"It was not! That bird's a curse!".

Lucie's whining protests only encouraged her laughter, as the image of Dawn flying face-first into Lucie's face was stuck in Eliza's mind.

Eliza had volunteered to deliver the food to the 'witch' that morning, giving her time to visit Lucie. She wore the same maiden dress and blonde wig as before, while Lucie wore the brown wig and Eliza's clothes.

From the night before, she was exhausted, and bags ran under her eyes, patted over by powder.

Lucie looked worse; a shallow face, her rosy cheeks gone white, and eyes drained from all light and joy. It made a pit of guilt form in Eliza's stomach, knowing that her friend was starving in her place.

Lucie knew the grandeur of palace life with filling meals, glamorous gowns, and light. Laying in this stinking, empty, and dark room was damaging her inside and out.

The two sat in tense silence for a moment. Lucie's shoulders were low, as she stared to the floor.

"You know we could return to how we were?" Eliza smiled. She never wanted to go back to the tower life, and it took a chunk of strength to offer it. "Would you want that?".

Lucie's head perked up, her eyes shining for the first time. She looked like she was about to say yes, that she would not think twice about it; but she did.

Eliza wished in that moment she could hear the conflict inside her friend's head, but Lucie's face said it all. Eliza knew that she wanted to say yes, but that was not what came out.

"No." Lucie whispered. She clenched her eyes shut, rubbing her face in her hands.

Eliza waited on a follow-up, a continuation, even another word. Lucie said no more, staring into space with her eyes to the floor. There was no sound in the room other than the clashing rain beating from the windows.

The tower room was dark, and shadows lined the walls. The two sat stiff, side-by-side on the crooked bed.

"You don't look good," Eliza mumbled. Lucie did not move. "Speak to me, please.".

Lucie flinched, and that pile of guilt felt like it would come flooding out Eliza's mouth. She did not want to get irritated, but it was hard to be gentle when you were getting no response at all.

The maiden opened her mouth to speak, before ignoring the question.

"How have you been feeling?" Lucie whispered, delivering a half-smile.

'There are two answers to this.' Eliza thought. She could say, 'fine', and return to the awkward tension, but that was untrue.

"I don't know how I'm supposed to feel." She replied. "It's bittersweet; I got to see my father again, but it's like each day is closer to the end.".

"Yes," Lucie mumbled, clutching Eliza's hand, "I'm sorry, if there's anything I can do—".

"You have done *more* than enough, trust me.".

Lucie looked uncertain, gently rubbing her fingers across Eliza's own. A strange feeling hit her, as words piled in her throat. She was unsure, about being open with how she felt.

"It feels like I have never understood who I was meant to be," Eliza whispered. "For a lifetime, I wanted to find my part in this world, yet I am playing yours.".

Lucie hummed in response. Eliza felt a flush in her cheeks, wondering if her friend had even listened.

"Does that make sense?".

"Perfect sense," Lucie answered, "You want to know what your own purpose is, but you cannot fulfil that whilst fulfilling another's.".

"Yes," Eliza nodded, hesitant. "That's why I went—".

Silence roamed within the room, and neither said a word. Eliza paused, shaking the thought away.

"Went where?".

Eliza froze, turning away. Lucie gripped hold of her arm. The two paused for a moment, Eliza half-stood and Lucie on the bed.

"Nowhere, it's not—" She paused. Lucie's glare stared sharply into her soul, and she knew there was no convincing her. "I went to the graveyard, as myself.".

Lucie's mouth fell, and she stood to her feet. Slowly, she marched towards Eliza with a glint in her eye.

"As yourself?" Lucie said, "You *didn't* wear the *disguise?*".

"No, but listen," Eliza took a breath, "I saw The King there.".

"You *what?*" Lucie gasped, "I told you not to go near *him*, you could have *died!* You could have been *caught!*".

"I didn't *know* he was there!" Eliza cried, "I was visiting my mother's grave, and I *wasn't* caught!".

"Fortunate that you weren't!" Lucie shouted back, frantically waving her arms. "Oh, Elizabeth! Can you not *abide* by rules for *once?*".

Dawn flew over and rested on her shoulder, protectively hiding her from the maiden. Eliza's cheeks flushed a steaming red, as she shot her head away.

She saw The Queen's chamber window at the high tower but could see nothing inside past the dark shadows.

"It felt right on my last birthday.".

"What?".

Eliza's head turned back. Lucie stood feet away, scanning her like a misfitting puzzle.

"Last birthday?".

She paused, shifting her eyes to the floor.

"I turned seventeen at midnight.".

Lucie said nothing, staring on in surprise. Her face showed no emotion, no thoughts.

It was a blank stare Eliza had never seen.

"How can you be brave, during all this?".

With that, Eliza's eyes widened. She thought, repeating the words in her head. She could not find an answer.

"How do you mean?".

"You act brave, but do you not feel it frighten you, what will happen?".

She had an answer for that, one she had never thought of before.

"It does." Eliza paused, "What does how I *act* have to do with how I *feel*? A solider could march a battlefield; but does that mean they do not fear what it holds?".

The maiden froze, averting her eyes to the window. A spotlight of pale light came over her, like an angel ascending to the sky.

"Yes," She whispered, "They fear it, if they are sensible.".

"Sensible isn't in my vocabulary, not these days.".

Eliza stared after Lucie's own gaze. Her eyes landed on the wardrobe, and a strange object sitting on top.

It glimmered in the light, like a piece of broken glass. Squinting her eyes toward it, Eliza crossed the room. She grabbed hold of the handle and pulled the mystery object down.

A blade, a sharp blade.

It had been brightly polished, and she noticed her own reflection in it. She ran her fingertip along the sharp edge, cowering away from Lucie.

"Why do you have *this?*" She asked, raising the point into the air. Lucie whipped around, turning speedily on her feet.

"Ah, *that.*".

"It is yours," Lucie answered, smiling with a newfound glint in her eye, "For protection.".

Eliza firmly clutched the handle. She flicked open the satchel and dropped in the blade.

"That will be useful," Eliza noted, nodding. Her eyes sparkled in the light. "Did I tell you a broke a man's nose the other day?".

"I should ask what you have *not* been doing, instead of what you have done." Lucie sighed, shaking her head. "The more you tell me, the more I regret this plan.".

Eliza smirked, lightly patting the satchel. She leant back against the wall, gazing after the flying Dawn.

"And your father, is he well?" Lucie asked.

She half-nodded. She was tempted to tell the story of how her father had accidentally tried to kill her but decided against it.

It could panic Lucie knowing that she had almost died more than once, and it was only day three.

Her arm reached into the satchel, as she fumbled through the contents of the bag. Carefully avoiding the unseen blade, she grasped the spine of the journal.

"Look at this," Eliza announced, smiling wide. "It belonged to my mother.".

She flickered through each entry, careful not to spoil the pages. Lucie smiled weakly, but her eyes were narrowed at the book.

Each page delicately inscribed with her mother's writing; Eliza smiled to herself.

"That's…nice." Lucie said, taking a step back. Eliza could sense the tension, slamming the book shut.

"What is it?" Eliza asked, "Do you not like it?".

"No, I said it was nice, but---".

A division fell between the two. Eliza's face furrowed, realising the problem. A long-lasting problem that they never addressed.

"But?".

Lucie gulped. Eliza's glare was unmoving, her eyes piercing into the maiden's own.

She prayed she were wrong, that the question would not appear. A question that was prejudiced in all its glory.

"There's none of *that* in it, is there?" Lucie winced.

Eliza's heart sunk. She knew that it was wrong to show Lucie anything belonging to her mother, knowing how she would react. The two stood inches apart, unflinching in their stand-off.

"Say it, Lucie.".

"Fine," The maiden sighed, "Is there *witchcraft* in it?".

Clutching the diary close to her heart, Eliza shot the maiden a glare. Lucie never trusted that her mother was not a witch, never wanted association with it.

Before Eliza's own arrest, the maiden held a privileged prejudice against witches.

"Why would you ask that?" Eliza sighed, rubbing the diary's cover. Even as she denied it, Lucie still held a distrust for witches.

"Witchcraft is a scapegoat, used against people like me." Eliza spat, "Do you believe that I would curse someone for fun?". Eliza knew, that if Lucie lived in the lower-class, the targeted class, her views would have changed.

"No, I know you better than that.".

"Yet, you believe the other women accused were guilty.". The light that shone over the two faded, into a darkness consuming their stand. Lucie rushed toward her, but Eliza stepped away.

"I see," Eliza began, "You know witches are not real, but you believe what The King tells you to.".

Lucie said nothing, and that was the clearest of answers. Nodding, Eliza turned away, opening the journal. She flicked to the next entry, which she had bookmarked with a stick.

Dear, Elizabeth,

Today's entry is not so lively. I am having trouble with our not-so-lovely neighbours now. They question me mercilessly, but I hope by the future, things might have changed. I am not typically affected by their remarks, but today it stung. They call me witch, a vile woman. That sounds terribly dramatic, but it is true. They are suspicious of the fact that your father married me so soon, and how I only recently joined the town.

It is so hypocritical, for example, they pressure you to get married young, but when you do, they call it suspicious? Well, here is a moral for you, Elizabeth. Do not be bothered as I over such remarks. Life is short, so live it as you wish to do so.

Your irritated mother,

A. S

"Elizabeth? Please.".

Eliza flinched, taken from her thoughts.

She had been dreaming about how once in her life, she had been in her mother's arms. That was a wonderful thought to have.

She looked up at Lucie, shaking her head. She stared over at her mother's neat writing, in thought. Her mother still sounded so sweet, despite the people making her life miserable.

"I forgive you.".

Tracing the lines, Eliza shut the diary. Her mother's words appealed to her in that moment, like a well-needed message.

'Life is short, so live it as you wish to do so…'.

Even while being stubborn, she repeated the words in her mind. Her mother had been right, life was too short.

146

Life was too short to hold a grudge, to hate when you could love. Internally, she was still hurt by Lucie's words. Yet, her mother's words overruled those by a milestone. Life was too short, not to listen.

"I never should have said that." Lucie sighed, creasing her eyes shut. "I was trying to be cautious, because neither of us knew your mother or who she was.".

"Until now." Eliza whispered, gesturing to the journal. "And no, there is not *witchcraft*. My mother wrote it herself, she was accused, like me.".

Lucie nodded, and the two sat in silence. Eliza's eye caught outside the window, and she saw The King walking alone outside.

He seemed to be thinking, pacing back and forth. Lucie followed, suspiciously staring down at him.

"There's our *royal highness,*" Eliza scoffed. Lucie stared at her, then him. He marched across the grass alone, unguarded once again.

"Come now, have some respect." Lucie said. Her voice was stern, and she did not seem sarcastic in the slightest.

Eliza froze, turning to Lucie with her eyes wide.

"*Respect?* I cannot respect an arrogant, ungenerous, lying, stealing murderer." Eliza announced. "How can *you?*".

'She's been raised in respect for the monarchy, not The King.' A voice reminded her.

"Not respect for him as an individual, but for the monarchy." Lucie murmured. "It's rude to disrespect the reign, not him.".

"I owe respect, do I? The *monarchy* owes my mother her life." Eliza spat. Lucie did not move, she sat with her hands folded into her lap.

"Elizabeth, I don't mean that; listen--".

Eliza knew how personally she was taking the remark. However, with such a statement, there were few other ways to take it.

"No, you listen. When I die—" Eliza's voice shook, cutting sharp. "When I die, stand at my tombstone, and look at my name, look at the hyphen between the years I lived. You look at that and say that I owed those people my *respect*.".

Lucie's eyes went gleamy and wide. She shook her head, marching toward her. Eliza expected an argument, a debate, anything.

Instead, Lucie threw her arms around Eliza in a tight hug. The two stood there, embraced, for a moment. She could hear Lucie's whimpering in her ear, slight and whiny.

"No, no." Lucie cried. "I don't want that; you *know* I don't.".

"Mm-hm.".

"I'm so *sorry*," Lucie whimpered, "For everything I said.".

"You said it still, what is it with you today?".

"I don't know whether it's missing my normal life, or living in this depressing tower," The maiden cried, "But life's too short to be hateful.".

11

The Cursed Locket

Lady Theresa paced the room, gesturing for them to raise their chin. Her cold face was brutal, scanning all three maidens with her squinty eyes.

"Hopeless, *especially* you.".

She gave Eliza a rotten look, tutting in her low face. Queen Grace was returning from a trip, and they needed to be prepared as could be.

The servant life had never once appealed to her before, but now, the grandeur was becoming quite appealing.

Everything was so neat and perfect, like a fairy-tale she could dream of.

"Miss Benson?" Lady Theresa queried, beckoning her over. With a quiet sigh, Eliza crept over to her. The old woman squinted her eyes, staring her up and down.

"Is that a *necklace?*".

Eliza's own head bent down, and she saw the locket inside her gown. It made a slight bump in the front of her dress, but it was unnoticeable, or so she had thought.

"Of course, it is a necklace," Eliza smiled, using her innocent tone. "What else could it be? A *hat?*".

Lady Theresa's eyes flamed. Faster than Eliza could see, the woman's hand grabbed the chain of the locket and ripped it out of her dress.

"Not so clever now, are you?".

She gasped as she the chain pulled tightly on her neck, rocketing her head forward. Lady Theresa leant in, pressing her sour breath into Eliza's face.

Cynthia cried out, yelling in the distance. It was all blurred out, all she could see was the rotten woman's face, as her blood boiled.

Lady Theresa's grip on the locket tightened, squashing it inside her dirt-filled fingernails. She pulled tighter, and further.

In a sharp sensation, the chain snapped. The glistening locket flung into the woman's grip as Eliza's hand reached out for it. A trickle of blood ran down her neck, from the slight cut the chain made.

"Let. It. *Go.*" Eliza growled. The woman held it in mid-air, and Eliza knew the only way would be to tackle her to the floor.

'Composed, Elizabeth,' A voice said, *'Do not give her what she wants.'*.

Lady Theresa's knuckles turned white, and Eliza was becoming desperate. The woman's eyes tore right into her, hurting more than her bleeding neck did.

The locket was the only connection she ever had to her mother, besides the journal. That locket had stayed with her from birth, she could not, would not, lose it now.

"Say please, Lucie." Lady Theresa taunted, dangling the locket in the air. Lady Theresa's tall frame towered above all the maidens, and she was unreachable.

'Say it.' Her mind said.

It would sound pathetic, for her to say 'please' to this woman. That was letting her win, and she could not let that happen.

'Say it.'.

She began to sweat, watching her prized locket fly. It dangled in the woman's grip, like a hypnotic stone.

'SAY IT.'.

"Please!" Eliza cried. She felt a wash of relief as Lady Theresa lowered it from the air, opening her fist.

Eliza reached out to take the locket, as Lady Theresa's fist clenched. She inhaled a sharp breath, and her eyes shot up. She gave Eliza one final, devious smirk.

She let out a pitched scream as her locket was propelled across the room. By an inch, the necklace slipped through her fingers.

With a loud clunk, it struck the coarse floor, the front flying off and breaking apart. It was broken, lying there on the hard ground.

It clinked and clanked with a sonorous ring, each end of the locket breaking off and shattering across the floor.

She felt her heart fall from her throat to the bottom of her stomach, reaching her hand out so forcefully it burned.

"No--" Eliza whispered, her hand clutching over her mouth. She fell to her knees, reaching out a trembling hand. It was damaged beyond repair.

The front was broken, and the chain snapped. Sobbing on her knees, Eliza buried her face into her hand. She took hold of the locket's broken piece, clutching it to her chest.

151

The world was blocked out in that moment. There were the mumbled words of Lady Theresa, who left the room with satisfaction. Then, the exchanging of conversation between her and someone entering.

Eliza did not know who had entered the room, she did not care. Nothing else mattered then. She cried silently into her lap, shaking like a frosted winter's day.

The other two maidens said nothing, and the blurred voices silenced for a moment or two.

A hand rested on her shoulder. Eliza froze, lifting her head. Her vision was blurred with tears, and she could not see the person, but their boots were like that of a guard.

'Thomas? No, he's younger than that.'. Her mind said, *'It isn't Edward either, he wears different armour.'*.

"You are a sight for sore eyes, you look disgusting…" The voice chuckled, but no one joined in. It was a voice she dreaded, one she internally kicked herself for knowing.

The King stood next to her. He wore a long red robe, all lined with gold jewels. The crown rested on his head, and his face had a sour smirk as he laughed at her state.

He reached out his hand to lift her up, but Eliza shook her head, putting pressure on her knee and lifting herself.

"Tell my *wife,* that Miss Benson is with me." Richard announced, nodding at the two maidens. Eliza's mind froze, as his words finally struck her.

"W-What?" Eliza winced, quickly wiping down her eyes. "N-No, my locket—".

"Hush, Benson.".

Mariah stepped toward them, awkwardly curtsying to The King. She gave Eliza an empathetic look, before taking a breath.

"Lucie, Your Highness?" She asked. "M-May I ask, why?".

"No, you may not." Richard answered, scowling at the maiden.

Eliza looked at the maidens for help, but neither objected to The King's orders.

Her arm was pulled to the door of the Queen's Chamber. She gave the maidens one last look.

He had walked out of the room and yanked Eliza behind him. Before she could object, she was being dragged down the hallway. The portraits of royals sat on the walls, staring right into her soul.

'Don't go near The King, Lucie said.' She thought, *'I can't be near him.'*.

She wanted to pull away, to run, but she knew that would only reveal everything.

"I need to return," Eliza said, stumbling with his fast pace. "The Queen, we need to be in attendance—".

"The Queen will understand," Richard grumbled, "I'll ensure *that*.".

In seconds, she was away from the chamber and entering a grand staircase. The stone steps echoed beneath the heels on her feet, and all she could see ahead was the fair hair of his head. He refused to look at her once.

The fast pace that they were walking at was straining her lungs, and she clutched her hand to her chest. Eliza wondered whether her life was coincidentally so eventful, or if she stirred her own problems.

King Richard remained silent, not sparing her a glance. She was trudged up the stairs and down another hall. This one had the grandest, largest doors she had ever seen.

"Why are you taking *me?*" Eliza asked, with her perfected Lucie-tone. With her free hand, she fixed the blonde wig on her head, and thanked herself for doubling the makeup that morning.

"For a *talk*," Richard spat, "I assumed you *knew* what for.".

There was a cold, tense atmosphere. It sent an iced shiver down her spine as she longed to stop walking. Eliza felt an uncertain feeling building in her stomach.

They met the door at the end of the hallway, bronze like the finest wood. The King unscrewed the lock and shoved the door open.

'Act like Lucie would,' She thought, *'How would Lucie act around a King?'*.

He tugged on her arm, sending her stumbling into the room. Eliza pretended to stand straight, wobbling in her heels.

Inside, the room was marvellous. There was a large bed with crimson covers and oak bedposts, and chests aligned to the walls.

A hunted animal's head had been stuffed and placed upon the wall, and sharp-ended swords sat on display.

There was a tapestry on the wall, appearing as a king on a throne and his people, decorated with red and blue.

"Sit." He ordered, nodding towards a chair. She scurried over and sat upon it, studying the arm. That chair alone seemed worth more than her house.

Richard followed, pulling over the seat across from her. Between them was a small table with goblets, as he lifted one up and poured wine into it. He reached out the cup to her, and she hesitantly took it.

The scarlet alcohol swirled within the cup, as she awkwardly sat it on her knee. Never once had she drunk alcohol, she could never have afforded it.

'Rich people drink wine all the time.' Her mind said. *'Don't react, act like you have done this before.'*.

He poured himself a goblet, resting his feet on the small table. Eliza felt a rush of second-hand embarrassment.

Kings, she thought, were supposed to be formal and sophisticated. It seemed wrong for him to act in such a manner.

She remained silent, focusing on the goblet in her hands. The silver cup caused her to sweat. To herself, she prayed to show no reaction.

Richard cleared his throat, as he downed his drink in one fast gulp, before slamming the cup onto the table.

'Is that how you do it?' She thought, *'Follow that, then.'*.

Imitating his movements, she raised her own cup. In one quick shot, Eliza downed the wine in one gulp, but the wrong way.

Eliza froze as her throat burned like an erupting fire. In a second, she spat the wine out, spluttering and coughing into her lap.

The King did nothing, watching her with a gleam in his eye. She spluttered and choked into her hand, gasping for air.

'This tastes like poison,' She thought, *'What if it is?'*.

"I-I am so sorry." She croaked. That was a lie, if anything she was purely embarrassed. However, as she had to keep reminding herself, she was playing Lucie's part.

Richard laughed, the hearty chuckle echoing in her ears. Her shoulders clenched as she sat firmly on the chair, careful to avoid another mistake.

She hated the man with every bone in her body, but her friend respected him, so she had to continue the act.

Eliza carefully kept her head low, but tried to make her voice confident, like Lucie would.

His laughter died eventually, changing to deep chuckling. He focused intently on her face, lowered towards her hands.

Eliza felt like she was in a hotseat, trying to keep composure whilst internally losing it.

"Can you withhold a secret, Benson?" Richard said. For the first time, Eliza felt intimidated by the man. Goosebumps ran down her arms.

'He's trying to intimidate you,' Her mind said, *'Remain unfazed.'*.

"Always." She replied. His eyes flashed, but he kept his calm, exactly as she did.

Richard removed his feet from the table, his hand on his chin. His brow furrowed, and he took a long sip of the wine.

The King's gaze still rested on her, like he was conjuring a war within his mind.

"Good, someone in this *cursed* place can." He scoffed, pressing his cup firmly against his lip. Richard stared towards the fireplace, the blazing fire reflecting within his eyes.

Internally, Eliza sighed with relief.

She was no fool when it came to standing her ground, but she could sense that he was not either.

His mind was like a storm thriving; he would kill you or kiss you depending on the weather.

Her fingers tapped gently on the arm of the chair, prompting him to speak. Eliza's own mind was desperate to know what was conjuring inside his head.

Whether it involved her or not, it was surely wicked.

"Your Highness does this secret involve—" Eliza inhaled a sharp breath, and his eyes darted towards her. "A specific person?".

He clicked his tongue, humming in response. A long murmur came from his throat, but no response. He lifted his fingers into the air, squishing them together.

"You know, I am at the heart of this country; I could overthrow any specimen that dares defy me." Richard growled, clenching his fist together.

Eliza nodded, encouraging him. She knew that his announcement was off topic, but any information she could learn was of benefit; regardless of how she found out.

"I could slaughter any man, with reason or without it." He continued, shaking his fist towards her. His lip was curled with fury, and his eyes turned a shade of coal. "I have before, and it leaves but a smear on my conscience.".

She smiled back at him, but her eyes fell. The man was so divulged into power, he no longer acknowledged morals, and he considered no one.

'Ambition can do great damage to a person,' Eliza thought, *'Or a carelessness for morality.'.*

Richard's fist slammed onto the table with a thud, making her jump out of her skin.

It was daunting for her to realise that he was so absorbed in his self-righteous proclaims, he barely noticed she was there.

"Yet, that *woman* proposes that I take no responsibility for what I have done. In my own lifetime, I lost it all and more, still that *woman*--" Richard's heavy breaths were all that was heard in the room, "She *dare* try to portray me as *a villain?*".

Eliza had leaned back, shifting her seat away. King Richard lifted a goblet, only to slam it onto the ground. A splash of wine splashed into the fire, provoking a roar. However, his words repeated in her mind.

"You lost it all in *your* lifetime? You are saying that all the lives, all the war," Eliza questioned, her pitched voice rising higher. "Is because of self-pity?".

The last part came out accidentally, and she stopped herself from reaching for her mouth.

Eliza knew she meant every word she said, that was the issue. She prepared for a storm of rage to flood at her, for to meet his wrath.

His eyes were focused on the fireplace. Auburn flames danced within his raven eyes, as his mouth stayed.

He was in great thought, or he had ignored her entirely; for once she could not tell.

"No, I do not *pity* anyone," Richard replied, a sharp warning in his tone. "To pity is an act of self-degradation, especially when against oneself.".

He shifted his gaze towards her, watching with intent. His manner was unreadable, and he stood frozen as he continued.

"I do not expect you to understand *that*.".

Eliza found no use in arguing back. She had said enough, and it was purely her luck he was too in thought to hear what she said.

Richard turned on his heel, pacing back across the room. He grabbed hold of a wood drawer and pulled it open, rummaging for something. With a slight smirk, he raised a small box into the air.

"Close your eyes.".

Eliza froze, as she reluctantly closed her eyes. She had no idea what the box held, but many options came to mind.

She narrowed it down to the fact that it could not be good.

Her ears became her strongest sense, as she listened to the tap of his feet across the floor. She felt him rest his hand on her shoulder.

'He's going to kill you.' Her mind said, as she shook the thought away.

She felt his hand brush the inside of her neck, and a weight landed on her chest. The iced metal sent shivers down her spine.

The edge of his fingers secured a chain at the back of her neck. Then, it dawned on her what it was.

"I noticed the *condition* of your old locket," He announced, as Eliza opened her eyes. The locket was exquisitely beautiful, a silver outline with a reflective, sapphire jewel. "Consider yourself fortunate that it broke.".

'It's clear why he's doing this,' Eliza thought, *'He wants something from me, from Lucie.'.*

"Cursed?" Eliza asked. He skimmed past her and lowered himself onto his chair. As she sat down, he gave a I-know-a-lot-more-than-you look.

"It was the locket of Elizabeth Spinner, wasn't it?" He grinned, staring right at her.

It gave her a strange nausea to hear her own name again, and her first instinct said that he knew who she was, that she should run.

"Yes, she gave it to me." Eliza replied, thinking on her feet. "I wore it as a sign of remembrance.".

He nodded, suspense in the air. She felt unafraid of him, in her own circumstance, but she had to play her part.

"Rumours have surfaced, accusing me of *targeting* this witch, claiming that this insufferable girl's arrest has more *meaning.*" Richard stated.

"That is why you brought me here," Eliza said, peering down at the locket. "You gave me this locket, to win me over, to get information from me.".

Standing up, The King marched across the royal chamber. He towered over her seat, leaning into her face.

"Precisely, Benson." Richard nodded, "Don't tell me you are *surprised?*".

"No, Your Majesty.".

He raised his hand, placing a finger to his lips for her to be silent. Richard's head shot behind him, searching. Strangely, he flinched, like he was afraid of an unseeable person.

"Is something wrong?".

Richard spun around, taking a long breath. He shook himself awake, placing a hand to his head.

"No, no.".

Eliza nodded, keeping her head low. His face was still, but there was a rage within his eyes.

The flames still danced, even if his sight was no longer on the fireplace, but on her. Returning to normality, Richard knelt with one knee.

"That witch will be the death of me. I spend my life searching for answers, yet I cannot rest until she is dead." Richard ranted, flinging his hands around aimlessly.

"Answers?" Eliza confronted. She hated putting ideas into his mind, but curiosity flooded from her mouth before it could be stopped. "Why must you pursue answers, if you do not need them?".

"That is not your concern, Benson.".

"I cannot help but think, Your Majesty.".

"A woman in your standing should not waste herself *thinking*," Richard spat, "I would argue that a woman should not *think* at all.".

Her mouth opened to protest but silenced before he noticed. Lucie would have shut her mouth after the first warning. Lucie would politely apologised. Lucie would have admired and passively listened.

"Yes, Your Highness." Eliza mumbled, hating the words she spoke. "My sincere apologies.".

Ignoring her, Richard reached up to grab her locket. He studied it, yanking her neck into her lap.

"Instead of wearing a cursed *piece of metal*, wear *this* instead.".

"Well, I—".

A thud came from the corridor, and the two of them froze. A smirk formed on The King's face, as the sounds got louder.

The door to The King's Chamber swung open with a crack, but Richard remained unfazed.

Queen Grace marched into the room; her cheeks flushed with rage. Her face was merciless, as pure anger lined her features.

Her faintly blonde hair had been pulled out of place, and she wore a sea-blue gown made of silk. A shimmering crown sat in her messed hair.

Eliza squirmed away from The King. A sly look was in his eyes, and he appeared unsurprised by the outburst. Mariah and Cynthia stumbled into the room, gasping for air.

"What is the meaning *of all this?*" The Queen yelled, strutting over to The King. In a flash, her hand whipped forward, slapping him across the face. A harsh crack echoed through the room, as The King's face flew sidewards, flushed scarlet.

Richard was startled, groaning in pain. The two rage-fused partners met face-to-face, as he grabbed her by the forearms and dug his face into hers.

"*Go on*, darling." Richard scowled, banging his forehead against her own. The two maidens turned pale white, and Eliza scurried onto her feet, rushing to meet them.

She ran across the wood floor, standing at Cynthia's side. The three ladies-in-waiting stood awaiting a command.

The no.1 rule for ladies-in-waiting, Eliza knew: *'Amidst or in the presence of higher standing, thou shan't speak unless spoken to.'*.

"Nothing happened, I swear on my life." Eliza whispered, tugging on Cynthia's arm. "What did The Queen say?".

"Well, she was terribly upset, but she does not blame *you*." Cynthia explained, whispering into her ear. "His Majesty has been deceiving her for years.".

The King and Queen were arguing under their breath, The King pointing daggers into her face and Queen Grace waving her arms around. Mariah glanced between the two royals, indecisive.

'I'm done for.' Eliza thought.

"You are a lying, horrid, *cheating*—" Queen Grace ranted into The King's snarky grin, murmuring some words Eliza was glad she could not hear from far away.

"I'm a *what*, my dear?" Richard sniggered, clenching his fist.

"A coward, and a cold-blooded one. You know what could happen *if* the inevitable truth was revealed." Queen Grace scowled, touching her nose to his. "You shall never admit it, but it *frightens* you, Richard.".

She could hear what they were saying, but it sounded backwards. Their words turned muffled and low, and her vision clouded.

The King inhaled sharply, grabbing Grace by her arms.

That same fire, rage still burned in his eyes. It reflected within the light and reflected the inner confliction of The King.

War formed inside his eyes, a violent shadow like no other. When war is not forming between two places, but inside one person; that was when you ran like daylight could not catch you.

"You have your long-awaited proof, the right to divorce me if you wish." Richard warned. His grip on her arm looked tight enough to reach her bone. "We'll see if you have the *gut*.".

It became clear, clearer than before. The man who called himself King, who relied on his title to save him, who knew his name was all he was worth.

He was nothing in reality's harsh glare; he was but the flaking remains of a man, clinging onto what little love he had, in his own wife.

"Seventeen years we've been married, and you still fail to realise how you need me. You think having an heir is of sole importance, that you need to have a pretty wife." Grace scoffed.

"And? You tell me this, why?".

"Someday you will see the truth. The most valuable thing you owned was having someone who loved you unconditionally, someone who genuinely cared; but was undervalued.".

Richard's eyes widened as he backed away from her, shaking his head. He did not appear afraid. Instead, his face lightened up with a sour smirk.

"*Au revoir*, darling. I have a thorough list of charming young women who would give a lot to be where you are." Richard laughed, shaking off the illusion that overwhelmed him.

"Is that a fact?".

"Indeed, it is.".

Queen Grace breathed in sharply, stepping away from her husband. The far-more-humanized woman seemed appalled at what had become of him.

164

She wiped at her eyes, turning her flushed face away from him. Grace started to march out of the room, waving a hand for the maidens to follow.

Eliza walked out last, exhaling a breath of relief. She turned one final time and saw The King smirking at her. In a quick move, she shut the door behind her.

Queen Grace stood with her face turned. The woman was crying, reaching for her swollen eyes.

Eliza knew, after everything, it was not her place to speak.

The other two maidens rushed over to Queen Grace, holding onto her hands and mumbling words of support.

Cynthia pulled the woman's hair from her sticky face, Mariah shushed her softly. Eliza stood, doing nothing.

'I've ruined Lucie's reputation, entirely.'.

Queen Grace had forever been sweet to the people, but as she cried, she glared righteously at Eliza.

It made no impact, for the feeling of guilt she had gotten incredibly used to.

It was that familiar empty feeling in her chest, and it was there every second of her life. Guilt.

Eliza had come to realise that when you rarely felt comfort, and instead only felt guilt and hurt, that feeling of hurt turns to a feeling of comfort.

Guilt was unavoidable, and it now became something she started to ignore; she had gotten used to it.

Eliza stood in that hallway, the guilty one. The *other* one, as she always had been, and forever would be.

That night, she had sat in a heap of her own wet tears.

Her temples throbbed as she thought, frustrated by the answers she was never told, and might never know.

She lay staring at the cold, brick ceiling above Lucie's bed, her mother's journal wrapped against her stomach.

Eliza opened it, skimming the pages before reading the next entry.

Account four.

Dear Elizabeth,

This day has been utterly terrible; it was your grandparents, George's parents, death anniversary. You will not know of grandparents, on either side, and it is a pity. I dare not speak of my own parents, for they quite despise me, as far as I would know.

However, your father's parents passed due to sickness a few years ago today, and they hated me equally. I will regret saying this, but I say your grandmother was a wicked old—.

Your ever-so-polite mother,

A. S

12

A Conflicted Captain

The following day, Eliza journeyed on another visit to her father. With her limited lifetime, she decided every moment she could spend should be a blessing.

The thought of dying itself still haunted her, but not while she walked.

When she did that, the wind brushed against her face, her feet could outrun her mind. It was distracting, beautifully so.

Yet, when she was alone at night in the shivering, isolated room, it all changed.

Figures of shadow formed in the corners of her eye. When she thought of the idea of execution, her world froze, time froze.

She could see it; walking up to the stake amongst those ugly, mocking people who made her life miserable for seventeen years.

He would be there, that fool of a king, delighted to see her death.

With one foot ahead, she tip-toed up the steps into the town. She wore the gold-blue maiden dress and wig, after defrosting her Lucie-persona. The satchel bounced on her hip, full of necessities.

The town was empty, and for the first time in forever, England was glazed white. The winter air left a soft padding of iced snow, crunching beneath her feet.

A soft smile graced her, as her eyes were captivated by the wonder. It refreshed her mind with delicate memories she had long forgotten. She chose to block out certain childhood memories, however special or sweet moments she did remember. Moments that were good.

One fond memory was of the first time she ever saw snow. Her nine-year-old-self hopped up and down, lifting the snow and blowing it into the air merrily, like any other happy child.

'Then you broke your nose.'.

That was a not-so-fond memory. In a childish giggle, she had thrown a snowball filled with sharp ice at a much older boy.

He tried throwing multiple back, harder, but she dodged them with an effortless laugh. The boy flushed with embarrassment, and he threw his fist at her.

It collided with her face, specifically her nose.

Shaking away the bittersweet memories, Eliza strolled on. The doors of houses had the same barriers, made of forest wood.

The cobblestone street had a suspicious liquid poured over it, and the uncertainty gave her nausea.

The commoners lived fearful lives, due to the misfortune of living beside the palace. Still, it never occurred that they would block their doors out of fear.

She continued her walk, keeping her head low. With the frozen weather nipping at her arms, she scowled into the air. A shuffle came from the distance, as Eliza froze.

"Morning." A voice greeted.

A hand reached her shoulder, as her head whipped around.

Edward smiled down at her. His grin was short and polite, as he lightly patted her shoulder.

'He appeared from nowhere, didn't he?'.

Her mouth fluttered wordlessly. His light chuckling could be heard from above her, and he cleared his throat mannerly.

"Good morning, Captain.".

"And what a fine one it is," Edward nodded, smiling to the snowy air. "However, it is strange to see you out at this hour.".

Eliza hummed a response, unable to work up words. The dainty snowflakes fell over their heads, settling on his deep hair.

"I like to watch the sun rising, it is a beautiful scene." Eliza whispered, staring at the tangerine sun's contrast with the angelic snow.

"And then?".

"On a stroll, before returning to my duties.".

Edward's eyes seemed lighter in the frigid day, and his formal blue knight-wear matched Lucie's dress. His hands wore white gloves, and the snow separated beneath his boots.

"Care for me to join you?".

Eliza paused, but hesitantly nodded. She was not supposed to be near anyone, but he was fine. He would not notice her change in character; he never spoke to Lucie.

The two walked side-by-side, as she raised her gown to her knees. The empty town surrounded them, and no one saw the peculiar sight.

"The town is deserted." Eliza pointed out, nodding to the barred doors.

"Indeed, not a face in sight," Edward mumbled, "And if there is, not a real face.".

Eliza paused, stopping dead in the snow. Edward gazed down at her, soft pieces of snowflake drifting past them.

"What did you say?".

Edward chuckled under his breath, narrowing his eyes right at her face.

"I am not easily fooled," Edward whispered, leaning close into her face. "Elizabeth.".

Her jaw loosened, and she took a quick step back.

"W-What did you call me?".

The heart inside her chest was screaming, telling her to run. She tried to, her feet wanted to move, but they felt sown to the stone ground.

'The King's Captain knows, his second-in-command. He knows.'.

"There is no use denying it," Edward said, stalking toward her. "While your appearance is convincing, I know mischief like the back of my hand.".

Once her mind processed the thought, her feet did move to run. Edward gripped onto her arm, his knuckles turning pale as bone. Her muscles clenched together, and her breath swirled in the winter air.

She remembered the dagger, hidden inside the satchel on her waist. Her left arm was free, if she could reach it, it would spare her time.

His face was calm, and his eyes stared into her soul. Still, there was a part of her that wanted to believe he was different. The burning rage that King Richard inherited was not there, instead, Edward seemed more human.

'Focus, Elizabeth, ', A voice said, *'Satchel. Blade. Strike. Run. '.*

Her fingers slipped into the gap in the opening of the bag, fiddling for the end of the blade. Their eyes met, and his grip tightened.

"I do not want to hurt you," He murmured, all light-heartedness gone.

"That's what they all say.".

"If you comply with me, I will comply with you.".

Her hand gripped the blade's handle, hidden inside the satchel. His plea made her pause, to wonder if she wanted him hurt.

"It's instinct to defend yourself," Eliza replied, "Who else knows about the plan, Captain?".

He released her arm. Edward stood with his hands against his head, taking a well-needed breath.

The wind blew around them, and the strands of her wig blew with it. She had avoided all eye contact with everyone, but with him, it was no use. He knew, there was no denying it.

"No one knows of your *foolhardy* plan," He answered, leaning in with a whisper, "Your friend, however, is aware that I do.".

Eliza sucked in a cold breath, turning to the floor. The goosebumps on her arms were livid, as she shivered.

"Lucie is not at fault, she wanted to help me." Eliza pleaded, gripping onto the front of his jacket, "I never should have agreed to this, but I needed to see my father again.".

Edward pricked her fingers from his clothes, averting his eyes to the ground.

For a split-second, she could have sworn there was pity in his eyes. A spark flashed into them, but it was dull. He raised his head once more, all pity replaced with a void stare.

"Come with me.".

He reached out and grabbed her arm, pulling her into a near alley. Eliza wished to protest, but she had a feeling of where he was taking her.

Her vision was censored by a black shade, and she stared above to see the sky, swirling in circles through her clouded eyes.

His tight hold yanked her along, and all she could see was the darkness ahead, and the walls surrounding.

In swift moments, he dragged her from corner to corner. They ran further into town, hidden by housing.

The streets of the city were unusually dark in the mornings, and the squawking birds were the only sound.

The tapping of their feet complimented it, his much heavier than hers.

Coming to a halt, they stopped in a crooked, shady lane. Edward stomped around to meet her. There was no emotion on his face, frighteningly so.

"If you're going to hand me in—" She was cut off by his hand flying to her mouth. His gloves rested over her lips, and with his other hand, he placed a finger over his own.

"That is *not* my intention," He whispered, slowly shaking his head, "I will, if you do not tame that voice of yours.".

His hand fell from her face, and she nodded in response. The captain took a long, deep breath while fidgeting with his gloved hands. He removed the glove that had sat over her mouth and wiped it down.

'Goodness, the man can't even bare getting a little saliva on his glove,'.

He took a breath, rubbing the back of his neck. She could tell that he seemed uneasy, like he was going to vomit or faint into the snow.

"I hate to sound disloyal, but The King has gone mad. The destruction he caused, what he *will* cause, is frightening. Rumours are that there is more to your arrest, that it is a far more complicated matter, and I agree.".

Eliza gulped. Edward stood with his hands against his hips, sighing aloud.

"Why tell *me* this?" Eliza asked. "That does not justify anything.".

"Excuse me?".

Eliza scoffed, shaking her head. In his eyes, there was a short gleam, reflecting minor fear.

"You have watched him take countless lives, knowing that all those witches were innocent women who longed for a chance at redemption." Eliza announced. "I find it hard to believe that you would care for *me* after all those lost souls."

"I never said I cared for you.".

173

There was a part of her that longed to trust him, for that chance. However, there was also the sceptical part, which said he could never be trusted.

"If you don't," Eliza laughed. "Why am I standing here?".

Edward said nothing, glaring at her. She knew she was testing him, and that if he wanted to, he could hand her in at any moment.

'He knows more than he's showing.'.

"How can you defend The King? Why did you?".

"I was naïve, I stood by what he said was right," Edward mumbled, "I never agreed with it, and now I'm attempting to change what I have done.".

Eliza hummed in response, clutching her hands together. Her eyes lit up as an idea dawned, and she suddenly stared at him.

"You know the truth, don't you?" Eliza asked, "The truth about The King?".

Edward sniffled slightly, raising his chin to meet her eye.

"Truth?".

The two stood silent for a moment, and a mutual atmosphere was in the air. A peace, for a split-second.

It was difficult to ask for the truth, when she did not know what there was to be true.

"No, never mind.".

"Tell me, Eliza.".

She paused. The knight met her eye, with a soft smile. For once, his eyes softened.

"Did you call me Eliza?".

"Ah, sorry." Edward turned pink. "When you mumble to yourself in the tower, you call yourself Eliza; I hear it when guarding the stairs.".

A stifled laugh escaped her mouth. Edward flushed a bright scarlet, rubbing at the back of his neck.

"*Shush.*" Edward scolded, awkwardly turning away.

"You listen to my rambling?".

"Don't test me, Spinner." Edward murmured. "Make no mistake that I would, *could*, hand you in.".

"You *could,*" Eliza drawled, giggling mirthlessly. "But you won't.".

He never asked about the 'truth' again, and she never pushed it. Edward had gotten too flustered to speak.

Besides, she had thought of all the possible truths, but there nothing that meant The King would have held a grudge against her, before everything.

'He's never liked father, what if there was a disagreement there?'.

"When *did* you work out our plan?" She asked, folding her arms to her chest. "No one else has, and they shouldn't.".

"I have a good eye for trouble. That day *you*, dressed as Miss Benson, fell down the steps, I could sense that a lady would not fall so easily." Edward chuckled.

Eliza scoffed, turning to the air. She stared up at the sky, watching as small birds flew over them.

They spiralled and swirled throughout the sky, crying out in their own animal callings. It brought a short smile to her face.

'Why am I so calm? He knows our secret, shouldn't I run?'.

"What do I do now?" Eliza asked.

He stared from her to the wall, like he was deep in thought. White dots reflected in his eyes, as the snow glazed the air.

"If I kept your secret, it could cost me my reputation, *my life*." He explained, "It is absurd for a knight, let alone a captain.".

She nodded, her lip quivering. His face was covered with shadow, and all she could see was the outline of his moving lips.

"That said, I remember when His Majesty refused me leave, to see my father on his death bed." Edward murmured, speaking to himself. "I felt outraged, but family came first, so I made an escape plan of my own.".

"Why? Do your family live afar?".

"Spain, which is where my parents live." Edward replied, "I was raised in this town by my uncle, for a chance at a noble-ranked position here, but my family heritage is Spanish.".

Eliza nodded, taking in the background information. It was unclear why he was telling her about his life story, still, she listened.

As he gazed into the frosted distance, he was reminiscing to himself.

"The King never liked me in the beginning, I figured why." Edward continued, "Due to that prejudice, I worked my own way to the top.".

"Good for you." Eliza smiled. Edward shook his head.

"I worked for every penny, and every title I own; that didn't make it easy," Edward rambled on, "To ensure my name was on his list, I had to be the only knight standing, the one who overthrew the privilege he was denied.".

"That is admirable, but why were you denied it?".

Edward paused, his eyes drifting down to hers. With an all-knowing smirk, he continued.

"I could ask you the same question," Edward said. "I was outcasted, insulted for where I came from, but I am proud of who *I* am. You were outcasted for not fitting their stereotype, for being different, but you are proud of who *you* are. We are two sides of the same coin.".

Eliza took a breath, turning to the ground. She knew she should have run, left the country, but her feet would not move; something longed for her to stay, to listen.

"Should I be *proud* of who I am?".

"Of course, you should be," Edward whispered, "It is a grave pity, that the people of our time refuse to accept what is not alike them. Perhaps, the future holds a life where we can have one.".

With that, neither said a word. A sweet moment it was, bittered by the drifting snow. She thought, the snow was a cleansing of the air. A renewal of peace, for everyone.

"Perhaps, I overshared too much there." Edward mumbled. "What I mean to say is, I want you to know that I understand. If you swear not to share what I just told you, I will not share your plan. Agreed?".

The knight reached out a gloved hand, coated in pieces of snow. Eliza carefully took hold of it, and the two shared a prolonged handshake.

"Then, I know nothing." Edward lightly laughed. "Nothing at all.".

His face remained neutrally stern, but his mouth twinged into a quick grin. Eliza could not explain why, or what, had made her form an alliance with the knight.

It was an unlawful acquaintance, but a genuine one.

"Thank you, I—" Eliza was cut off by an echoing crack, the crunch of footsteps from a distance.

Edward's head whipped behind him, as he clutched his right hand to his sword inside his belt. Darkness overshadowed them, and all she could feel was Edward's stance behind her.

Eliza's heart skipped a beat, and her eyes darted from Edward to the misty fog. His face was stern, refuelled with the lawful fight we always had.

"Who is there? Reveal yourself," He demanded, his voice a threating chill. "Or I shall save you the effort.".

His spare arm protected her, holding her back. The freezing mist ahead of them showed no sign of an intruder, but the crunching of snowy footsteps got louder.

Edward pulled the sword fully from the hold, holding it ahead of them. The silver split through the dark, and Eliza hid behind his shoulder. The two cowered from the shadows, clinging to one another.

"A final warning; *reveal yourself!*" Edward yelled.

The peculiar smoke blew past them, sending a chill down her spine. Cold, frigid air filled the scene, and as she clung to him, she felt Edward's arm begin to tremble. As uncertainty loomed the air, her grip on him tightened.

"Stay here," Edward lowly murmured, shifting his face to hers. "I will investigate, but if I shout for you to *run*, then you *must*.".

"That's a promise.".

Nodding, Edward stepped away. He put one foot forward, slowly pacing through the lumps of snow. The fog consumed him, until his blue figure disappeared into the abyss.

Crack. A sharp sound echoed, like a piercing screech in her ears. Eliza's ears perked up, at that familiar striking sound.

"*Duck!*" She screamed, crouching down to her knees. Eliza held her head in her hands, burying her head into her bent legs.

All she could see was black, until a wave of sound infected her ears. Her face shot up, with her jaw fallen.

Edward screamed out a strong, pain-wrecked roar. She watched as he stumbled backwards, with a skin-splitting arrow piercing through his jacket and straight into his flesh, ripping into the shoulder her hand had rested on.

"*Captain!*" Eliza screamed, thrusting out her open hand. Through blurred vision, she saw her pale hand and Edward, fallen out of the fog.

He fell to his knees, whimpering in agony. The sword he had held collided with the stone ground, making a loud clank.

No words escaped her mouth, she stood with her eyes watering at the gruesome sight. Crimson drowned his jacket's shoulder, staining through the material in a cruel, stomach-sickening way.

179

With a grunt, he shifted slightly. Eliza watched in awe as he forced himself onto shaking legs, while groaning in bloody, unbearable pain.

"Get my," Edward took a shaky breath. "Get my s-sword.".

Eliza quickly complied, gripping the sword's handle. Edward had two hands clutching his bleeding shoulder, with the arrow still sucked inside his flesh. Spots of red blood scattered his jaw, as he gasped for breaths.

If anyone had to defend them, it was her.

Turning to the fog, she saw a spine-chilling sight. There was a figure standing there, wearing an anonymous black hood. Their face was covered, but a bow and spare arrow were tucked inside their cloak.

The figure was familiar, and when she got a look at the hood, her heart froze. A wave of sickening déjà vu hit her.

'The assassin.' She thought, *'The King's attempted assassin.'*.

The hooded figure stalked toward her, and her feet stood where they were. She had no control over herself, and her hand raised itself into the air, steadying the sword.

Both hands gripped the weapon. She raised the sword above her right shoulder, prepared to strike with all her life's training.

"*Stop,*" Edward grumbled, a shakiness in his tone, "T-They will try to *kill* you.".

"Wouldn't be the first time." Eliza said, glaring at the hooded assassin.

The shakiness of her hands was increasing, and she feared that the sword would fall, that it would split her own shoulder in half. A strand of blonde wig blew in her face, covering the assassin's stand.

The assassin stepped into morning's view, as a shining white shone over them. Eliza's breaths hitched, her lip shivering.

"You might have scared a whole town, and it's king." She spat, speaking more to herself than to the figure. "I don't fear you, whoever you are.".

A dark chuckle came from beneath the hood, as two wrinkled hands gripped the cloak.

"That's my girl." The voice laughed, gently pulling the hood back.

That voice, it was one she knew. Her eyes widened, as carefully, Eliza lowered the sword.

"*Father.*" Eliza whispered, barely muttering the dreaded word.

George Spinner stood in the mist, with the shady hood wrapped around his lanky figure. His same old face, and gleaming brown eyes.

'That cannot be right, it can't be him. My father wouldn't do this.'.

An instinct flooded her, as she dropped the sword. Eliza ran over, gripping hold of him, tighter than ever before. His gentle hands rocked her in his arms, as she sobbed into his shoulder, all emotion flooding out.

Even she did not know why she cried. She should have been livid, screaming at the top of her lungs. Instead, she clung to him like the world would not dare pull them apart.

In Edward's words, family comes first.

Her father cared; he always did. He was there, when no one else was. He never missed an occasion, and they only had each other. She hated him for what he had done.

Her blood should have been boiling, but she was his blood, his child. Nothing in the world could make her hate him, when he was the one who raised her in the world.

Their warm embrace was held for a second, before Eliza pulled away. She stared into his eyes, like she knew who he really was.

"*You* tried to kill him—" Eliza whispered, her face gone an iced pale, "You are *not* a murderer, I *know* you are not.".

Her father was silent. Eliza's lip trembled as tears fell. Her father, the gentlest, strongest man she ever known. The man she had idolised from childhood. An attempted murderer.

"Did you *kill* anyone?" She whispered, shifting her gaze to the floor. She noticed another tear in Lucie's maiden dress, cutting a sharp slice through the silk fabric.

Edward struggled to his feet. His jacket and white shirt were stained in crimson, and his face had gone a deathly pale colour.

Eliza skipped over, realising how she abandoned him. She slithered a free hand under his uninjured shoulder, gently supporting him.

"T-Thank you, Eliza.".

"You're welcome, Edward.".

'When did that change? He called me Spinner, I called him Captain.'.

"Yes," George whispered. His eyes stared into hers, a sadness swimming within them. "It was an act of *vengeance*.".

Not an attempted murderer. A murderer.

Eliza's eyes met the floor, cringed and swollen. Edward slipped and stumbled to the floor, cursing under his breath. She swung down with his pull, prompting him to stand.

"*Vengeance?*" Eliza asked, steadying to her feet again. There was one thought in her head that she wished she could abolish, but it was still there.

'He murdered someone,' She thought, *'He is guilty as any killer.'*.

"King Richard, his knights. They stole your mother from me, my *wife*, and now they want to steal you, my *only* daughter." Her father pleaded. "Elizabeth, I wanted them to feel that pain, that pit of guilt and betrayal from the ones who swore to protect their people. What good have they ever done for us?".

He gestured to Edward, limping on the ground. The gory sight of the knight was difficult to see, but her father did it effortlessly.

Eliza shook her head, taking her eyes from the wounded solider. The sadness in her father's eyes was replaced with a murderous gleam.

"Not all of them are bad, father.".

Her father's face contorted into a disgusted look. His hand reached out to grab hers, but she pulled away.

"When have you seen a good knight?" Her father asked, with a confrontational tone.

She stared at him, saying nothing. A silence roamed the air, filling their void alleyway with tension. Her father raised his bow into the air, and the spare arrow from his pocket. Eliza's eyes furrowed, watching him.

Her heart skipped as he raised it, connecting bow and arrow to strike. His weapon was directly aimed at the crouched Edward, prepared to inevitably hit its intentional target.

183

"I am ensuring they cannot *harm* anyone else, that they know *pain*.".

"*No!*" Eliza screamed, sprinting towards her father. He gasped as she gripped his bow, shoving him away from the impaled Edward.

She wrapped her foot around his leg, tripping him over. The bow launched the arrow, only to see it soar off into the fog.

Her father flung out his fists, trying to push her aside. Her father whacked his arm into her stomach, sending Eliza flying onto her backside. She tumbled backwards, gripping her ribs.

Eliza collided to the ground with a thud, as an intense pain came from her muscles. She gasped for lost air, wheezing in her chest.

He dropped the bow, and it clunked against the stone floor. She sat knelt against the stone, as it scraped into her scarred knees.

The pain in her ribs suffocated her, and she reached out the palm of her hand, crawling over the ground.

She struggled to her feet, her legs shaking. George Spinner froze, still in shock with his disappearing arrow.

"I will *not* let you hurt anyone else, Father." Eliza whimpered. "These are innocents, it is *unfair*.".

Family first, until your only family was an assassin with a shady cloak.

"You were an innocent; did they take mercy on *you?*" Her father scoffed.

"No." Eliza said, turning to Edward. "They didn't; but he did.".

Her father stared over at the fallen knight.

"There are good people amongst the bad," Eliza said, "And equally, there are bad among the good.".

Her father bowed his head, staring across the alley.

"He helped you?".

"You could say that.".

Her father turned his gaze to Edward and walked over towards him, the cloak flouncing behind him. He supported his hand underneath the knight's shoulder, and using his upper arm, pulled him to his feet.

"Thank you, Spinner." Edward murmured, sighing in relief.

•

That day, Eliza and her father had dragged the wounded captain to their cottage.

Despite his protests, she insisted on him testing her promising medicines, and her father had bandaged his piercing wound.

Once he was bandaged, dressed in fresh linen, and bloated with bread, her father had sent him out with a pat on the back. Not the shoulder.

Eliza had stayed with her father for dinner, while he told her everything about his assassin life.

There was an uneasiness between the two, while she confronted him about the killing of a guard.

He explained that the knight had been a killer himself, and an evil one.

That he had overheard him making fun of her, calling her the tower-witch. She thought that was no excuse.

However, he pleaded with her that he would never do it again. That he was wrong and should never have done it. She agreed with that.

In the end, she said she did forgive him, despite the haunting thought of him killing someone with that frightening, dark hood.

While he had been stirring the dinner, she had managed to read another page of her mother's journal, as she sat at her kitchen table where it was written.

Dear Elizabeth,

I know he is going to find me, that boy-king. I am afraid, I truly am. It has been haunting me for days.

I have tried to convince your father that we should leave this town, but he says that would only raise suspicions.

Besides, he has his farming and market-selling to do in the country, he says.

That caused a row between us last night, and everything has been tense since then. He says that the people will do nothing, that they have no power. I say that they do, and that they will hunt me down and arrest me, I know it.

Alas, do not blame your father. He loves you, as much as I do. Your bond is so strong between the two of you, I admire it.

Well, this letter may not be as light-hearted as the rest, and I may sound crazy, but I know they are after me. Even if I am the only one that believes it.

Sincerely,

A. S

186

13

Three Words

Cynthia banged on the door, as loud as her slight knocks could be. Eliza ran from one side of the room to another, flinging clothes and accessories across Lucie's small bedroom.

"Lucie, must you take so *long?*" Cynthia whined. After the previous days' events, Eliza had found herself sleeping until noon.

It was only her once-in-a-lifetime luck that she was not needed until then by the wildly impatient ladies-in-waiting.

Eliza had been startled awake by their calling, reminding her that they had planned to go on a walk. She did not remember agreeing to it, but she did.

She scampered over the pile of gowns, all shades of rosemary pink and delicate blues. The restrictive blonde wig had barely been tugged over her head, and the usual blue-gold maiden dress sat only on her hips, waiting to be adjusted.

"Lucie! Make haste!".

She wiggled into the dress, hopping up and down. Her makeup, the key factor, was only mid-way done.

Stretching the gown over her chest, her arms tugged on the ribbon at the back, tightening it to her waist.

Eliza threw her arm over to the table and poured the silver tins of makeup from her satchel.

First, unscrewing the tin, she rubbed lightening powder onto her face. Then the others, emphasising certain features, onto her cheeks, eyelids, and jawline.

The dust-white powder made her normally pale complexion even paler, to fit Lucie's 'beauty standard'. She unscrewed tins and discarded the lids as time cut short, before Cynthia got suspicious.

Rubbing every cream, moisture, and powder onto her skin, Eliza looked at herself in the dusty mirror.

Surprisingly, her smudged attempt at applying makeup did not fail. Her lips were lighter, and her face was emphasised into looking more rounded, presentable.

Dusting herself down in front of the mirror, she tidied the wig until it looked as realistic as could be.

Her blue maiden dress, stitched in the front, and dark blonde wig were set. She lifted the satchel, pulling it onto her waist, and slipped on the flat shoes. Eliza took a long breath.

"Coming!" She called in her maiden-tone. Unlocking the door, it swung towards her.

"There you are!" Cynthia exclaimed, "I thought you had *died* in there.".

Eliza, keeping her eyes low, gave her a weakened smile. The two maidens stood ahead.

Cynthia's hair fell curtly at her shoulders, in blonde curls. Her eyes twinkled in the light, and gladly, she looked much happier.

Mariah stood behind, laughing at the younger's enthusiasm. Her hair was fixed into a low bun, as wavy strands fell in her face. She appeared lost, gazing after Cynthia with a look of soft pity.

Cynthia grasped hold of Eliza's hand, pulling her from the room. The two maidens nodded to one another, strutting towards the staircase, pulling her behind them.

Pinpoint light split into the hall, due to the barred windows that blocked sunlight. Eliza scurried along, trailed by Cynthia's tight grip.

They strolled up the staircase and into the light, dresses bouncing at their feet. The stone echoed against Cynthia's heeled shoes, as she speedily skipped up the steps.

"Would you slow down, dear? You fly at the speed of an *arrow!*" Mariah groaned.

'An arrow, that's ironic.'.

The maidens were unaware of how she spent her free day, and that she was still shaken from seeing an arrow pierce through a man's shoulder.

Edward could bare it, but she felt sickened when her father pulled the bloody arrow from his shoulder.

Dry blood covered the man's arm, and there was a deep wound left behind, like a scarlet rabbit hole in his skin.

"Sorry, my nerves have been terrible all morning." Cynthia sighed, her eyes dulling.

Mariah's face dropped, and she placed a hand on the girl's shoulder. She gently pushed her to walk on, strolling across the floor and to the staircase into town.

"Enjoy the day, while it lasts." Mariah said, putting on a smile.

"I leave to be married tomorrow," Cynthia cried, "I will never return here, and Gabriel--".

189

Cynthia's eyes filled with tears, before she quickly wiped them away. The three stood beneath the steps, eyeing each other.

"Why do you let him treat you that way?" Eliza asked, unable to restrain herself. It was a concept she never understood, why Cynthia would grin and bear such horrible treatment.

"What choice do I have, Lucie?" Cynthia whimpered, rubbing at her eyes. "It was my fault; I shouldn't have refused.".

Mariah sighed, lightly rubbing the maiden's arm. Eliza could not help herself, like most times.

'I'll never understand why she'd put herself through this, but I can try to.'.

"No, it is not your fault," Eliza protested. "Why spend your life with an arrogant twit who hands out wilting roses?".

Cynthia flushed pink; her watering eyes gone wide. Eliza never meddled with romance, but she knew what was right and wrong.

"Oh, Lucie." Cynthia sobbed, "I'm afraid it is not that easy.".

"I don't know the in-and-out of romance, but a wise man told me," Eliza smiled, "People are like cups.".

"Cups?".

Smiling, she raised two hands into the air. Cynthia stared at her, with a look of blatant confusion.

Eliza remembered the moral of the story. Her father had lectured her on it, years before.

"Some cups are tall, some are small." Eliza said, demonstrating with her hands. "If you pour gallons of water into a small cup, what will happen?".

190

"The cup will overfill.".

Giggling, Eliza nodded. She turned again to Cynthia, weighing her hands up and down.

"Yet, if you pour a gallon of water into a tall cup, it will fill just right." Eliza continued, "If your pour too much love into a person who cannot hold it, it doesn't work; like how the small cup overfilled.".

Cynthia's eyes transfixed on her, nodding along. Mariah's sad eyes seemed to brighten, like she knew the moral before it came.

"And if you pour all your love into a tall cup, it will fill perfectly." Eliza smiled, "If you look at a half-filled cup, some will say it is half-full, others will say it is half-empty.".

The two maidens nodded along, gazing from one another to her.

"You make excuses for Gabriel, you see that even if his cup is not full, it is half-full. Gabriel does not appreciate you; he sees that your cup is half-empty." Eliza said, "That is why, in love, both cups must be full, and both people must contribute.".

Mariah and Cynthia stared at her, bewildered. She saw Cynthia's eyes begin to fill with tears. In an instant, the maiden threw her arms around Eliza, pulling her close.

"Thank you, Lucie.".

Awkwardly patting her on the back, Eliza smiled toward Cynthia. She was not sure if her cup-talk made sense, but it had the right affect.

"Who knew you were so clever?" Mariah laughed. "Didn't I tell you, Cynthia? There is something different about her, for the better.".

Cynthia pulled away from her, wiping her tears away.

"I do not believe I can change what will happen to me, but I can try." Cynthia nodded, "Regardless, I'll never forget those words, Lucie.".

The three stood in the delicate tension, smiling in their confined space. Shaking herself straight, Cynthia gave them a nod, before going into town.

"That will mean a lot to her, even if she has to leave," Mariah said, turning to Eliza. "I'm proud of you, Lady Benson.".

Nodding, the two followed Cynthia up the stairs. Her wig blew in the winds, along with the loose fabric from the tear in the gown.

Reaching the top, all three entered the outdoors. The town was more populated than before, as fruit and vegetable stands beckoned for customers, and children played across the stone.

A tall, mousy-haired woman stood with a young boy at her side. In his fist, he held half of a wooden sword. The top half was missing, broken off.

Cynthia took hold of her and Mariah's arm, linking arms with the maidens. As they daintily strolled along, amidst the booming voices and harsh winds, a rotten-looking crook caught her eye.

'Broke-nosed Joe.' She thought, a light smirk on her face.

A piece of torn cloth had been wrapped around his nose, and an up-to-no-good snarl was on his face. He lent against a brick wall, his red-haired mate by his side.

Turning back, she saw that Cynthia had ran off to speak to a man in the town. Her and Mariah stood side-by-side, taking in the village scene.

"Lucie, might I give you a well-meaning word of advice?" Mariah asked, glancing at her. Eliza nodded.

"If I were you, I would avoid The Queen for now." Mariah took a pause. "I mean no harm, but you have worked alongside Her Majesty for two years, and we really wouldn't want to lose you.".

'I knew it, The Queen hates Lucie now.'.

The exquisite necklace was hidden inside her satchel, resting on her waist. She could not bring herself to wear it or break it. It would be a waste to break, and besides, Lucie could sell it for a good fortune.

Eliza took a heavy gulp. She felt that same guilt, knowing she was tearing apart Lucie's reputation. Or worse, her employment.

"I never intended to hurt Her Majesty," Eliza replied, softly. "The King dragged me from the room, I couldn't say no.".

Gaining the Queen of England's trust would be no easy task, after she had lost the trust, she never had.

The dusted sun shone on them, but instead of summer light, it was an iced grey. In their part of England, terrible weather was typical.

"I know that, but she does not." Mariah answered, looking sympathetic. "What did he want from you? He has no reason to speak with us, we only serve his wife.".

"Well," Eliza paused, "It was about the witch, and what I know of her.".

"I see." Mariah nodded, "I understand why she was hurt. It made her think of when she first married King Richard. Those were rough times.".

"Rough times?".

Mariah's eyes fell. She appeared in thought for a moment, before shaking her head.

"Indeed." Mariah said, "They married at eighteen, and all was well, until…".

"Until it wasn't." Eliza finished, gazing at the castle. "Did they not get along?".

"It took time for her to adapt to royal lifestyle, as it would for any outsider." Mariah continued, "The King had no concern for her, instead meeting with ladies in court. When she found out, it scared us all. I feared she would kill him.".

Eliza had never thought of The King and Queen's early years. They were married for over fifteen years, so she assumed that it was good.

"Then, why didn't she leave?" Eliza asked, turning to Mariah. The maiden gave her a confused look, shaking her head.

"A woman cannot leave her husband, certainly not if she is royal." Mariah scoffed. "The King would not let her leave him. He needs an heir, and therefore, a wife.".

Flustered, Eliza turned away. She should never have asked the question; it was obvious how little she knew of royal customs. Internally, she prayed Mariah took no heed of it.

From the corner of her eye, she saw Mariah's pained gaze, staring after Cynthia. The maiden spoke to a much-older nobleman. She stuck her finger at his chest.

"Father listen to me.".

Cynthia's father had a bright-red face, like he had been slapped across the country. She was clinging to his chest, on the edge of tears.

194

"That horse-faced *imbecile*," Mariah ranted, turning to Eliza. "The poor dear has tried convincing him to let her stay, to let her marry a different man; but he will not allow it.".

"It isn't fair," Eliza sighed, "She should not need his permission.".

Cynthia's wailing echoed across town, as people turned to watch. Eliza's blood boiled, not only at the girl's father, but at those treating her situation like a show.

"I thrive here, it is my home. I cannot go with Gabriel." Cynthia said. Her voice croaked with fear, like a slow-shutting door.

"You offer nothing except embarrassment to the family!" Her father yelled, "You will do as I say, and leave tomorrow with Gabriel.".

The buttons of his waist jacket were pushed to their limit, as though they would fly off his pudgy frame. Cynthia stepped toward him.

"No." Cynthia said, earning a gasp from the crowd. "I will never be enough for him, I could give him all I have, but my glass will always be half-empty. I want to find someone who will see my cup is half-full.".

Her father grabbed onto her, like Gabriel did, leaning his growling face into her own. Eliza's mouth fell at her statement, but a small pride filled her heart, for the girl she barely knew.

"You blame him? It is no surprise he run off with other ladies, you have set your childish standards far too high!".

"It is not a high standard to want to be loved, father." Cynthia said. "And I cannot spend my life making excuses for him.".

"Love is no concern in the matter. It has no financial benefit, the sooner you learn that the better for us all." Her father lectured.

Eliza's foot jumped out towards the girl, but she was pulled back by Mariah. The more she pulled, the tighter the woman's grab on her arm was.

"We need to help her, Mariah.".

"We cannot, it is not our place.".

Cynthia's father was scornfully watching his helpless daughter. Tears streamed down Cynthia's face, as she covered them with her hand.

"Go on, *cry* like you always do!" Her father mocked, cruelly.

Eliza's heart ached for the girl. She knew the feeling of being mocked, humiliated by your own town. It had happened more than once.

Sweat reflected from her forehead. Mariah's face revealed no emotion, but her eyes shimmered in the light.

Then, Eliza turned to her right. One man's laughs were throaty, like he had a bad cold. An idea dawned on her, and her face lit up.

"It is not *our* place to help," Eliza whispered, leaning over to Mariah. "Others, however?".

A mischievous glint rested in her eye, as she strolled across the town. Mariah hissed, reaching to grab her.

The villagers, with their scruffy jackets and brown caps, stood ahead of her in a crowd.

She kept a solemn look on her face. Her mouth curled ever-so-slightly into her cheek, watching her right side.

The people glared at her, as she shuffled into the crowd. There was one person she needed, the attention of one. If she caught their eye once, that would be enough.

One man scolded her, another remarked. Their ugly, displeased faces watched her.

A large-looking man stood ahead of her. She tried stepping past him, but he nudged her away. She gave an impatient sigh, tapping her foot against the cobblestone.

The man paid no attention, his bearded chin turning the opposite way. Her eyes landed on her own feet, then on his.

With a smirk, Eliza rolled her blue gown to her knees. At the speed of light, she crushed her foot down onto the man's shoe.

He let out a yell of agony, clutching his injured foot. Eliza shrugged, jollily continuing past the crowd.

She pushed past more commoners, and they parted like a flock of birds. They were brave enough to mock an innocent girl, but they knew better to mess with a maiden who would break a man's foot.

'Or perhaps his nose.'.

Reaching the end of the swarm, she stared at the shady corner at the edge of town. Two shadier men stood, grinning spitefully at the scene.

One foot in front, she stepped across the cobblestone. Her dress flew out ahead of her, and she caught the eye of two villagers.

Her eye spotted Mariah, throwing her arm out to her. The older maiden shuffled through the crowd, less roughly than she had.

'Don't waste your energy. This man needs a lesson, and I'll happily do it; or not.'.

She saw that one puff-faced redhead had spotted her. His fat finger thrust out at her, patting his friend's shoulder. She smirked, strolling through. The other man had noticed, and his eyes went wide.

'Broke-nose and Redhead, we'll see how much nerve those crooks have.'.

Eliza walked quicker, as the crooks marched toward her. They shoved people out of their path, she danced gracefully through them.

'Time it, Elizabeth. Wait for it.'.

She reached Cynthia's father, and leant against the wall behind him. Broke-nosed Joe had a dirty grin, his smirk widening as he got.

The two men had appeared from the crowd. Redhead's eyes were shadowed, and his face was not smiling.

The frostbit sun shone on the two as they entered the light. She tapped her finger to her chin, giving the men a mischievous grin.

"Do your worst." Eliza muttered. She slowly walked backwards, closer to Cynthia's father, until she was inches from him.

Broke-nosed Joe was decided, eager for revenge. He let out a yell, bringing his hand into a knuckled fist. He swung it out, aiming for her face.

Eliza ran to Cynthia's father, grabbing onto his shoulders. She swiftly swung his body around to face Joe, ducking behind him. Joe's face turned to terror, but it was too late.

Joe's fist collided with the man's pudgy face, smashing against his jaw. Cynthia's father was rocketed to the ground, his arms flaying helplessly in the air. Eliza threw her hands off his shoulders, pretending to be shocked.

'Fool.'. She thought, *'How do people still fall for those tricks?'.*

Redhead screamed, pulling on his hair. Joe's jaw fell, as he stared in shock at the injured man.

Cynthia's father groaned in pain, clutching his flushed cheek. He leant on his side, coughing up splattered blood.

Eliza's face appeared to be horrified, but she was completely satisfied.

Cynthia stood amidst the crowd. Her face turned pale white, but the slightest smile was hidden beneath her hand.

"N-No, I was aiming for her—" Joe mumbled, pointing in Eliza's face. Her act appeared to be working, but beneath her hand there was the pettiest of smirks, and only he could see it.

"You tried to attack me!" Eliza objected. The convincing person she was, she managed a few fake tears, appealing to the town's emotions.

A few nodded. Fake tears ran down her face, as she skipped over to Cynthia, who took her arm.

"You should be ashamed, making the lady cry!" One man shouted, darting his finger at Joe.

"*Crook!*" One hearty woman cried.

Following, villagers screamed at the man. Joe's face dropped, as she stumbled into the brick wall. Cynthia's father lay clutching his face, murmuring under his breath.

Mariah stood frozen in the crowd, and she gave a nod of approval. Broke-nosed Joe cowered away, panting.

A tomato came rocketing through the air and smacked against the man's face. He screamed, covering his face in his hands. Thick pieces of tomato splattered over him.

The juice leaked from his greased-hair and stained on his white shirt. Young children giggled in delight, following their parents.

Pieces of rotting food came from every direction. Potato peels sat on Joe's head, and the tomatoes made his face as red as Cynthia's father.

Cynthia heartily laughed, doubling-over with a wide smile. The girl disregarded her father, who was lifted by his colleagues.

"Dirty thief!" One man roared.

Young children rummaged into the barrels of rotting food, searching for out-dated vegetables. Joe was now surrounded head-to-toe by vegetable juice, muck, and flies.

A roar of laughter erupted as he tried to run, only to trip over his feet. The scowls of his face were permanent, and he smelt strongly of stinking tomato and muck.

The whole scene smelled like rotten egg, mixed with a muck-covered tomato. She felt Cynthia tug her arm, pulling her from the crowd. The maiden did not turn back, but she still giggled to herself.

Mariah noticed, and rushed over to join them.

Mariah linked onto Cynthia's free arm with a whisper. The three walked as a trio, gracefully leaving the scene.

The coarse-bricked houses surrounded them, and they walked quickly towards the castle. Eliza sighed leaving so soon, but Cynthia needed away.

They went to the right of the castle, squeezing through the alley between the castle walls and the forest, Trees brushed past her arm, and a shadow loomed over them, with sun splitting through.

Cynthia's smile stretched from ear-to-ear, as she held both Mariah and Eliza close. Her hopeless giggles never ceased, as she led them to the castle gardens.

The better she got to know the maidens, the more she realised the lives they truly lived.

Lucie spoke of them, but only briefly. Eliza wished she never assumed that they lived spoiled lives, that all was perfect.

Cynthia was a soft soul, who strived to please all. She carried a grace with her and a pleasant smile.

It was strange to imagine that this girl, who was small enough to be a preteen, was to be married.

"Lucie, that trick was brilliant!" Cynthia exclaimed. She shook Eliza's hands wildly, her tone raising with every word.

Eliza was thrilled with her approval from both maidens, and an unstoppable smile met her face, as she followed into the flowered gardens.

The beautiful flowers lay inside walls of hedge, organised into colours. The emerald grass was beneath their feet, and despite the winter, it felt as heart-warming as a warm summer's day.

Cynthia skipped onto the grass, flicking off her heels and raising her gown. Eliza laughed along, with a genuinely free feeling in her heart.

She tugged her gown to her knees, running through the grass with the purest feeling of joy. Mariah strolled slowly behind them, chuckling lowly to herself.

"Cynthia, your *ankles* are showing!" Mariah gasped, chuckling to herself.

"Life's short, Mariah!" Cynthia laughed, smiling widely to the sky. "I had a change of heart; I want to be free! If a man sees my ankles, so be it!".

Eliza kicked off her flats, feeling the grass crunch under her toes. She laughed, tears of happiness streaming from her eyes.

She ran onwards, spreading her arms out in the air. The wind brushed her face, and the scent of clean grass filled her lungs.

'This. This is living.' She thought, *'Perhaps, before I was only surviving. What if living is much more than that?'.*

For once, she felt on top of the world. Her wide smile ached her cheeks, as the grass split between her feet.

The world spun, and her gown flew in the air. Her satchel flew, beating against her hip.

Dizziness was overwhelming, but that freedom of feeling was something she would treasure forever.

Losing her balance, Eliza toppled backwards, landing on her backside. Cynthia had done the same, arching her back and spreading out her arms.

'Could you ever be happier than this?'.

Mariah kneeled onto the grass. She did not scold them, or remark at all. Instead, she gave Cynthia a weak smile.

"Prissy." Cynthia smirked, sticking out her tongue at Mariah. The older maiden laughed, returning her playful look.

Watching, Eliza thought of Mariah. The oldest of the maidens, the woman was sophisticated. It was obvious, how she cared for Cynthia as her own. Eliza had regarded her as a parental figure for the upcoming lady.

"That was *dreadfully* improper, Miss Cynthia." Mariah joked, imitating an old woman's voice. "Lady Theresa might *whip* you with her cane.".

Cynthia laughed aloud, wiping her eyes. Her tears were no longer upset, sticky tears. They were warm, fuzzy-feeling tears.

"Mariah, you cannot imagine how much I will miss you." Cynthia laughed, "*If* I leave.".

"And I you," Mariah smiled, "Wherever will I be without you?".

The younger girl gave a comforting smile, reaching across the grass and grabbing Mariah's hand, squeezing it.

"You will be wonderful, as you are." Cynthia smiled. "And I will return, even if I must drag Gabriel across the sea.".

Mariah gave a reassuring smile, but Eliza knew forced smiles when she saw them. Inside, she could sense the woman's hurt.

Eliza saw the tower in the distance. The height and rough structure still sent a chill down her spine, in the worst of ways.

'Lucie is in there,' She thought, *'Hopefully.'*.

No one said anything for a moment, and the young girl pulled her hand from Mariah's. Seeing the tension, Eliza spoke.

"That tower, what was it built for?" She asked, nodding her head to the building. "Is it not strange to have a tower built for prisoners beside the castle?".

Mariah and Cynthia turned to one another, narrowing their eyes toward her. Cynthia scoffed.

"You don't know why that tower was built?" Cynthia asked. Eliza shrugged, chewing the inside of her cheek. Again, both maidens stared like she was a puzzle.

"Well, are you sure you want to know?" Mariah whispered, giving Cynthia a warning look.

The girl crawled onto her knees. She seemed in storyteller-mode, acting with her hands.

"It was built because of—" Cynthia was cut off by Mariah, as she leant into Eliza and turned her voice to a whisper. "Princess Rue.".

Eliza nodded for Cynthia to continue. She had never heard the name, Rue, before. Mariah cleared her throat, eyeing Eliza then Cynthia.

"Her proper title was Princes Ruelle." Mariah explained.

Cynthia nodded along, making faces and gestures at Eliza with a smirk.

"Then, she was Richard's sister?" Eliza asked, piecing the story together. The two maidens laughed, as Cynthia sat cross-legged on the ground.

"*King Richard*, and yes." Mariah corrected. "She was the first child of King Rupert and Queen Katheryn, and older sister to our king.".

Eliza nodded, staring at the tower. She had assumed The King was an only child, never thinking that he had siblings.

Cynthia smirked, again raising her hands to act out her storytelling.

"Princess Rue was good, but she and King Rupert fought over the good of the people." Cynthia explained, "She hated his views and treating of his people, so she tried to escape from the royals at a youthful age.".

Eliza smiled, listening intently. She did not blame this princess for trying to escape the royals, and their toxicity.

"Alas, Rue only got to the seashore before she was taken back to the kingdom." Cynthia said dramatically, "When she arrived, her father ordered for that tower to be built, for her to be imprisoned inside.".

Mariah gazed off at the tower, her eyes drifting from it to the woods, as though she could still see the princess running.

"So, the tower is used as a temporary dungeon for prisoners The King does not know what to do with?" Eliza asked.

The young girl nodded, taking a well-needed breath. All three sets of eyes were on the tower, and the story came to life.

"Eventually, she was allowed out, and all was well. Until her mother and father died a tragic death while on a trip, killed by enemy soldiers." Cynthia said.

Eliza thought back on when she saw The King at his mother and father's grave, and how he spoke to them.

"The death caused rows between the two royal siblings, and after the coronation of King Richard, Princess Rue ran a second time!" Cynthia shrieked, raising her voice to highs and lows. "She was never found.".

Eliza felt a strange feeling, as her eyes widened in disbelief. Cynthia nodded, shrugging in a humble manner.

"*Never* found?" Eliza asked, "She disappeared? That's it?".

"That's it." Cynthia giggled, "*Poof!* She was gone!".

Eliza was stricken with disbelief. It was mind-boggling how, after many years, the princess remained unfound.

Princess Ruelle could be on the other side of the world. It was hard to believe that someone could disappear, never to be seen again.

Then again, this princess was proof that it could be done. That sparked a new idea into Eliza's mind, after long thinking that she would never get away. It had been done, and it had worked.

•

After the day, Eliza collapsed onto her bed that night. Pulling off her wretched wig and gown, then pulling on her nightgown, her eyes were crossing over.

Her arm sluggishly sunk into her satchel, pulling out the diary. The words were blurred, and her eyes felt like heavy weights, but she had to read it.

Slowly pushing herself up, she raised the journal to the window to extract a little moonlight, Eliza began to read what words she could see.

Dear Elizabeth,

I cannot explain. Yet, be wary that I know they are suspecting me. They are coming, and now your father knows it. If anything happens, if I go to the stake, I love you. You are so small right now, and it pains me that any infant would be stolen from their mother.

I love you, now, then, and always. You have your father, and he will take care of you, I know.

They call me witch, they say I am practicing witchcraft, they target him too.

Please do not be angry at anyone for what they do to me, if they do anything. I want you to live as wonderful a life as you can, as you deserve to.

206

It is too late for me, but you still have a life to live, and I hope in your time, you never have to feel how I do, suffer how I do.

I love you,

A.S

Eliza had fallen asleep, with the diary lying flat on her face. Sticky tears ran down her cheeks, as her light snores filled the room.

She had read each word, tracing them delicately with her finger.

'I love you.'.

She read each word, except those last three. She had fallen asleep before reading those. Still, even in her dream, she had not forgotten them.

She never would.

14

The Agreement

Eliza sat silent on the chair. Cynthia and Mariah sat on either side of her. No one said a word.

Queen Grace paced back and forth, in a moment of stress and hopelessly muttering under her breath. The Queen's Chamber was silent, except for the hushed breaths of all three maidens.

"There was something different this morning, *he* was different," Queen Grace muttered. "I know he's plotting something, but what?".

"Do not fret, Your Majesty," Mariah hushed, "The King is quite stressed with the rumours, perhaps if you spoke to him?".

"*Rumours?*".

"Yes, Your Highness.".

Queen Grace marched over, a fear glistening in her eyes. Eliza could swear she never saw the woman so distressed. With that, Cynthia had cried twice in the past hour.

By dusk, Cynthia would be gone with her fiancé. That left only Eliza, or the real Lucie, and Mariah.

The Queen had not acknowledged Cynthia's state, or that her belongings were stacked in trunks at the end of the corridor.

She had not noticed at all.

"I heard of no rumours, while abroad." Grace sighed, looming over Mariah. "What trouble has he stirred now?".

"Well," Mariah paused, "There is speculation surrounding the witch and her trial, have you not heard?".

Queen Grace winced at the mention, avoiding Eliza's intent eyes. The woman stared out toward the tower.

"Spinner?" Grace sighed, "Yes, I'm afraid I have.".

"The people are curious why The King holds her in the tower," Mariah continued, glancing to Eliza and Cynthia. "Does he not plan to have her executed?".

"I cannot be sure," Queen Grace replied. "He won't speak to me, certainly not about that. I feel that I'm useless to him, that being The King's wife is only a title now.".

Mariah's face crumbled, staring towards the floor. Cynthia's head sat on her hand, as she stared into oblivion.

It was a tense day. Cynthia's departing brought a saddening atmosphere, but that worsened when The Queen stormed in, ranting about The King's plan.

"He made arrangements of preparing a carriage, but where would he be going?" Queen Grace asked the air.

Eliza chose not to answer, skimming her eyes across the floor. Queen Grace had been avoiding her all morning, she could tell.

"That reminds me," Queen Grace whispered, a sharp anger in her tone. "Do you know what secrets he hides, Lady Benson?".

"No." Eliza answered. Purposely, she kept her eyes low.

Grace did not look convinced. She rolled her eyes, her blue gown flourishing as she walked toward her.

The crown on her faint hair shimmered in the light.

"Do *not* lie to me." The Queen scowled, leaning over her. In that moment, she resembled Lady Theresa, but younger. "You *know* his plans, don't you?".

"If I did, you would too." Eliza announced, a slight warning in her tone. "He interrogated me about the witch, no more, no less.".

That was not the truth, but it was not a lie either. Silence returned to the room. Queen Grace could not see it, but Eliza saw a small smirk on Mariah's face.

"Perhaps, The King wants to surprise you?" Cynthia asked. The two maidens turned to her, as she spoke for the first time all morning. "It could be a good thing, that he is so distant.".

Queen Grace shook her head. She continued pacing back and forth, clutching her chin.

"I am aging, soon, I will not be able to give him an heir; a son." Queen Grace cried, burying her face into her hands, "*That* is why he is distant, he has given up on me.".

No one answered that. Staying silent was easier than agreeing and being sent to the stake.

Eliza never cared for the monarchy, but she knew that all former rulers had at least one son.

King Richard and Queen Grace did not have children. Therefore, there would be no biological heir, male or female.

"There must be an eligible heir somewhere." Cynthia said, "A long-lost relative, perhaps?".

Queen Grace's eyes watered as she blinked. It would be disgraced if she gave The King no heirs at all. The people would stir rumours, and the royals would suffer great embarrassment.

"There is one, but…" The Queen's voice trailed off, staring into space. "No, it is impossible.".

All three maidens glanced at each other. Then, it clicked.

'Princess Ruelle.' She thought, *'If she ever returned.'*.

If the princess returned, she could claim the throne, but only if King Richard were dead. She would be royal-blood, and the rightful heir.

"An heir will come, but that is not the problem at hand." Mariah said. "What can we do to help, Your Majesty?".

The Queen shrugged lightly. The woman was fighting back tears, Eliza could see. In a way, the unmarried girl understood.

Eliza dusted down her blue-gold dress, the silk running gently through her fingers. The wig still sat neatly on her head, matched with the maiden's headband.

"No, Mariah." Queen Grace mumbled, "I need to sit down, that is all."

In comparison to the maidens, The Queen was glamorous. Her gown was patterned with flowers and richness radiated from her. Even her composed walk outdone the maidens.

To Eliza, it was clear what had drawn The King to her at the beginning. She was beautiful, even with age.

Queen Grace plopped herself onto the plumped pillows, gazing off into the fireplace. She pressed her hand to her head, and strands of undone hair fell messily into her face.

Eliza sat with her whole-body tense. No one dared move or speak as The Queen thought. There was an uncertainty in the air, and it was unclear whether Grace would cry or scream.

"Your Majesty, I need to inform you that—" Cynthia took a deep breath, "That I am leaving, tonight.".

Queen Grace grumbled in response. Cynthia's eyes started to water, and tears trickled down her face. The girl's pinkish face reflected in the firelight, puffed and sticky.

'That is the third time she has cried,' Eliza thought, *'She's distraught.'*.

Mariah lent her hand to Cynthia's. Her other reached to the girl's face, brushing her tears away.

Queen Grace's eyes focused on the fireplace, ignoring all three ladies. The Queen was distracted, but Cynthia was hurting.

"Did you speak to Gabriel?" Mariah whispered, swooping Cynthia's hair from her face. The young girl shook her head.

Mariah continued gently stroking Cynthia's tears away, whispering words of comfort. Eliza stared awkwardly to the floor.

Sounds of marching boots echoed from the hall. The three maidens and Queen flinched at once, as repeated banging came from outside.

"What is happening?" Cynthia whimpered, shifting her seat from the door. The footsteps grew louder, and Queen Grace's eyes grew wide.

The doors flung open, rebounding across the floor. Two stern men stormed in, wearing gold-lined jackets. The tallest of the men stepped forward.

"Matthew." The Queen whispered, standing from her chair. She swept across the room, gripping hold of the man's hand.

Matthew was a cold-faced, raven-haired man. He had dark skin, buckled boots, and appeared to be a well-dressed attendant.

"Lady Grace," The man greeted. "His Majesty ordered that you come with us, and that your ladies pack any valuables you *independently* own.".

The Queen's brow furrowed. Eliza knew that there was something not right and noticed the untrustworthy feeling the man gave.

"And why should I do that?" The Queen asked, folding her arms.

Matthew clicked his tongue, turning away. It was clear the man was pressured.

"The King has been granted permission for a divorce." Matthew announced, avoiding The Queen's look. "You forfeit the title, Queen, and no longer hold authority.".

Queen Grace's eyes widened, as she stood with a lost look. She took a long breath.

His words rang in Eliza's ears, repeating themselves. The King and Queen were to be divorced; she never even thought of that, it never happened.

"D-Divorce?" The Queen winced. Matthew stood beside her, his face in a stricken frown. Mariah marched toward them. A spare guard gripped her arm. Scowling, she sat back down.

"I will speak to Richard," Grace announced. "This cannot be right; I will prove it.".

"I cannot allow you to leave," Matthew replied. "I am ordered to accompany you while you pack, and escort you to your carriage when you are prepared.".

Eliza sat shocked, watching the scene continue. An arm nudged her, as she turned to Mariah.

"Do something, anything," Mariah whispered, pleading with her voice. "*Please*, we could lose our positions over this. Make it stop.".

Sighing, Eliza stared at her. Mariah begged with her eyes, digging her nails into Eliza's arm. She stared from corner-to-corner of the room, unable to think of a solution.

"I don't know how to stop this," Eliza whimpered, meeting the maiden's fearful eyes. "I'm sorry.".

"You do know, Lucie." Mariah pleaded, "I saw what you did for Cynthia, how you thought on your feet to help her. I do not care how horrific or extreme it is, just *do* something.".

Eliza nodded, scanning the room. Two guards, an ex-Queen, three maidens. Her eyes drifted to Cynthia, and something clicked.

"Out of my way, Matthew" Grace demanded, but the man stood balanced. "I might not hold a Queen's authority, but I am still his *wife*, for now.".

"My command was to remain by your side, and I shall see The King's order through." Matthew refused.

Eliza slowly shuffled over to Cynthia. The girl sat chewing on her nail, dazed and distracted.

"Will you do something for me?" Eliza whispered. Cynthia turned to face her, hesitantly nodding.

Eliza knew if her plan worked, she could kill two birds with one stone. Taking a breath, she prepared for the absurd proposal she would make.

"Faint." Eliza murmured. Cynthia's face widened. If they were not quick, they were done for. No in-between.

"*What?*" Cynthia whimpered, her mouth opening wide. "You want me to faint?".

"Pretend to faint, or die, your choice. Fall to the floor and play dead." Eliza explained. "It will distract the guards, trust me.".

Cynthia glanced over at Mariah, who discreetly winked. The three maidens shared a look, calculating their plan.

"B-But…" Cynthia cut short.

Lady Grace was shoving her finger into the man's chest, refusing to comply. By the second, the ex-Queen's rage burned, and time ran out.

"If you do, The Queen can escape," Eliza said. "And, if you faint and need a doctor, how could they allow you to leave tonight?".

Cynthia's face turned a paler-white, as she slowly nodded. The girl straightened her posture and gave a determined smile. The plan was set.

"*Three...*".

Eliza began counting down. Cynthia took a deep breath and pressed her hand to her head, pretending to feel woozy.

"*Two...*".

Lady Grace clenched her fists, scolding the man. Eliza blocked out the woman's protests, focusing her eyes on Cynthia's shivering face.

"One...".

Cynthia stood to her feet, wobbling back and forth. She clutched her hand to her forehead, coughing into her arm.

"Now.".

Cynthia's eyes shut, her legs collapsing to the floor. The maiden tumbled backwards and hit the ground, her blonde hairs sticking to her wet face.

Eliza winced, as a painful thud filled the silence. Cynthia lay unmoving on the floor, her lips parted and hands crooked, like a broken doll.

Grace let out an echoing gasp, clutching her hand over her mouth. The two guards shoved past, sprinting across the room, and kneeling beside the girl. Cynthia's eyelids closed over, and her face went snow-white.

She had tilted her face to the side, and her legs spread out inside her dress.

Matthew pressed his fingers to her throat. The spare guard brushed her loose hair from her face.

Eliza caught Grace's eye.

She nodded suggestively to the door before giving a short smile. Grace glanced from her to Mariah, as her face softened in realisation. Narrowing her eyes at Cynthia, she nodded, returning the smirk.

Noting the guard's distraction, Lady Grace turned across the chamber floor. She exited the room gracefully, standing tall and postured. In the blink of an eye, she was gone.

Her feet could be heard marching across the hall, in search of her mad-driven husband.

Eliza nodded to Mariah, contented with their plan. She could not imagine what was happening within Cynthia's mind, but the girl's state was believable, while it lasted.

Even if it were outlandish, her plan had succeeded. If phase-two went accordingly, then Cynthia would be spared time before she left.

There was a murmuring of voices from the hallway, and both maidens turned to the door. A man's voice came from the unknown, and she prayed it was a guard.

Then, a familiar voice spoke.

"Why the hurry, *dear?*" The voice taunted. Slowly, Grace stepped backwards into the room, with a fist gripping her forearm.

King Richard entered the chamber, shoving Lady Grace inside. He kicked the door shut behind him, scanning the room. His eyes landed on Cynthia, with a cruel laugh.

"That's *unfortunate.*" Richard chuckled, acting with fake concern.

The King seemed in a good mood, opposite to everyone else in the room. Grace tugged her arm from his grip, squinting her eyes at his face.

"What is the meaning of all this?" She begged. "You cannot divorce *me.*".

"I can, and I did.".

'*Phase-one failed,*' Eliza thought, '*Let's hope that Cynthia doesn't.*'.

He hummed in response, sweeping past her. The two guards were knelt beside Cynthia, ignoring The King and ex-Queen's arguing.

Living within the castle, the guards must have been used to endless quarrelling from the royal couple.

The King stood dressed in a forest green jacket, tinted with gold to match the crown. Extravagant as always, even his shoes had golden lining.

"*Why?*" He replied, mocking her. "Is this a surprise? You did me no *good,* not ever.".

Grace scoffed. She reached out for his arm, but Richard swung it away. The Queen had been right. He was different, but she could not see why.

"No good? I was loyal to you, I held my tongue when you asked, I abandoned my own family for you, what more could *I* have done?" Grace protested. There was a desperation in her voice, pleading with him.

"It is not what you could have done, it is what you *failed* to do." Richard answered, spitting out the word, failed.

The Queen's face turned a sickly-green colour, matching The King's jacket. Her lips were fell into a frown, as she wiped at her eyes.

'*Who could blame her?*' Eliza thought, '*With this divorce, she loses everything at once.*'.

"My father was right; I was *wrong* to marry *you,*" The Queen cried, "You have become the very man he warned me about.".

Richard's face gave no emotion, he stared blankly at her face. It appeared that words did not reach him.

"Then go.".

The King's mouth was stern, and his eyes were dull and dissociative. He stared right through her, emotionless and cold.

Everyone in the chamber, except Cynthia, had turned to watch him. His eyes sent chills down Eliza's spine, as they froze on his wife.

"Go?" Grace queried, with barely a whisper. Eliza expected him to burst into rage, to give a snarky remark. He did not.

"*Leave*, Grace." He declared, void. "Get *out* of my country.".

The Queen took a breath, flickering her eyes from him to the maidens. The mood had changed, and along with everything else, was still.

Mariah nudged Eliza, and she shot her head to look. The maiden nodded to Cynthia, and Eliza followed her stare.

Matthew reached his hand in underneath her back, and the other under her legs. With a grunt, he carried her in his arms.

Cynthia had her head lolled back and her arms limp. If the guard had common sense, he would see how peculiar it was that she was unconscious for so long.

The King and ex-Queen ignored him, their gaze on one another. Grace's eyes stared into his, like she hoped to reach him, to find his humane side.

"Richard, I will leave, but only if—".

"*If*? It is not a choice; it is an order from your king.".

"My king?" Grace laughed, humourlessly. "What about my *husband?* You become a different man, a man I do not know, when you call yourself king.".

Matthew briefly nodded to The King, before carrying Cynthia from the room. His guards followed, speeding past the mad-looking King.

"Richard, tell me what this is all for." She pleaded. Eliza could tell she was appealing to his softer side, if he had one.

"Need I tell you?" Richard sighed, "You speak against me, defy me, contradict me and above all, have not given me an heir.".

"Fine, that may be true." Grace said, "Yet, that is not the true reason.".

Richard's face hardened. He stepped away from her, staring on in disgust. A familiar fire burned in his eyes; one Eliza had seen before.

"I'd choose my next words carefully, if I were you." Richard spat.

"Oh, I *will*.".

Richard turned to leave, but she grabbed his arm. The roles had reversed.

He entered the room pulling her arm, and he would leave with her grabbing his. For once, she had the upper hand on him.

"I know too much for your liking, don't I?" Queen Grace drawled, "It is a threat to have me around. You know that if anyone uncovered the truth, as I have, it would ruin you. It risks losing the thing you depend on most.".

Richard growled, edging away from her. The lines on his face creased, like an angered wolf preparing to slaughter its prey.

Eliza flinched at the tone of both royals, not realising how tight her grip on Mariah's arm was. Grace was treading on thin ice; but not because of her tone, or what she said.

It was because she was right, and he knew it too.

"It is not my secret to tell," Grace whispered, "Yet in these times, you cannot risk that I know and always will.".

The King pulled his arm from her, staring to the floor. The cruel look was no longer on his face. Instead, there was nothing, no emotion.

Eliza felt bile rising in her throat, and her stomach felt like it was turning upside down. No one spoke, no one dared to.

'What is there to say?' She thought, *'All has been said.'*.

Moments passed, and there was nothing. Grace spun on her feet and pulled open the door to the closet behind her. She reached in, pulling out dresses and jewels into her arms.

Mariah followed, pulling Eliza alongside her. Eliza felt The King's gaze, landing on her. While she was distracted, The Queen pulled a trunk from the wardrobe, firing in all her belongings.

"I am not giving you the satisfaction of throwing me out," Grace announced, smirking toward The King. "I'm leaving *you*.".

Eliza spotted Richard from the corner of her eye. While keeping her eyes low, she caught him signalling to her.

Richard nodded his head towards the door. Eliza stared from him to The Queen. In the pits of her stomach, she wanted nothing more than to avoid him, but she knew that would only make matters worse.

Mariah noticed their exchanged glances. The maiden nodded to her, giving an empathetic smile. Sighing, Eliza turned to the ex-Queen.

"Might I be excused, Your Highness—" Her voice cut as Richard gave an irritated cough. "I mean, Lady Grace?".

The Queen clicked her tongue, murmuring in response. Eliza supposed that meant yes, and Mariah smiled softly. Not a smirk, or a grin, but a comforting smile. One that said, 'It's ok.'.

Eliza took a breath, recollecting herself. Each time The King asked to speak with her, it risked everything. However, she knew there were few who defied The King, and still had their head.

She walked slowly across the room, purposely slowing herself down. She knew living Lucie's grand life was better than the tower, but when speaking with him, there was no place she would rather be.

"*Make haste, Benson.*" Richard hissed, eyeing Grace.

He stood outside The Queen's Chamber; his attitude changed. No longer bad-tempered or upset, but proud.

"Finally." He laughed, taking her hand in his own. Eliza froze at that.

He shut the doors behind her, leaving the alone in the corridor. Her eyes rested on his jacket, instead of his face. Eliza could tell he was waiting on something, that he wanted her to say something.

"*Well?* Are you not pleased?" Richard scoffed. Eliza's face went blank, and her mind ran wild.

'Pleased? What is there to be pleased about?'.

Whatever it was, he expected her to know. Saying nothing gave away nothing, but it certainly made him impatient. He squeezed her slight hand, placing his much larger one on top of it.

"The divorce was finalised." He continued, "Remember *now?*".

Eliza went from nodding to shaking her head. It was not that she had forgotten, but she did not know what to remember. One hand was clutched in his, the other poised behind her back.

She tried to put herself in Lucie's mindset, but that was useless. Lucie would have known no more about this divorce than she did, after it was only finalised that morning.

"Forgive me, I am feeling under the weather," Eliza answered in her posh-sweet-Lucie tone. She prayed that he would send her away if she were ill. "Why am I to be pleased?".

'When did the, saying nothing, stop?'.

King Richard rolled his eyes. He scanned the hall for any guards, before leaning into whisper.

"Our agreement, Benson." He groaned, squishing her hand in his grip. It was painful, like he was making up for the fact he could not squish her. "This is only the *first* step.".

Whatever Eliza had expected, she was not expecting that.

She forgot many things, but she was sure that she never made any agreements with him. The dark walls loomed over her, squashing her in like she was a bug beneath them. Like the maidens, she must have forgotten she agreed to Richard. That was it, it had to be.

"Goodness," He groaned, giving an exaggerated sigh. "Let me *refresh* your memory.".

Eliza nodded, realising it was obvious she had no idea what he was saying. Not that she did that purposefully, but it meant she got an explanation. It was a win-win.

"You spoke to me, asking of a higher position in court. You wanted to be taken seriously, to prove you could be greater than a lady to The Queen.".

She did not remember that. Eliza thought on her discussion with The King, but besides his all-powerful-king monologue, they barely spoke.

"Then, weeks ago, I offered you a deal, didn't I?" He asked, and instinctively, Eliza nodded back. On the inside, her heart sunk, if it were possible. Her only saving was that she did not know the deal's contents, but one thought sunk into her mind.

"…You refused it at first, saying you could never agree. Then, you came running back, like most do.".

She was not disguised as Lucie, weeks ago.

That meant that the real Lucie made a deal with The King, and that hit her like a ton of bricks. Eliza had not been arrested for that long, which meant Lucie had done the deal before she was in the tower.

"…When you finally agreed, we decided that you would give me the information I needed, which you did.".

Eliza nodded, like she knew what he was saying. On the outside, she showed no surprise to it.

"…And I can save you from being sent away for marriage, like your fellow lady-in-waiting.".

That was true. Lucie had been on her trip to France, to meet a suitor. Lucie dreamed of being married. It did not make sense, why Richard would save her from it.

"…You came to me and told me all you knew. That allowed me to continue my, investigation.".

Her stomach sickened with suspense. His words repeated themselves in her mind; that word repeated itself.

'Information. Lucie gave him information.'.

224

In her head, she wanted him to stop. She did not want to hear any more. It felt like time was slowly passing her, and all she could do was listen and endure.

'Please, tell me I'm wrong. Tell me it's not that.'.

"…You spoke of all you had seen and heard in your lifetime, giving me somewhat useful information.".

All she knew was The King had been searching for information for weeks. Certain information; about her.

Eliza denied her solutions, and her mind searched for practical ones, for excuses she could give. Still, there was a part of her that knew what would come. That part of her mind that saw no point in denying things and told the obvious, even when she did not want to hear it.

"…Information on that witch, Spinner.".

Eliza's heart tore. Simple as that.

Lucie had given him information, about her. That was why he had been searching, why he knew where to search. It was all from Lucie.

"I needed to know from an inside source, which is why I recruited you, and our plan worked well for us both. I got the information I needed, and…".

Slowly, she nodded. Not to him, but to herself.

"I will have a new wife, who can give me an heir and in exchange can rise to the highest position of power." Richard smirked, pausing.

Richard pressed his finger under her chin, lifting her head. His eyes gleamed in delight.

"And that darling little wife, her story will be a perfect fairy-tale," Richard smirked. "The Queen of the land, who found true love, as the fairest maiden of them all. Yet, a fairy-tale is never complete, until the witch is defeated.".

He lent in, his smirk coming into view. That cold, vile smirk she hated.

"Isn't that right, my *dear* wife-to-be?".

15

Lucie's Confession

Eliza had not gotten any sleep that night. She tossed and turned in bed, and her eyes stung with restless sleep. In fact, her entire face had been puffed, as Lucie's tiny room felt like it was closing in on her.

Her mind prevented her from sleep, and in the pitch-black, she had reviewed everything. That was her only way of understanding it.

With King Richard's brief reminder, she knew what Lucie did not tell her. Her heart hurt at that, and stress drained her energy.

From what The King had said, it all made sense. Until it did not.

King Richard needed information on her, and Lucie was the ideal candidate. She was close to him and could be persuaded.

Coincidentally, Lucie was under stress upon learning that her father was sending her off to marry.

Richard was desperate for an heir, that Queen Grace had not given him.

If he married Lucie, she could give him an heir, and she would get to stay in England with a successful marriage.

'Win-win', In Eliza's own words.

Shaking the thoughts away, she stood facing her tower. The harsh wind blew onto her face, but her gaze was colder, far more threatening than any weather they faced.

Eliza's rational side was gone, and she was out for blood. It was not as simple as Lucie had told a lie, or tripped her up, or made fun of her.

Her only friend had traded information, about her. She had done it long before Eliza was arrested.

That meant Lucie knew what was going to happen to her. Lucie let it happen, and never even warned her that it would.

Eliza's head tilted down, watching the grass blowing in the wind. She wore that same maiden dress, and her satchel sat on her waist. In her hands, she had the silver tray, with stale bread and water.

Her mind had gone numb, along with her heart. Betrayal was a feeling that blinded a person, she had read that somewhere.

Eliza marched with the satchel bouncing on her hip, her eyes narrowed and dark.

She could see Edward standing on guard, watching her approach. The tower got closer, until she stood beside the guard.

"Move.".

Edward gave an affronted look. Clearing his throat, he sheepishly laughed.

"Who hurt *you?*".

"*Many, many* people.".

Edward bit the inside of his cheek, clicking his tongue at her. He shifted uncomfortably, peering to see any passers-by.

"Did someone find out?" He asked, leaning in with a whisper. To her surprise, he looked genuine.

'Lucie looked genuine too, once.' She thought, *'How can I trust him?'*.

"No." She replied, irritated. "And if they did, what would it matter?".

"It would matter a great deal," Edward said, raising an eyebrow at her. "When did you become so careless?".

She could sense he was not convinced.

"Listen, I need to speak to Lucie." She mumbled quietly.

"I figured," He replied, stepping out of the way. The door creaked open, and he held it for her to walk through. "Be quick, and Eliza?".

She paused, peering around her shoulder. Edward stared her up and down, sighing heavily.

"Nothing," Edward muttered, pulling the door closed. "Go on.".

The door shut with a bang. The stone echoed beneath her as she stepped across, climbing the stairs. The silver goblets wobbled on the tray, and her grip tightened.

The stairs spiralled beneath, and peering down, she saw how high up she was. She stopped at the door.

A wave of nostalgia hit her, and a feeling did too. Not sadness, or fear. It was a feeling, but one she could not pinpoint.

Her fist raised to the barred, wooden door.

'Open it.'.

She could not bring herself to, despite how she tried. It was easier said, than done.

Her hand shook. She bit her cheek, taking a moment.

It was not fear stopping her, but a self-awareness of what she would do. Swiftly, she reached for the lock, unscrewing it.

Pressing her hand to the wood, Eliza pushed the crooked door open. It swung to reveal the room, and one overexcited raven.

Dawn flew before she could see it, landing promptly on her shoulder. That bird, daft as it was, knew when she was near.

'At least someone cares.' Eliza smiled to herself.

Lucie, dressed in Eliza's own clothes, marched over. She paused, noticing the deranged look in her eyes.

"Elizabeth?".

"*Save it.*".

Eliza shut the door. Lucie treaded backwards, holding up her hands. The girl smiled like it was a joke, with an insufferable smirk.

"Are you *alright?*" Lucie giggled.

Eliza was not even smiling. She was very-much-not 'all right'.

"Isn't that the question? You tell me.".

Lucie stopped laughing. Eliza felt smoke coming out of her ears. In that moment, even the slightest twitch of Lucie's face sent her rage into a frenzy.

Dawn flew from Eliza's shoulder. The raven circled the ceiling, flying from corner to edge. Lucie played with her hands, avoiding Eliza's eyes.

'Playing the innocent card,' Her mind said, *'As always.'.*

It was strange to feel so much hatred for someone you cared for, Eliza thought.

"Well," Lucie began, realising she had to answer. "You don't look good, you look upset.

Eliza shook her head, laughing. She laughed, but not in a friendly way.

The room surrounding them was dark, and the wind crashed against the windows. A deep shadow loomed over her, opposing to Lucie's light.

"Why do you *think* I'm upset, *Lucie?*" Eliza shouted back, spitting the words out.

Lucie jumped, stepping even further back. Her eyes were wide, shimmering in the light.

"I don't know..." Lucie whispered.

Eliza, blinded by hate, could feel no remorse for frightening her. She did not genuinely think she was. Lucie was extremely talented when it came to acting the victim.

"*You don't know?*" Eliza replied, mocking her. "I'll tell you.".

Eliza stormed right up to her. She gripped onto the girl's arm, forcing her to face forward.

"You *lied* to me, Lucie. You lied to me, and I—" Eliza winced, her rage turning to hurt, "*I trusted you!*".

Lucie's entire face fell, and Eliza could spot the exact moment where she realised. She dug her nails tighter into the girl's arm, seconds from drawing blood.

"N-No…" Lucie sighed. "I promise, I can explain—".

When she did that, something clicked in Eliza's mind. That face of fear, it was an act. She had saw Lucie do it, for sympathy or favour, one hundred times before.

"I've seen your sympathy act," Eliza spat. "Tell me the truth, did you agree to *marry* him?".

Lucie's face, faster than she ever seen, fell from fear to a neutral look. The girl pulled her arm away, revealing white scrapes on the skin.

"Yes, I did." Lucie began, her voice calm. "I thought *you* would *understand*, Elizabeth,"

Eliza masked her surprise, but internally, she was shocked by the change in attitude.

The manipulative act became clearer by the second. She swore not to fall for it.

"Understand? You knew he wanted me dead, and you said *nothing*." Eliza scoffed, covering the hurt. "Is your father's approval more *valuable* than my *life*?".

Lucie's face was void, unclear of emotion. The glimmering eyes, trembling arms, frightened expression. It all dulled.

"No," Lucie answered, gazing up at her. "But what about *my* life?".

Eliza did not expect that. Her head started to pound, as she stumbled away. She could not see how Lucie could justify it, at all.

"*Your* life? How is that more important than me *dying?*" Eliza shot out, her words turning into cries.

"I have a *life* ahead of me. My father was sending me to marry a stranger in France, to ship me off to France. My life would have been *wasted.*" Lucie explained, waving her arms around.

Eliza stood with her jaw fallen. No tears ran, she was not sure she had any left.

"I *had* a life ahead of me, before *your* scheme!" Eliza shouted, turning her hurt to rage. "Does that mean *nothing* to you?"

Lucie said nothing, averting her eyes to the left. There was nothing happy about the room, only bitter tension.

"It does, but—" Lucie paused.

"*But*, what? There are no 'buts' when it comes to friendship." Eliza corrected, "Either you are loyal, or you're not.".

Lucie nodded, sighing heavily. Eliza was sickened that Lucie could agree to that, after she had been anything but loyal.

"I needed to marry well, Elizabeth. When Richard offered, it meant that I would get that and more. My father would *finally* accept me," Lucie explained, "I did not know it would go this *far*.".

'*Didn't know it would go this far?*' Eliza thought, '*Of course you didn't.*'.

"...I did not know *why* he needed information, I thought it was to do with your *mother*." Lucie continued, "I saw an opportunity, and I took it.".

Eliza stopped dead at that. She had a feeling in her stomach that Lucie did know. Still, she would never admit that.

"My *mother?*".

"Yes, because she was a--." Lucie paused, "A witch.".

If Eliza's blood had been boiling before, it was on fire. When it came to the witch-ideology, Lucie believed The King. She sided with him, and his absurd ideas.

"My mother was no *witch*, she was innocent, like me." Eliza warned, edging closer to her. "Do you truly believe Richard's claims?".

Lucie's eyes fell. Eliza knew the answer, but she wanted to hear it.

Rain poured outside, thundering against the windows. Shadow now draped over Lucie, instead of her. It was a dark, gloomy day.

There was still a question, digging at her mind. It rose in her throat, aching to be asked.

"Do you *love* him?".

Lucie's soft eyes shot up, staring right into Eliza's. Her mouth dropped, prepared to speak. Except no words came out. She waited. Lucie could not give an answer.

The girl's cheeks flushed, and she buried her head. Eliza's fists clenched. There were unsaid words, and she needed to get her point across, before time ran out.

"Fine, be a coward.".

"I'm *not*.".

"No?" Eliza scoffed. "Then, why don't you set the record straight?".

Edward told her to be quick, but she had not done that well. She was too distracted, and as the words rose in her throat, her vision turned dark; shadowed.

Tears blinked in Lucie's eyes, as she clenched them shut. Eliza watched carefully, as the maiden's frustrations became clear.

"Richard knows who I could be, what I am capable of." Lucie growled, gritting her teeth. "Richard trusts me to aid him, and I *will*.".

"Richard had a *wife*." Eliza spat. "He is manipulating you; he can't *love*.".

"No, you're *wrong!*" Lucie shouted, in a desperate cry. "I have no *choice,* and even so, he will *learn* to love me. You never understood my life, how love was never an option for me. Marriage is a social *standard*, and people like me do *not* do it for *love*. We suck it up and *learn* to love!".

Eliza wobbled backwards, surprised by the sudden outburst. Lucie's breaths filled the room, as her eyes turned bloodshot, and teeth clenched.

"Oh, *well I beg your pardon*." Eliza scoffed. "You live a life of luxury, have everything you'll ever need, never went starving in your life. Yet, you must get married; *how terrible it is!*".

"You don't understand, you *never* did.".

"Do I not?" Eliza scowled. "Go cry to your royal *husband* about it, because I could care *less*.".

Lucie turned her back, her fingernails grinding into the palms of her hands. The maiden's face flushed a flaming red.

"I did what I *had* to do," Lucie sighed. "Good grief, I thought *you* would be the one who understood.".

"I trusted you with my *life*, and you abused having that power. You were mean, you were selfish, *and I—*" Eliza stopped. A flush of rage came over her, a glimpse of red. Her voice turned to a scratchy scream; anger filled. "And I will *never* waste another *ounce* of *my trust* on someone like *you!*"

The girl's face turned pale, and her eyes skimmed Eliza head-to-toe. Lucie's chest heaved, and she shoved her away.

"Is that right? Well, I will never waste another minute of my time with *a witch like you!*" Lucie screamed, her nose inches from Eliza's own.

"Fine!" Eliza shouted back. "*Good riddance!*".

The two girls separated, glaring at one another. Lucie's entire body was clenched, into a tight tension.

"Richard was right," Lucie yelled, pointing her finger into Eliza's chest. "You're *nothing* but a filthy *witch*,".

Eliza scoffed with a mocking-laugh. Lucie smirked at her, staring her up and down with a sick grin.

"…And I hope you get what you deserve." Lucie murmured.

That struck her, right in the heart.

Lucie pulled on her head, yanking the wig from her hair. She fixed out her blonde waves, shaking herself with a smirk.

The girl headed for the door, but Eliza got there first. She threw herself over it, her hands over the lock. Lucie shot her a glare, growling up against her face.

"Out of my *way*." Lucie snarled, hopelessly pulling at Eliza's arm. She would not budge, and her friend's light grip had nothing on her.

"Tell me, what *did* you tell Richard?" Eliza shouted, panting as she held on to the door with every strength she had. "Did you feel *any* remorse, betraying the one person who stood by you?".

"I told everything. Your spell books, your potions, your mother…" Lucie drawled on, "He made me *realise* you were trouble, a damage to my reputation and my *life*.".

"Your father could have told you *that* years ago.".

"I should have listened.".

It was clear the two would not come to an agreement, and neither of them wanted to.

Lucie pulled forcefully on Eliza's arm. It was painful, but there were still more questions she had to ask.

"Those, potions and spell books, were studies for medicine." Eliza clarified with a snarl. "I was trying to cure my father.".

"*Why*? You knew those medicines might never work; it was *useless* hope." Lucie scoffed.

"That is one thing *you'll* never understand." Eliza growled, gripping onto the girl's shirt. "When you have *nothing*, you savour every crumb of hope you have.".

Inside, Eliza knew there was still a part of her that did not want this. The part that wanted them to make it up, to have Lucie by her side again.

"Now, you have stolen a *daughter*, an *only child*, from her *father*. How does that feel?" Eliza asked, sniffing. "If I *die*, there'll be no one there to remind him to take medicine. To wake him in the mornings, only to encourage him to rest. To spend every moment of their life worrying about him, because that's what you do when you care for someone.".

237

Lucie's eyes flickered, for a split-second moment. Then, her face hardened again, like a coarse stone.

"Wouldn't any *reasonable* person have done what I did? You were suspected no matter what.".

"A reasonable person," Eliza answered. "Not a good one.".

One part of her wanted to hug the maiden tight, to give her the benefit of the doubt and reconcile as always.

Another part wanted nothing to do with the conceited, betraying, rotten maiden.

She realised Lucie had been speaking to her. Or rather, spitting at her.

"...Richard knows the potential I have. All my life, I have been underestimated, do you know how that feels?".

Eliza, in fact, was barely listening. She was too absorbed in her thoughts, looking back on many moments.

"No, *you* don't, because people overestimate you. They think you're such a threat, that you'll curse them in their sleep...".

It was not she wanted to stay with Lucie, but that she did not want to be alone again. For the most of her childhood, she was, and it was terrible. Eliza wanted someone, but not Lucie.

"...Alas, soon you will see. When you reflect on your life, and all the unfortunate events of how it's turned out...".

That was why she forgave Lucie all those years. If she were reasonable, she would have lost Lucie years ago, but that fear of being alone was what kept her there. That was what kept her by Lucie's side.

"…In the end, look at us. I am to wed a king, bring pride to my family and to be the mother to the future king…".

Eliza had been alone all her life. Lucie did not know how that felt.

"…You're on death toll, hated by everyone and whining for your *father*…".

Eliza had zoned out, in a daydream of hard slaps of truth and hopelessness. Her eyes watered, and heart felt numb.

Lucie was well-liked. If she lost Eliza, it made no difference. It became clear that she and Lucie valued one another differently. She was Lucie's main friend, but it would make slight difference if she were not.

"…And you can paint me as a villain, but this is all on you…".

Eliza snapped back to reality, half-comprehending what the girl had said. Lucie gave her a mocking glare, smirking pridefully to herself.

"…If having a grand, fulfilling, and successful life is villainy to you, then believe me, I *never* want to be your version of a hero.".

Lucie stormed up to the door, gripping onto the handle.

Eliza's posture had sunk, along with any hope she had. The numbness in her heart and soul was deafening and silent, all at once, like a sonorous ring in her mind.

Lucie froze, with her hand trembling in mid-air. In truth, Eliza had given up.

It was over, and she was no better than she was at the beginning. In fact, she was worse.

She pulled the restrictive wig from her head, wiping the smudged makeup from her face. A smear of powder marked her hand, with streaks of red tint. Lucie stood with her hand on the door, watching.

"Shut the door on your way out, Lucie." Eliza whispered, close to silence.

Lucie cautiously nodded, as genuine fear struck her face. The door creaked open, before slamming shut.

She was alone, and it made her wonder, when was she not?

Was the loneliness there all along, or a slow creep through her heart? Like a reminder of who she was, and who she would forever be. A bleak headstone on a pitch of grass, marked with her name.

Eliza felt her knees wobble, and her whole body trembled. Like a snapped piece of wood, she fell to the floor, her knees slamming against the wood.

Clutching her hands to her face, her throat croaked and burned. Tears ran from her eyes, as a scream bubbled in her throat. Yet, she made no sound.

Her face was severed red and creased streaks lined her skin. Eliza sobbed into the palms of her hands, as creaking, soft cries escaped her.

The realisation had not hit, and it was better that way. Eliza took a deep breath, her throat croaking and hitching.

She had accomplished nothing. She had gotten no further than when she first entered the tower.

It all felt surreal. Here she was, back in the tower as a prisoner. Except, it felt scarier, she felt more claustrophobic within its walls.

Elizabeth Spinner had gone right back to where she started.

The King's opponent, the village outcast, the loud-mouthed girl who never bit her tongue. She was gone.

For the first time, she could admit it.

Richard had won. He had left her with nothing to fight for, nothing to lose. The once spite-filled girl without a care in the world withered into dust.

That man stole everything, including her only friend.

And all it took was a ring, or two.

16

A Heart of Rue

She woke up in a flood of sweat, and nightmare. The lack of heat in made her freeze to death, and her fingers felt numb, purple.

It had been few days from she returned herself to the tower. Yet, it was much, much worse. She felt like screaming into oblivion, after speaking to none for days on end.

All she could do was prepare for the inevitable. She knew Lucie would not tell Richard their plan, for the fear of being arrested.

The main thought was, why would Lucie plan for them to switch, if she were working for Richard all along?

'...And I hope you get what you deserve.'.

Those words never left her. She had examined, evaluated, and began overthinking them. Eliza could not help but ponder if she meant it.

One part of her said no, that Lucie would never say that. The other said she did mean it, and that she was a fool for ever trusting her.

That 'other' side took over a lot, those past few days.

Her face was sticky and dry, in crimson spots and rash. She had rid of that dreadful wig and put on a white nightgown.

It hung loose on her and heaped in the back, when she pulled it tight to her figure.

The white sheets surrounding were crinkled and half-fallen from the bed. Her bare foot, uncovered by the mattress, was a ghostly white. Eliza groaned, lying back down.

Lucie, Richard, her faceless mother. They haunted her dreams for those past nights, and aside from the nightmares, Eliza barely got sleep at all.

Her thin, shallow face had bags drooping from the eyelids. Her arms felt weak, and she was not motivated whatsoever to leave bed.

Dawn swept overhead, adding to her dizziness by spinning in circles. The raven landed on her headboard, pecking its neck down. Its beady eyes stared into her soul, unblinking.

"Go 'way." She grumbled, stuffing a pillow over her face. The pressure felt like it would suffocate her. She could feel Dawn's bird-feet pricking at her fingers, lifting them up and down.

Frustrated with the lack of attention, Dawn squished Eliza's finger inside its beak, biting down. She screamed, rocketing, and tossing the pillow to the floor.

Dawn fluttered through the air, and Eliza clutched her bitten finger, scowling at the bird.

"*Ow!*" She squealed, flinging her finger in Dawn's face. It had two faint marks, reflecting the bird's bite.

Sighing, she flung her legs over the edge of the bed, sitting with her arms folded. It felt like each day was repeating itself.

Eliza was succumbing to nothingness. The day before, she lay on the stone floor, making shadows with her hands. Even that was no fun, and no smiles came.

She had eaten, slept, breathed, and sobbed. Gobbling down the small-portioned stale bread, which was barely enough to feed a raven, became the best part of the day.

Standing to her feet, a shiver of cold came over her. The room surrounding her was bland, dark, and ice-cold.

As she examined the tower, she wondered. This, as the maidens told her, was the tower designed for the lost princess.

She could imagine a princess, resembling Richard, having those sleepless nights that she was. The only difference was, in favour of royalty, the princess got out alive.

She took a trembling step forward, her muscles aching with every flinch. If she could urge herself to walk, to do something, she might feel a little happier.

The haunting room made her want to throw herself onto the bed and cover her head with the sheets. She had a strange, self-conscious feeling in it.

Unsure whether she was paranoid or not, Eliza swore she could hear a voice in the room. A frightened woman, screaming a name she could not interpret.

The sound came from behind, whispering into her ear. Yet, each time she turned, there was nothing.

Shaking, Eliza took another wide step across the floor. Her nightgown swished past her ankles, and Dawn circled like a wave of black smoke. The floorboards creaked beneath her weight, croaking.

A shiver went down her spine, then a weight pressed into her shoulder. Like a slight hand, clutching her collarbone, caressing her in comfort.

There was nothing.

Eliza's breaths reflected over her nose, in the frostbite cold. Her heart pounded inside her chest, as she searched for the source of the weight. It could have been air, a simple gust of wind. That was all.

The windows were not open.

That same, ear-piercing sound haunted her. A female scream, sounding from a distance. The thought left her wondering if she had heard it at all.

Pulling her foot into the air, she took another large step. Her knees cracked as her leg stretched her body following. Two steps were better than one, or not getting out of bed at all.

Reaching a stand, Eliza straightened her posture. Her eyes ran from one end of the room to the other, daring the spirit, or ghost, to touch her shoulder again.

She stood with her head high. Her shoulders arched back, and she waited. Nothing.

"Who *are* you?" Eliza murmured, eyes clenched shut. She knew she was testing something, that might not be there, but a little hope was better than none. A little hope that someone was guiding her.

There was no answer, and she did not expect one. Still, she waited for that same gentle touch. For the weight of the spirit to come again.

A bang echoed through the room. Eliza flinched, her pupils widening. Her eyes scanned the room, from the windows to the bed; until she spotted it.

Her satchel, which had hung against the mirror rim, had fallen to the floor. The bag's contents spilled out, and one object had slid across the wood. One she recognised.

"The journal," Eliza mumbled. Her eyes turned to the ceiling. "Mother…".

Her question had been answered.

Eliza stood. Her breathing was off course, and her hands shook. The journal lay feet ahead of her, but her own feet felt glued to the floor. Her eyes wandered across the room, searching for any paranormal activity.

Colours and mists floated in her vision, but she was sure they were in her head.

The true spine-chilling factor was that someone was there, that a spirit roamed the tower room.

"Mother, are you with me?" She whispered. Either that or she was seeing things, but a pinch of hope that she was protected, was comforting.

Forcing her stiff legs ahead, Eliza trembled towards the abandoned journal.

That faint, distant mumbling was still there. It sounded so high-pitched; it became inaudible.

"Is *this* what you want to show me?" Eliza asked, edging closer to the satchel. As she got closer, she noticed a white spot, from the bag.

It appeared flat on the floor, but leaning nearer on her toes, it became in view.

It was a torn, dirtied piece of parchment with scrawled writing. The piece sat slightly beyond the journal, like it had been ripped out.

Eliza, unsure what to expect, took her decisive step. She crouched with a crack of her knees, the nightgown brushing against her toes.

Her hand graced the piece of parchment. She could not lift it, and her heart stopped in that moment.

It was too strange, in coincidental timing, that specific parchment fell out. Her sceptical mind was ravaging with excuses, meanings, and possibilities; few of them making sense.

The parchment was spotted with dirt, with sentences cut short by the tearing. There was a hole, cut with a sharp edge.

There was something important; that parchment was important.

Her shallow fingers landed on the letter, and the edge of her nail traced it. She reached forward, crawling on her knees.

An iced sensation ran down her spine, and she knelt on the stone with one arm out. Her entire body pale and greyed, scarily frail.

Shutting her eyes, she swept out her hand and gripped the paper's edge, pulling it into the air. It flayed helplessly between her fingers, like a leaf in the wind.

Eliza could not understand why she shook, or why her gut felt like it was squirming inside her. She knew only that she needed to be there.

Dawn flew over, perching on her shoulder. The raven peered its neck down, scraping its beak against the paper.

"Should I?".

The raven did not reply. Her heart sunk, as if she had expected an answer from the nonverbal animal.

Then, Dawn's eyes shot to her. Its eyes were never-ending swarms of black holes. The raven gestured its beak to the paper, then to her.

Eliza's mouth fell, and she stuttered over words. Her eyes, dark but no match to Dawn's, were alarmed.

"Did you just *answer* me?".

Dawn's eyes drooped. Eliza was speechless. Never, in all the years they had been together, had the bird shown any understanding, or emotion. The raven, eyes squinted, let out a loud squawk.

Its head poked to the paper, then to her. She received the clear hint.

"Yes, I'll read it *now*..." Eliza mumbled, lifting the parchment to her chest.

Dawn, nodding its approval, flew from her shoulder and rested on the windowpane. She took one, steady breath.

After that, her chest swelled like she could not breath at all. Her eyes started on the first word, steadying the parchment.

Elizabeth, if you find this, I am so sorry. I am going to stuff this parchment in the back of the journal, and if you find it, know that this is the true story. Please, if you are able, read this and to understand. I cannot live this lie any longer, and I need to tell someone, in case my fears come to life.

That introductory paragraph had been written above a scrawled letter. Her eyes urged her to read on.

My name is not Anne Spinner.

My true name is Ruelle Raford, Princess Ruelle Raford.

I grew up royal, and I ran from my title to marry your father, to be rid of the corrupted lifestyle. Richard, my younger brother, is currently on the throne.

248

The first time I escaped, my father found me and locked me into a tower. Years later, he and my mother passed in an accident, leaving Richard and me. The control went to his head, and he became violent towards his people with his dangerous ideologies. It was unbearable, and I escaped a second time, but I was smarter then. I took on the fake name, 'Anne Spinner', and your father helped me escape.

When you were born, I wanted to move far away, but with his farming work, we couldn't risk it and end having no funds at all. After I escaped, Richard went cold-blooded, hunting me down. I was never accused of witchcraft; I was never a witch.

As for Richard, the man he has become, I do not know at all. Blood-thirsty and in undeserved power.

There have been so many lives taken, and I fear my own shall be. Richard would never have the gut to kill me. However, I feel he would have someone do it, if he wanted. He is no longer my brother. Simply a lost cause of what could have been a good king. If Richard does not bear children in future years, you are eligible to the throne. I trust you will make the right choice, if you ever find this letter.

Do with this information what you will, as I trust in my own blood. And please, don't allow Richard conquer England if you can help it, never let him get to that stage, he cannot outrun himself. I love him dearly; but I do not know him anymore. I wish I did.

The page fell from Eliza's hands, floating down to the dusted floor. It brushed against her rough knees, and her hands remained frozen, crooked in mid-air.

Her heart made a thud, for the first time in what felt like forever.

Eliza's mind was blank, blurred. Words rang in her ears, that same mumbling.

The mumbling, the high-pitched scream, the name. All those voices in her ears came to life.

A wave of memory rushed over her, and her vision began to blur. That voice in her ears rang.

Her head felt like it was floating, and her eyes shut. A wave of sleep-like hallucination brushed over her, as her head spun. A scene played in her mind, one she distantly remembered.

The world spun, slowly closing over.

Her vision faded, like a slow-burning memory.

Memory, a distant memory.

•

A woman was leaning into her face. She had mesmerising, ocean-blue eyes and fair waves brushing past her ears. The woman was speaking to her, hushing her, but no sound came out.

The woman's head shot back and forth from her to the distance. They were in a room with scratched stone walls and cross-hatched windows.

It was her father's room, the room in her cottage home.

The woman was knelt on the floor, holding her in her arms. No audible voices could be heard, but the pounding of footsteps could be sensed from far in the distance.

Every second, the woman clutched her against her chest.

Her soft scent, and tight hold on her was a familiar feeling. She was nuzzled against the woman's blouse, and all was good.

She saw herself being pushed backwards, quickly, from the woman's arms.

No longer did she see the blouse, but instead two tiny feet ahead of her, her own feet.

She wore a cheap, cotton garment and bitesize boots.

She saw the woman again, being pulled away by rough hands. She realised she had been torn from the woman's arms. No sound came, but she could feel slight tears running down her face. The woman was screaming, reaching a desperate hand out to grab her. Both the woman's arms were gripped by the stranger's hand, forced behind her back. The woman fighting for her had a scarlet, agonised face, using every breath to reach.

Two pieces of metal came into view, the body-armour of two nasty guards. That was where the stranger's hands came from. They both pulled the woman away, who was still begging.

A third person stepped into view, shoving past the guards. The woman had been tugged away, out towards the door. She could only see the torso of the third person, a crimson-gold jacket.

She felt herself being lifted into the air, up to the new person's chin. The grip on her was tight, squishing her with a harsh poke. The sweet-smelling, nurturing woman was gone, missing.

She could see the woman's mouth stretching wildly but could not hear the words being said. The woman, who was previously gentle, now had blood-thirsty eyes directed at the man.

Her own small eyes turned from the woman to the man holding her, to identify him. It started with his chin, then her tiny head lifted further.

A young man with a shining crown was holding her. His face was disgusted, scowling at her cheap cotton. He had dark eyes, and fair hair, resembling the woman. Except, as a male version of her.

251

He dropped her onto the bed, clearly irritated by her small self.
Faster than she could see, he darted out of the room, gesturing to
his guards. The woman was forced backwards by the knights. She
fought, kicking, and screaming like a wild animal.

It was too late, and the woman was pulled away. The shadows of the
corridor buried her, and all to be seen was hr hand reaching out
one last time, before her sound came back to life.

Her ears cracked, and a wave of sound intruded into her ears. The
mumbled voices of the guards were heard, and the woman's voice
overpowered it all. A scream that sounded like the scraping of a
blackboard, coarse, like her throat was breaking.

"ELIZABETH!".

•

Eliza's chest fell and rose again, as she scuttered backwards on her
heels. Her pupils had drastically widened, and hands shivered
uncontrollably.

Memory, harsh and unresistant, crashed into her like thundering
waves. Her childhood, her mother, that dreadful day. All at once.

The woman from her vision, she knew, was her mother. The faint-
brown hair, soft blue eyes, gentle scent. Everything opposite to her,
but she still felt the connection.

The third-person, crown-wearing young man. That was King, or
Prince, Richard. He looked only to be around eighteen, what he
would have looked like at his bride-to-be's age.

Eliza's mind was ravaging, only starting to comprehend all the latest
information.

She, an outcasted commoner, was the hidden daughter of Princess Ruelle. An eligible heir, if there were no sons to take the throne.

That was strange to think, after believing she was a nothing, a nobody.

Regathering herself, she ferociously rubbed at her eyes as they burned. Her ears rung like she was beneath the town belltower. Thundering and crashing waves hitting her eardrums.

The screaming was her mother's voice. It was the sound she could not hear in the memory. Her mother had been yelling and breaking her own voice, just to be near her.

Elizabeth. That was the name echoing in her ears.

Her ghostly legs ached for her to stand. She pressed her hands to the floor, lifting herself painfully to her feet.

Dawn's blackberry eyes were studying her, its beak pointed sharply in her direction. No words came from her mouth, instead remaining clogged in her throat, unable to speak.

"*I-I...*" She stuttered, trying to speak. Her entire body shivered, standing in the freezing, shadowed tower room.

Taking a recovered breath, she stood straight. She needed to stop herself shaking, from causing her muscles to go painfully tense. Eliza recuperated, staring into the distance.

The castle stood outside the tower, and she found herself walking towards it. Her feet crept across the room, and she cautiously reached the window, clutching the bars.

One of the highest windows, and the largest, was The King's. Her eyes shadowed over, turning dark.

The harshest truth of them all hit her in that second.

Richard, the so-called monarch, had arrested his own sister with his guards. Eliza remembered what her mother's letter had said. He would never have killed her himself; he would have his guards do it for him.

It became hurtfully obvious; her mother was never executed. Her own brother had her murdered in cold blood.

He killed her mother.

The King, who was trying to kill her, had killed her mother.

Ruelle claimed he would not have; Eliza begged to differ.

Then, another repulsive truth came. If he was the brother of her mother, that came with another harsh realisation, that she had not noticed. He was her uncle, and she, his niece.

They were related, and he knew that while arresting her, while planning to have her executed.

'Then, why would he want to kill me?'.

The darkness filling her eyes was replaced, but not by light. She slowly felt her blood boiling, pure anger filling her veins.

He killed her mother. He was the one responsible. He was the reason she never truly had a family.

He took that from her.

All Eliza could see was red. The castle ahead of her, the windows, the broad sky. It all turned a faint red, and rage boiled inside her, ready to burst.

There were many things she needed to mentally unpack, to comprehend and consider. Yet, she decided it could wait, it was unimportant.

Rage blinded her; shock could wait.

Slamming her fist against the glass, Eliza shot around on her heel and stormed to the mirror. Her reflection stared back at her, bloodshot eyes, and a flushed face.

When she in the mirror, she could no longer see herself. Her dark eyes, her ghostly-shallow face, her raven hair. It was not her own, yet it was.

The idea she was related to him sickened her; it brought a churning in her stomach. Staring at her own reflection, her features became more evident.

All she could see was him, his shadowed, fiery eyes identical to her own.

Fire burned in her eyes, emphasising the red. Eliza's vision was already blurred, but all she could see was the blazing redness, and a reflection that was not her own, except it was.

She could not explain, or start to know, what was happening. Subconsciously, she knew it was her reflection, that she was standing there.

The rage, the hurt, the fight in her heart. That said otherwise. Eliza was out for blood, exactly like before. Except worse, far, far worse.

Her blurred vision darted at the mirror. A figure formed behind her, a ghostlike shadow.

Richard stood over her reflection, in a shadowy mist. The shadow would not fade.

He stood there, dressed in fine robes, and a golden crown. The crown he never deserved.

'It's not real, he's not real.'.

Her breaths hitched, as she desperately tried to shake herself awake. It was a hallucination, a sick nightmare.

Staring in that mirror, it was undeniable. Their sharp smirks, blazing eyes, shadowed features. She was his blood, his relation.

"I'll never be like you!" Eliza screamed. Crying herself into a frenzy, her hand swung out before she could stop. Her fist flew, striking the smirking figure, the reflection.

Her fist smashed against the glass, and it shattered with a crash. Pieces of mirror scattered across the floor, and blood started to ooze from her knuckles.

Eliza pulled her bloody fist to her chest, clutching it in her spare hand. Only half of the mirror remained, cracked, and sprinkled with shards of glass.

She could not believe what she had done, she did not want to.

The broken part of the mirror revealed wood, that her fist had cracked against. Her reflection was now distorted, in what was left of the mirror.

Her eyes fell to the pieces of broken glass, eyes wide and aware. For that split-moment, things became brighter.

'Nothing's bright anymore, Eliza,' A voice said. *'These are the end times, for you.'*.

She could not get off-track; she knew what she was doing.

'Think, Elizabeth.' Her mind said, *'Think of what HE did, to all of us.'*.

Dawn shifted. Its beak was pecking at the window bars, eating bits of dust. Massaging her crimson-stained knuckles, she peered over.

"Dawn?".

The raven seemed unfazed by her tantrum, like it had not happened. It took her a moment to be sure it did, that she had not gone mad.

Dawn nipped at the bars. Suddenly, the window cracked.

Eliza crept over, instinctively reaching for the windowpane. The second she did, it cracked again, and flung open.

She gasped, watching the window fly wide. A gust of wind hit her, refreshing and forceful.

'It's open.' She thought, turning to Dawn. That was when she realised. *'It was always broken. Dawn broke it.'*.

She thought back on when she and Lucie stood in the tower, and Dawn came crashing through the window.

It opened then, and one of them had eventually shut it, but why did she never remember it could be opened?

Her eyes studied her bird, nodding to the window and back. Eliza understood then, and a plan came into mind. Except, this time, it was not a plan without a plan.

This was her plan, and it was one that would work.

Her eyes turned to the castle, darkening once more. Her mind decided what she would do, and there was no turning back. She stared to her feet, watching the satchel on the floor. That faint redness came back to her.

Eliza knew what she was going to do, it was set in stone.

Bending down, she gripped the satchel. Rummaging inside, her palm felt the item for which she searched.

257

Dropping the bag, she clutched the blade in her free grip. The sharp knife glimmered ahead of her, and she returned to the mirror.

Her stirred reflection stared back at her, and she gave one look from the knife to herself.

Over those days in the tower, one thing she learned was that it was better to do without thinking first.

That was something she would have frowned upon a year back, but much had changed in a year.

Eliza raised a strand of her waved, greased hair between her fingers. She stretched it out, feeling the pressure in her roots. Shutting her eyes, she steadied the blade in the air.

Snip.

A strand of hair floated to the floor, her hair. She let go of the lock, now only falling to her chin, instead of her waist.

She took no joy in cutting her hair, but it would help the anonymity. The main reason: she no longer wanted hair at all.

Nothing that resembled her to him was worth having, and her hair was one of those. Taking a larger clump of hair, she raised the blade higher.

Crunch.

Then, she could see her own ears, sitting out of her short hair. She squinted her eyes, avoiding looking at herself at all until it was done.

Snap.

Another clump of mahogany hair to the floor. Her eyes darted up to the mirror, half her hair almost cut off. Redness flowed through her, and rage boiled within her.

This was his fault, all of it.

Everything and evermore, it was all his fault. She hated him for that.

Snip.

"I *tried*, didn't I?" She whimpered, tears of frustration brimming her eyes. Strand after strand was gripped and cut, falling to the floor without a sound. "I obeyed their idealistic *rules*, didn't I?".

Her hair was uneven and messed, but that could not be helped.

"Yes, I was reckless, but wasn't *I* a good person?"

Titch.

"Did I ever deserve *this*?".

Hair, deserted and curled, circled around her bare feet. Tears of rage, hurt, and all in between ran down her face. She studied herself in the mirror; she could not recognise herself.

Crack.

Staring herself down, she knew she looked pathetic. Her throat gulped and pleaded, and her face was blistered, puffy and swollen.

Then, studying herself, the pitiful feeling started to embarrass her. Her heart ached and pounded in her chest, and she scowled at her own reflection.

"Well, *so be it*." Eliza growled, her features turning still and cold, "If they want me to be a *witch*, a curse on society, I will be. I will be their ideal tragedy, the lost cause. The only me they will ever care about is the me they *hate*. Trying to be good is useless, because it *isn't* in their agenda.".

Crunch.

That stricken realisation hit her with a thump. Those words had spilled out without her realising. Yet, every word was true.

She tore on her final strand of hair, studying it, before slicing it in half. Her blood-shot eyes flickered back to the mirror, as her hands reached for her head.

Her hair was now at her long chin, blowing in the air. It was sticking out like electricity. Shakily, Eliza nodded to her reflection.

"I'm a *paradox* to this society, someone that was born in the wrong time. Still, I know what I *will* do." She whispered to her reflection, "I have my *own* task to complete, and so help me, I'm doing it myself, *my* way.".

Eliza turned from the mirror, knowing that if she stared at what she had done for long, the tears would flood again. She dropped the blade, and it hit the ground with a clunk.

Walking over to Dawn, she nodded, brushing away the last tear she swore she would ever have. Her own clothes were in a heap on the floor, scattered amongst one another.

She grabbed hold of the tacky nightgown, pulling it over her head and tossing it to the discarded hair strands.

Eliza reached for the chestnut skirt on the floor, and stepping into it, pulled it on over her bare legs. It was easier than Lucie's clothing, as she had tailored her own garments.

Next, she reached for the white corset-blouse, lifting it to her chest and stretching her arms into the shoulder straps. Fastening it at the back, it remained suitably against her.

Dusting herself down, she reached finally for her trusted navy hood. The shimmering pendant fastened it, and she was set.

"Now, if anyone ever *cares* to know about Elizabeth Spinner, and what she ever *dared* accomplish in life," She announced, to herself.

Nodding to Dawn sadly, she lifted the satchel, stuffing the journal inside. Eliza braced her hips against the windowpane, staring at how far she had to go. It was a long distance to the ground; one she might never make.

Perching Dawn onto her shoulder, Eliza stomped one foot onto the window bar, as wind blew her loose hairs away.

"…Tell them I *tried*.".

17

A Royal Wedding

It was a long way down.

Eliza looked to the pit of the tower. Grass breezed at the bottom, and the wind crashed against her skin. Her chopped hair blowed in the gust. There was no right way down.

The ground beneath her swirled, and she felt sick to her stomach. One leg was thrown out of the tower, clinging to the windowpane. The other knelt inside, preventing her from falling out.

There was no one in sight. No guards, maidens, or people. She never thought that it was a feast day, but then again, it could have been Christmas for all she knew.

"This is *insanity*.".

If a strong breeze came, she could have been toppled from the window. An idea struck her.

"Then again, what isn't these days?".

Eliza swung her leg inside the tower. She ran to the bed and crouched down onto her knees.

One strange object sat underneath, for unbeknownst purpose.

A muscle stretched painfully in her back, as she thrust her hand underneath the bed. Feeling the bumpy, shrivelled feel of the item, she pulled it out from underneath.

A chestnut rope scattered across the hidden floor. Eliza tugged, as it came out in connected lengths.

"This'll do the trick.".

Eliza hastily pulled the rope into her bundled arms, trailing it across the floor. She and Dawn exchanged a look.

The rope barely extended from the window to the bed, too short for a who-knows-how-tall tower. Dawn made a squawking sound, fluttering away from the rope.

"*Shush,*" Eliza scolded. "I can't afford you making *noise*, not now!".

Dawn gave her a blunt look. One that judged her for scolding it, when she had been wailing her eyes out hours before.

She heaved the rope out of the window, letting it hang in the wind. Eliza pressed her waist against the windowpane, leaning out.

The rope made it halfway down, and there were only a few inches left. Carefully, she threw the last of it, gripping the end.

The weight left rotten splinters on her hands, with a burning sensation. Eliza dragged the end of the rope over her shoulder, before tying it to a hook in the window.

"Will it last? *Un-*likely." Eliza cocked a humourless grin, flaying her arms in the air. "One life, right? What have I to lose, besides the obvious?".

Gripping the rope, she swung it around the hook. It curled against the metal, leaving only a loose strand.

Dawn's eyes stared into her soul, cocking its beak away from her. Running the rope among her fingers, Eliza kicked pressed one foot into the windowpane, gripping the frame.

She pulled herself up, so that she was standing on the wooden bar. Eliza stood tall, arching her back, taking in the view of the castle.

The wind brushed her face, causing her skirt to blow above her knees. That was one of thing she had been shamed for her entire life, flaunting her ankles.

Once, she had purposely lifted her dress to her hips, dancing around just to make them scold her. That ended with her being dragged home by the ear, like most things did.

Reminiscing on childhood memories was the one thing that brought her the closest-feeling-to joy.

Shaken from her thoughts, Eliza pushed herself out as far as she could, her head dangling over the naked grass.

She was higher than ever before, closest to the sky.

"You should join me, Dawn." Eliza said. "I am never returning *here*.".

Eliza awaited the raven's flight, for when it would perch her shoulder.

"Dawn, you cannot stay there *forever*," Eliza sighed, "You'll rot, and have to eat dust-bugs."

There was no answer. Dawn soared into a loop and swept past her shoulder. The raven began flew gracefully, beating its wings against the winds. The raven flew into her chest, before swooping again into the air.

Dawn was ecstatic to be free, gliding across the horizon. Eliza watched, a weight sinking in her chest. Seeing her pet so free, happier than life, she realised how long it had been kept from the outdoors.

Due to her, it had been locked away its entire life.

Curling out her finger, Eliza gestured for Dawn to come. The raven merrily swept through the air with a squeak, landing in the palm of her hand.

Her heart ached in that moment, telling her not to do it. Yet, it was better for Dawn to have its freedom, to be happy.

"If you want to go, you can." Eliza spoke softly, letting go of the bird. "You deserve to be free.".

Dawn nuzzled into her hand. Its bristled hairs brushed against her skin, spending one, final moment.

The raven began to flutter its wings, swooping into the sky once more. She could sense it was for good.

"Stay safe in this wide world, you daft bird." Eliza whispered. *"Au revoir!"*.

In the blink of an eye, Dawn soared in the distance, headed for the sky. The bird rocketed towards the sky, doing cartwheels in the air. It turned into a black dot, then nothing more, disappearing into the world.

Despite the looming sadness in her heart, Eliza felt a motherly pride. It was not a forever goodbye, only a temporary. Her trusted pet would return to her hand someday, all she had to do was hold it out.

Eliza balanced on the windowpane, ready to start the climb. Her knees cracked as she bent, twisting her body to lay on her stomach.

Eliza's legs curled around the rope, leaving scratch-marks along her thigh. Her feet tightened around the rope.

Letting go of the windowpane, she lowered her hips off the wood. Her entire body was clinging to the rope, as she climbed herself down.

"Don't look down, *don't*—" Eliza's eyes shot to the ground, and her heart skipped a beat. A wave of nausea came over her, forcing her eyes shut.

Her thighs loosened, lowering her down. Visions intruded her mind of falling to her death or being spotted. She could not agree which one was worse.

Her body was cautiously sent down, as the satchel bounced on her lap and her hood blew in the wind.

Forcing confidence, her movements speeded up, knowing that she could be caught any moment. Slipping down the rope, her muscles ached with how tightly they clung.

Eliza felt that she was choking on her own saliva, breathing in the fresh air.

Strands of hair blew past her face, and all she could see was the brick wall of the tower.

A dream-like, strange feeling hit her, as she realised how close she was. When her thighs were being torn by the rope, and her hands ached for a break, she was there.

There was a short distance between her and the grass. The rope had a few bare inches left, not enough to hold her.

Eliza took a risky breath and let go of the rope.

A surging swoosh ran through her stomach.

She let out a scream, realising she had let go with her hands instead of her legs. Flying, her own scrawny legs stuck out over her.

In a heap, Eliza impacted the grass with a thud. A surge of pain flooded through her, landing on her backside.

Her satchel flung through the air and whacked into her stomach.

"Why does everything have to end with me *landing on my*--" Eliza stopped herself, wobbling to her feet.

'Remember what you're here for.'.

She fixed her satchel onto her hip, checking the hood still hid her face. Her mind was set, without a second to turn back.

One foot ahead, she marched across the grass. Eliza stopped at the gardens, smiling at the flowers.

Each one was a rosemary, or honey-lemon. One flower had its head chopped off and was now a helpless stem. It was amongst a bed of flaking, frail roses.

Eliza noticed a rosemary flower lying at her feet and bent to pick it up. Twirling the stem between her fingers, she opened the pocket on her blouse. Eliza plopped it delicately inside.

'Rosemary is for remembrance.' She thought, *'I read that somewhere'.*

Covering the flower, Eliza journeyed on through the gardens. Not a soul was in sight, and she started to wonder if it was all a dream.

It was more likely to be a dream, than it was to be real.

She met the brick wall and ran her hand along it. The sharpness scratched her fingers, but she had learned not to notice.

Turning the corner, she strutted down the same alley she had with the maidens, past the bristling hedges and looming trees.

The town was in sight, and she peered around the brick wall. All she could see was the cross-hatched, crooked wood houses, and no more. No people were in the village at all. It was deserted, and empty.

A sigh of relief came from her, but it did not match the feeling in her chest. Her heart became alert, suspicions arising.

Eliza pressed her foot into the stone, slowly stepping out from her hiding. She crept across the village, eyes looking left to right.

'It must be a holiday.'.

A metallic clank came from across the ground. Eliza went stone-cold, prepared to sprint. Peering to the sound, her heart relaxed with relief.

Edward stood against a castle wall, fidgeting with his armour. He cursed under his breath, guarding a large double door. With the gigantic size of the castle, she had to create a mental map to remember where he was guarding. The church.

'Why would he be guarding the church?'.

Skipping across, she carefully approached him. Her advantage was that he knew about her previous plan, and might be willing to cover for her, with a bit of convincing.

His eyes shot alert, upon hearing her footsteps. Edward's face had shadowy bags underneath the eyelids, looking sleep-deprived to the maximum.

"*Eliza?*" Edward said, as she reached his side.

Eliza faintly laughed. Edward's dark hair was curling over his shadowed face, like it had not been fixed in weeks.

"I'm not escaping, if that is what you think." Eliza murmured, a glint in her eye. "Not *yet* anyway.".

His eyes continuously glanced between the church and her, nibbling on his lower lip. Eliza peered into the blurred church window.

He stepped into her view, covering the glass.

"A *likely* story." He drawled out, with a hint of sarcasm, "Trouble follows you from sea to sky; I know from experience.".

Edward slugged out his shoulder, showing it was wrapped in a brown-stained cloth. He awkwardly shifted it into place, eyes wincing from pain.

Eliza said nothing, nodding. Her face remained void, staring to the ground. He shuffled above her, adjusting his armour over the wounded shoulder.

'If he knows what I'm here for, he'll take me back in a heartbeat.'.

"Fine, you caught me." Eliza scoffed, raising her hands above her head.

"I should hand you in, if I were *spiteful* enough," Edward warned, gripping onto his sword hold.

Eliza stood on her toes to see into the church window. The glass was coloured and blurred, showing only the heads of people.

There were crowds, standing at the walls and the doors.

All were dressed in their Sunday best, and standing stiffly in the stuffed church.

Eliza ducked down to avoid being spotted, while watching the people.

"Stop that," Edward scolded, shoving her away from the window. His fingers poked into her chest. "I told you that you cannot *be* here, you need to go back to the tower.".

Eliza's eyes turned to him, cautiously watching his moves.

"*Go back* there?" Eliza scoffed, "I'd rather *execute* myself.".

Edward's hand swiftly reached for his sword. She gave an affronted look.

"It is not *safe* here, especially for you." Edward mumbled, glancing into the church. "Trust me, I know.".

"*Why?*".

Edward gripped her shoulders and pulled her to his chest, pressing a finger over her mouth. A roar of commotion echoed from the church, the sound of cheering.

Eliza's face lent into the glass, her breath marking the colour-tinted windows. She could see the formally suited-and-booted attendees of the service, and the walls lined with blazing fires for light.

The pews were wooden and chipped, bending under the weight of the villagers. Brick walls caved the people in, and golden ornaments were placed across the crimson room.

Her eyes scanned the place, watching the scene through blurred glass. It was rare that the people crowded together for occasions, even on a feast day.

Gazing to the altar, her questions were answered.

Richard and Lucie stood there, clutching one another's hands. The King was dressed in the finest white robes, lined with sparkling gold. His hair was slicked back, and beard trimmed, while the crown shimmered on his flat head.

Lucie, undeniably beautiful, had her hair in a low bun. Her face glowed in the candlelight, and a veil ran down from her head to her toe.

Her dress was a white gown, with puffed sleeves and a low front. The maiden was not smiling, her face was firm, as she stared into her to-be-husband's face.

Eliza stepped away, her eyes falling to the floor. She saw it coming. Still, it hit her like a ton of bricks.

"They are to be married, today?" She whispered, turning to Edward.

He solemnly nodded, giving a sympathetic look. He stared into her eyes, watching her slowly lose it, slowly fall apart.

"Yes, and none of us have had any sleep, with your friend and her demands." Edward scoffed, glaring into the tinted window. "We told her it was impossible for the marriage to be arranged in a week, but she made it possible, by depriving us of sleep and social life.".

Eliza shook her head, following his gaze.

"We aren't *friends*.".

Edward nodded. Eliza stared up at him, watching as his eyes widened in alarm. Fear struck him, slowly creeping on his face.

He gripped onto her arm and swung her across the ground. Eliza stumbled with a yell, being tugged behind his back.

Her face collided with the metal of his armour sending a striking chill into her cheek.

Staring into the window, she saw all the crowds of people stood to their feet. The well-dressed villagers' dumbfounded faces stared at her, pointing fingers in alarm.

"They spotted you." Edward gasped, pushing his arm out ahead of her. She froze on the spot, gazing all around for a way out.

The commotion from the church could be heard for miles, and the creaking of the open doors echoed through the air.

"*Follow me!*" Edward yelled, tugging on her arm. He made a jumpstart onto his feet, tightly gripping her. Eliza felt her feet run faster than ever before, as they both ran from the scene.

All she could see was Edward's arm yanking her forward, his legs bolting across the stone ground.

Eliza screamed as she dodged the rows of houses surrounding them, leaning in unnatural bends.

She could hear the roars of the villagers, her feet pounding off the ground. Many times, she had to duck to avoid signs, and barrels in their way.

Her shoes scratched off the coarse brick, as she threw down her neck to avoid a dangerously placed sign. Her sight ferociously went from left to right, whipping back and forth with her hair.

The ground spun beneath her, as the scent of rough ale filled her lungs. The far-off screaming of the people and Edward's feet filled her ears, like a hammer striking a board.

Her eyes landed on the sight ahead of her, noticing that he had lead her the opposite direction of the castle.

They were headed for the far left of the city, as the cobblestone streets got shorter.

She gasped for air, sprinting as her skirt flew up and her satchel hit her hip. Eliza noticed the barrier ahead, a plank of wood fence that separated the city and the training grounds.

The separation had been created by King Rupert, who insisted on having space to train his knights and store war-equipment.

"Duck!" Edward yelled, tugging her arm to the floor. Instinctively, she half-ducked, crouching her knees. Edward did the same, running half-crouched as he forced her under the fence, the wood grazing her hair.

Eliza had no time to breathe as she was pulled on. Mud splattered from the ground to her skirt, staining her bare ankles.

Edward ignored it and continued running. The commotion of the people was no longer heard, as they ran through the outskirts of town.

She was brought to a hasty halt, as Edward let her go. He gasped for air, clutching his injured shoulder.

"T-That way." He coughed, nodding to a small hut. They were surrounded by fields and muck.

The training area had sheds, barrels full of fencing swords, stools for spectators and barns for horses.

Eliza stood on her toes, gazing over to the hut. It was tiny and confined, splattered with dried muck. Her eyes noticed crude markings made in the wood, by immature specimen.

"I cannot leave you here," Eliza replied, groaning as she did, "You'd freeze to death.".

Edward shot her an exhausted look, before mumbling below his breath. She reached her arm under his arm, heaving him to his feet.

Eliza hoisted him along, stumbling over to the hut. She was unsure why she chose to help him, but it was an act of courtesy, after he saved her from the scrawny hands of the village folk.

If she went back to the village, she would be killed, or worse.

"We can rest in the shed, for now," Edward groaned, tugging on her cloak. "'Till we work out what to do.".

Gripping onto the shed door, she pushed Edward along, who was doubled over behind her. Kicking the door open, it swung with a creak.

Edward ran into the hut, immediately shoving past her. Eliza slammed the door, leaning against it with a long breath.

From across the room, she could hear Edward grumbling, clutching a bucket.

"Captain?" She mumbled. "Are you alive over there?".

Edward threw his head into the wood-barrel bucket, spluttering on his knees. Thick, lumpy vomit spilled from his mouth, as his choking filled the room.

"*Yuck,*" Eliza cringed, earning a glare from the knight. "You shouldn't have left bed this morning, you look terrible.".

The wooden shed had makeshift red banners lining the walls, made of carpet. Barrels of ale were balanced at the back, and an unstable-looking table sat in the centre, dirtied with stain and carvings.

"I'll manage, I always do." Edward grumbled, gesturing to a dusty stool. "Sit.".

Stools without legs were slugged against the wall, and a spiteful portrait of a monarch was hanging loosely from a nail, with the quote, *'Vivat Rex'*, carved onto the frame.

Eliza sighed, arching herself from the door and to the stool. She slugged herself onto it, sighing heavily to the air.

"On a little executionary date, are we?" A voice called.

Her head shot to the shadowed corner of the room, noticing the legs of a figure relaxed onto a shelf.

Edward's face raised from the barrel, sickly-yellow vomit dripping from his chin. The corners of his face curled up in annoyance, as he marched over to the corner.

Swinging it out, his fist disappeared into the shadows. The voice let out a childish scream, their feet dangling like a ragdoll.

"You scoundrel, *why are you here?*" Edward roared, his face stretched and tight. The figure was raised into view, helplessly flaying in the air.

Thomas squirmed in Edward's grip, wincing away from the knight. His cheeks were a flushed red, coming into the light.

"I-It's my right to be here! I am as much of a knight as you are," Thomas cried. "...*Captain*.".

Edward laughed, letting go of Thomas' collar. The young knight squealed, falling onto the floor.

Eliza smirked, as Edward shoved past. The Captain plopped himself down onto a stool, resting his legs on the table.

He reached with his good arm for a goblet standing on its head, twirling it amongst his fingers.

"Since you're so adamant to live up to knightly duties, get me a drink." Edward smirked, nodding his cup toward the knight. "That's an *order* from your captain.".

"Make it *two*." Thomas grumbled, slugging across the room. His face was pale and deprived, covered with spots.

Eliza sat with her cheek against her fist, eyeing both knights with disinterest.

The stuffy shed quickly got on her nerves, its tight walls curling in around her.

Thomas filled two goblets to the brim with ale, raising them to his eyes and measuring their amounts. He slid one over to Edward and stomached his own in one gulp.

"You didn't answer my question," Edward mumbled, swirling his drink. "Why are you here? All knights are on duty.".

Thomas sunk onto a stool, spreading his legs out wide. He murmured a response, shrugging.

"You think The King would care? He's preoccupied with his *bride-to-be*." Thomas scoffed, rolling his head back against the wall.

A smirk formed on Edward's face, lightly chuckling in response. He gave Eliza an all-knowing look, narrowing his eyes towards the knight.

"Unless you are planning to run down and object the wedding, be a man and get over it." Edward said, drops of ale dripping from his cup.

For a moment, Thomas' eyes lit up. Opening his mouth to speak, his hand clutched the goblet.

"I cannot get over it, I never will." Thomas dreamily sighed, staring into the ceiling. "Being her second option is enough for me, with the chance that I could be her first.".

"Bold of you to assume you're her second option." Eliza mumbled, earning an irritated look. The talk of Lucie brought back memories she would rather forget, and she subtly averted her eyes.

Edward laughed, swinging his feet down from the table. He stood up against Thomas, reaching for his arm.

"Kid, she would have sold you for a penny and two figs," Edward reasoned, "She was not interested, in the *slightest*.".

Thomas' eyes fell, and he shrugged his arm out of Edward's grasp. Sinking back onto the stool, he downed another disheartened drink.

"You'll see, one day," Thomas mumbled to himself, "I'll prove you wrong, *all* of you.".

"I'm not one to speak, but she hates your guts." Eliza scoffed.

Edward rolled his eyes, his back turned to the sulking knight. Eliza gazed up at him, crossing her arms.

"If you agree to comply with me, I have a plan to get you out of here." Edward said. His hand reached out, open for her to take. Her hand leant out, hesitant. It was inches away from his, from sealing the deal.

"I agreed to a plan before, worst mistake I ever made.".

Edward smiled, clenching his fingers into a fist. The two met face-to-face.

"Then, you will have to trust me." Edward said, taking hold of her hand. He shook it, smirking.

"Why help me? It risks everything for you.".

"I made an oath to my father on his death bed, swearing to never harm an innocent. Yet, under influence, I stood by laws that shamed that promise." Edward whispered, staring off into the distance. "I am a hero by no means, but in all, a good man.".

An exaggerated cough came from the back of the room. Thomas, shooting the two a disgusted look, stood from his seat.

"You are a disgrace to knighthood, that's what you are." Thomas growled, shoving a pointed finger into Edward's face. "Real knights abide by law, and don't help insufferable *witches* like her.".

Edward gave a cruel laugh, turning around to the young knight. Thomas' eyes went large, glistening in the light.

"What would you know about being a real knight, kid?" Edward demanded. "Morals come before law.".

Thomas stammered over words, slowly nodding in shame. Edward dropped the knight effortlessly, turning back to her.

"I will help you flee this town, and you must run as far as your legs will carry." Edward announced, resting his hand on her shoulder. "We will deal with the rest.".

Thomas' eyes were squinted at the captain, a nasty snarl on his face.

"*We?* I am not helping her." Thomas scowled, gesturing to Eliza. His eyes stared her up and down, in utter hatred. "I say we turn her in to The King, give her what she deserves.".

Edward raised his hand to his head, cursing under his breath. He gave an irritated look to the young knight.

"It was not an offer; it was an *order*." Edward spat, "Unless, you wish for me to show The King that *darling* letter you wrote for his wife.".

Thomas' face turned a sick-white. He shook his head, backing away. Edward scoffed, gripping onto the sword on his belt. Nodding to her, he gestured to it.

"Can you fight?" Edward asked, pulling the sword out of its hold. He swung it through the air, prepping for trouble.

Eliza's brow raised, as she reached for the nearest barrel of swords, pulling one from the bucket. It was a silver, sharp fencing sword, alike to the one her father owned.

Raising it into the air, she elegantly sliced it through, twirling it effortlessly through her fingers. Thomas flinched; Edward stood amused. Bringing it to a halt, she held it in mid-air, inches away from Edward's nose.

"Impressive." He smirked, pulling his own back. Thomas rolled his eyes, pretending to fidget with his own sword.

"For a *girl*.".

Edward sighed, giving her the, he's-only-jealous-and-he-knows-it, look. His eyes peered through the peephole in the door, watching for any passers-by. Turning back, he pushed the door open with a nod.

"Here are the rules; stay behind me, and please," He stared over at Eliza, "…Stay alive.".

18

The Final Salute

The trio stepped out of the hut, with Edward on stand-by.

"This place *stinks*," Thomas groaned, kicking muck across the field. "What idiot had the *bright* idea of building a training ground *here*?".

Edward pressed his hand down on Thomas' sword, pushing it back into the hold. Eliza stood adjusting her hood with her sword-free hand, making sure it covered her face.

"It was *your* father; didn't he have some bright ideas?". Edward replied, with a hint of sarcasm. "*And foolish ones*.".

The younger knight's face flushed pink. Eliza let out a light laugh, watching the smoke blow out of his nose.

"No, he was involved, but it couldn't have been his *idea*." Thomas scowled. "My father was a *proud*, brave man.".

"*Proud*, is right." Edward said, "He never did stop talking about his mighty achievements, about thriving in *glory*, and all that.".

"He *died* in glory!" Thomas yelled, gripping Edward's bandaged shirt. "I swore to myself when he died that I would live up to his name, and I don't appreciate you portraying him as a fool, *when he was anything but!*".

Thomas took a loud gulp, sucking in his lip. He kept face, standing with his back tall, but she could see through it. Never had she seen a person filled with such whole-hearted anger, so suddenly.

Edward stood with a solemn face; his gaze fallen to his feet. He showed no reaction to the outburst, no shock.

A tension filled the space, as all three stared at one another.

"Fine," Edward whispered, "I apologise.".

Thomas took a step back. He rubbed harshly at his eyes, hitching breaths. Nodding, he pushed past Edward and Eliza, his forearm covering his eyes.

Eliza glanced behind her, watching as he slugged away. He stopped at the fence, leaning against it.

She was no expert, but Eliza could sense his hurt, without knowing what had surged his sudden rage.

"What *was* that?" Eliza murmured, "I've seen a dozen angry, but never like that.".

Edward sighed, beginning to walk over towards the fence.

"The result of something my typical remarks tend to forget," He whispered. "The kid takes a lot to heart, he's not as tough as he acts.".

Eliza gave a blank stare, watching the captain examine his own words. Fastening his belt, he gestured for her to follow.

Skipping to his side, she walked with her sword swerving through the air. The crunching of the grass beneath their feet, the echoing winds; it all gave her an uneasy, explosive feeling.

"What *now?*" She said, averting her gaze to his face. His strong chin was tilted upwards, confidence radiating in his stride.

He looked over to Thomas, and for a moment, she feared he would abandon her completely.

"I do what I pledged to," He announced, "Protect the people, from others, and themselves.".

There was no direct answer in his claim, and what little trust she had left in people shifted inside her chest. Eliza realised how both knights had their sword in a tight hold, fittingly attached to their belt.

Staring at her own clothing, she pulled her skirt out at the waist, carefully lowering the sword inside it. She tied the metal against her leg with a loose strand.

The metal pressed against her skin, but it was better to take the risk, than visibly carry a sword in her hand. They met the fence, as Edward creaked it open.

Thomas was first to march through, hurrying to get his blackmailed job over. Eliza, watching him walk off, thought of an old saying her father once said, in all his wisdom.

'When a person is hurting, the greatest lamentation one could give, is time, and the healing it may bring.' She recalled.

Trapped inside her bittersweet recollections, she had not noticed the taller knight, leaning down to her face.

"Are you alright?" Edward asked, lightly shaking her shoulder.

Her eyes widened like misty-blue stones, as she helplessly mumbled a response to the awaiting knight.

"Yes," Eliza sighed, shaking her thoughts away. "I'm fine.".

The two, and Eliza, stomped across the brick alleys. She peered over their shoulder blades, rushing to stand at Edward's side.

"We will cross the town, and guide you out to the forest," Edward began, nodding to Eliza, "Please, keep your face covered.".

Thomas smirked, poking his snarky face in hers, still scarlet from his raging outburst.

"Yes, *please* do." He scoffed, "People will know something is not right, if they see *him* with a girl.".

"I beg your pardon?".

"Don't deny it," Thomas taunted, laughing to himself. He turned to Eliza. "Witch, when have you ever seen him with a girl he's not arresting?".

Edward gave him a stern look, shoving the younger away. Eliza rolled her eyes, wondering if returning to the tower would be a better option, than spending her day with the fool.

"Don't call her that," Edward spat, "Remember, it is our duty to help the innocent.".

Thomas' grin widened. He flickered his eyes between Edward and Eliza, slugging an arm on her shoulder. Eliza tensed, shifting away.

"Oh, *I* see." Thomas laughed, "It all makes *perfect* sense now.".

"What are you *suggesting?*" Edward scowled, raising a finger to the knight. "You tread on thin ice, kid.".

A gust of wind blew past them, as creaking signs swung in the distance. The bitter scent of ale was in the air, in the most-crooked part of town.

"I see why you are helping the witch, why you are letting her escape." Thomas snickered. "You *care* for her, don't you?".

Edward turned pink, narrowing his eyes at the knight. For a split moment, his eyes caught Eliza's.

"Don't interrogate me, Thomas." Edward muttered, shutting his eyes. "Learn to stay in your place, and it'll do you good.".

Thomas snorted a reply, shifting a snobby chin to the side. Edward gripped the knight's shoulder, shoving him along. Eliza knew he tried to hide it, but she saw the flaming red in his face.

The cobbled streets echoed beneath them, as Thomas ran his hand over the sharp walls.

Wooden signs hung overhead, as the sky darkened to a grey shade. Thomas slowed his walk, humming jollily under his breath.

Eliza felt a brick hit her foot, before a spinning sick-feeling washed over her. She tipped forward, falling through the air in a swish.

The ground spun, as she did. In seconds, she fell head-first towards the ground.

Edward's arm swooped down, and seconds before she hit the stone, a strong arm gripped her. Eliza wobbled, balancing on bent knees. Her fencing sword was still in hand, and she sighed in relief, seeing it only inches from striking her chest.

"Close," Edward mumbled, glaring over at satisfied-looking Thomas. "*Too* close.".

Eliza's blood boiled, as she noticed the younger's foot inches from her. Edward's face turned grey, his eyes like snake-like splits.

"*Are you mad?*" Edward yelled, his veins bulging out of his temples. His face was a bright red, turning purple at the cheeks.

He heaved his free arm underneath her waist, tightly hoisting her to her feet. Eliza shakily stood, gripping onto his collar.

The sword inside her skirt temptingly pressed against her skin, as she strolled toward Thomas.

284

"Have you not heard the village rhyme, for messing with a witch?".

Her fist clenched, and there was a strong urge to punch his face. An idea came to mind; less gruesome, more effective.

"Here is a tale to spread far and wide of a witch, and a boy, who dared to strive.".

A smirk met her face, mumbling beneath her breath with an undeniable grin.

"If the boy shall refuse to be tame, they will hex his soul and flee his name," She whispered, seeing the fearful spark in his eyes. Eliza knew that all she did was recite a rhyme she had heard, years ago.

When King Richard began witch hunting, the children of the village made their own jolly rhyme, picking on others as usual.

"If he dares do his fellows wrong, they shall sing their wicked song.".

The village children, unaware of the extremities and risk they put themselves under, made their own song for witchcraft.

"If his sword is swung too late, they call for him to meet his fate!".

Thomas stepped away from her, pretending to laugh. His voice shook, and she could sense the uneasiness she brought.

"But who are they, might you ask? They are the curses of our town's witchcraft.".

She felt Edward grip her arm, pulling her behind him. Thomas kept his eyes on her, sharply.

"Their spells, curses and castings are grim! Witches' cauldrons are filled to the brim!" She sung, giggling humourlessly to herself.

He clutched one arm to the other, shuffling himself along. She gazed at the signs hanging above, and a determined Edward, tugging her through the city's nooks and crannies.

"Listen close, listen here, witches are the ones to fear! They'll steal you from your nesting bed or cast a spell over your very head!".

Edward pulled them to a halt, pressing her against the wall. Recognising the homes, she realised how close they were. Bristling winds blew past, as the smell of rotten apple cores entered her mouth.

"Witches in the back, witches in the front, witches we are destined to hunt! Alas, do not make the mistake we did! Witches will find you; they already did!" Eliza sung, smirking cruelly at the knight.

She felt no genuine happiness, but a slip of satisfaction from frightening him.

"That's enough," Edward scolded, shaking her. He leant in, whispering; "Don't encourage him.".

Sighing, Eliza agreed, giving one final look to Thomas. The boy's lip was trembling in a restless manner, his eyes shining in the light.

Getting closer, she could hear distant shouting, perking up her ears. Sounds of screaming and rage and stamping of feet.

Eliza threw her hand over her mouth, in a flood of surprise. Thomas' head poked over her shoulder, as she felt his jaw lower like a line missing the hook.

People were everywhere, elbowing and shoving into one another. Children clung to their parents, and two men stood closest to the wall, slamming their fists into each other's faces.

The villagers were a mob of beige and crisp white cloth, like a flock of distressed birds.

The loud voices filled the space, and it was clear something was wrong. Eliza scanned the town for the two newly-weds, but they were nowhere to be seen.

"It's a *pandemonium*." Thomas whispered; his mouth fallen to the floor. Edward nodded, turning back to them.

"Stay behind me," Edward lowly warned, motioning to Eliza. "Take hold of my arm, and I'll guide you, while you keep your head low.".

Eliza hesitated, lightly reaching out her hand. With a nod, she gripped hold of his arm and fixed her hood. Thomas clutched his sword, prepared for the worst.

The noise was unbearable, and the tension vibrated painfully in her ears, like a banging drum. Eliza could only see people nearest, from balloon-faced men to wailing children. Her sight was a flash of people's clothing, and she turned to see Thomas, who's chin sat over her shoulder.

His face was greying-white, as his cracked lips quivered in the air. He shot gleaming eyes from Edward to the crowds, like he was awaiting the punchline to a cruel, tormented joke.

Her feet followed Edward's, as he shoved past the hordes of people. A few angsty, crude words of abuse were shouted their way, as Edward effortlessly cleared their path.

"No, no we can't do *this*." Thomas trembled. Eliza froze, feeling two hands grip her arm.

The knight clung to her like a shaking leaf, his head whipping from sea to sky, in the claustrophobic crowds.

His shivering breaths brushed her own pale face, as she was thrown into the crowds, like being sucked into an ocean.

All she could see was the backs or fronts of people, from the tidiest of waistcoats to stained white linen.

Eliza felt her heart racing inside her chest, as her hands shook.

Raising her own arms from beneath her hood, she elbowed people out of the way, making their task easier. Thomas had let go of her arm, amidst the screaming, the chaotic atmosphere that would never end well.

Edward's grip sent a striking pain into her hand, and her hood faded out her vision. Eliza's head pounded like a thousand shattered glasses, and she focused directly on him.

"Where are we *going?*" She yelled over the noise, squeezing Edward's arm.

"To the *other* side of town, where we can avoid this *chaos!*" Edward shouted back, unable to look at her.

Eliza felt the rough arms of rougher people being shoved against her, as they pushed through the crowds.

Edward inaudibly yelled at the pedestrians, clearing their path like a sheepdog and its sheep.

Glancing behind her, Eliza saw nothing but beige and white. Thomas was gone, sucked into the ugly, squashed crowd.

"Where's *Thomas?*".

She could see the edge of the central town, and they were inches from freedom. A few more shoves, and she would be free. Edward's mouth was drooling wide, and his eyes sparked open. The Captain turned left to right like a crazed dog, awakened in alarm.

"*Kid!*" Edward yelled, freezing. "For goodness' sakes, he's got *stuck!*".

She stood on nerve-aching tiptoes, scanning overhead for the young knight. The dark and frizzled hairs of commoners blended in the mob, but her eyes settled on fair-haired knight.

"*There!*" Eliza shouted, pointing her finger over a scowling man's head. Dust blew into her eyes, making them sting like open cuts, but she focused on the knight. They lost him once, it would be a shame to do it twice.

Thomas' half-seen face was petrified, as he slammed his fists into the crowds in his path. The boy struggled for air, and as Eliza stared further on, she spotted his target.

King Richard towered over the crowds, roaring with scarce lungs. His face was stretched and his eyes wide in blinded hatred.

A sword sliced through the air, parting the distressed crowds like frightened bugs.

His exquisite wedding robes had been drenched in muck and a spine-chilling crimson. The King was out for blood as his sword penetrated the air, and the frightening factor, was how far he would take it.

Lucie clung to his arm, tears streaming down her cheeks. Her face was smudged and rash, as she desperately tugged on her husband's arm.

Richard, spitting at her face, swung his elbows into her chest, sending her rocketing from his path.

Thomas, not too far from them, had his arms reached out. When his eyes saw Lucie, they gleamed with fright. When he stared at Richard, his eyes turned cold, with bubbling hatred.

"He's trying to save her," Edward sighed, "He's so blinded by affection, he's going to get her hurt.".

Eliza's eyes drifted from Richard to Thomas. She realised how, if Lucie had chosen the knight, how simple life would have been.

The knight was an arrogant twit, but there was no denial, he did care immensely for Lucie, in his own strange way.

Both nodding, Eliza and Edward shoved past the people. They fought toward the knight, hoping to save him from making the wrong decision.

Turning to her side, Eliza only then noticed. She and Edward's hands were tightly intertwined, gripping one another with such intensity, the pain was comforting.

"*Thomas!*" Edward yelled, ignored by the younger knight.

Eliza watched Thomas get closer to the couple, yelling Lucie's name. People roared at him, but he had blocked it all out. His eyes were on her, but hers were on her husbands.

The villagers surrounded them, and all Eliza could do was stand and watch, hoping for the best.

Thomas swung his fist out and gripped Lucie's arm. She looked horrified, flicking him away like a pesky flea.

"*Richard, please! They are only a child!*" Lucie cried, screaming at the top of her lungs. Richard sliced his sword recklessly, coming seconds away from striking a young boy.

He turned with his sword raised, his eyes landing carefully on Lucie, then focusing on Thomas.

When he saw the knight, his eyes fired with rage. He squinted at Thomas' grip, clinging to his wife's arm.

Richard's sword was propelled high over his shoulder, and Eliza knew what would happen long before it did.

290

"*No!*" She screamed, tears welling in her eyes.

A storm was building up inside her. The uneasiness, the iced chill of winter, the frantic screaming, her pounding head.

It made her wish it were all a dream, that none of it was happening.

The harsh reality hit her like a blast of frozen wind; it was happening.

"*Lucie, move!*" Richard roared, as his sword swung down towards the floor, and he thrust it out to separate the crowds.

Life stopped in that split-second moment, and Eliza felt herself freeze.

There was no stopping it, no preventing. She was too far for that.

Edward's fingers tore into her skin like burning needles, gripping her hand tighter by the second.

Thomas dived in front of Lucie, his knees bending and launching him over her body. She let out a deafening squeal, clutching onto his shoulders.

Slicing through the air, Richard's sword aimed for the crowds.

His face fell into utter shock, as instead, the point of his sword swung towards a knight, and his wife.

Eliza's heart stopped beating, like it ever had.

The sword pierced through Thomas' knight-wear, and through him. The weapon lodged itself inside his chest, sending him rocketing backwards.

Edward let out a grave roar. His entire body curled, as his fist reached out and he screamed, a throat-ripping scream. Eliza's hand, in his, numbed. The pain was non-existent, for her.

She was yanked forward, aimlessly pulled along by Edward. She could tell he was not thinking, his only goal to reach the wounded knight.

Lucie ducked, running to Richard's side. Tears ran freely down her face, as she cuddled it into The King's chest.

Thomas' legs collapsed to the floor, his hands shaking and stained in crimson. Hopelessly, he lay flat on the ground, with Richard's bloodied sword sticking from his chest.

The noise silenced in that second. All to be heard was Edward pushing his way past, and Thomas' whimpering.

Reaching him, Edward dropped her wrist in the mid-crowd, sprinting over and kneeling at Thomas' side.

"*Kid...*" Edward whispered, his hands wavering over the sword.

Thomas lay on the stone, his skin splashed in his own blood. His shirt was stained in scarlet, his eyes had gone dull and dissociative.

"*A-Am I—*" Thomas voice broke, as his eyes clenched shut. His transparent tears blended with his splattered cheeks, turning red instantly. "A-Am I going to die, Captain?".

"No, kid." Edward comforted, tears glistening in his own eyes. "Listen, talk to me, tell me something, *anything*."

Edward ripped his bleeding bandage off his own shoulder, tearing it into pieces with his teeth. He shakily wrapped it around Thomas' wound, as the boy cried in agonising pain.

She watched Edward's face turn distraught, his face paler than before. For the first time, she saw genuine tears in his eyes.

"I-I want my mother, *please*." Thomas begged, gritting his teeth. "S-She will know, she can *h-help*.".

Thomas' hands trembled over his wound; his head tilted back. He groaned, as his shivering fingers tried to pull the handle, to no prevail.

A woman burst through the crowd. She was dressed in a ragged dress and dirtied white apron. Her face was full and red, but her eyes were a piercing blue, alike Thomas' own. Eliza's heart tore, as she recognised the woman; Margaret McGlynn, Thomas' mother.

Margaret flew onto her knees, clutching hold of her son's hand. She cried along with him, her face paled and lost for words.

"My *boy*—" She croaked, pressing her free hand against his cold face. "*Please, Captain, help him*.".

Thomas' eyes flickered, as his head began to slowly tilt to the side. His face turned a sickish grey, and his arms started to fall limp.

"*M-Mother,*" He croaked. The boy reached a trembling hand to his mother's face, stroking the tears away with his thumb. "*I-I*.".

"Shush, it's alright." Margaret whispered, her voice breaking. "L-Look at me, Thomas.".

"*Please, please,*" Thomas cried, straining his high voice. "C-Captain make it go away, *make the pain stop*.".

Eliza's eyes floated to Lucie, who stood with sticking tears on her face. Her hands clutched her mouth in shock, as she clung to Richard.

Her crystal gown was covered in muck, while her blonde hair had been loosened out of its tie, leaving only rough waves.

"*C-Clara.*" Thomas croaked; his face stretched out in pain.

The boy shook his head, like he was fighting for life. Every second, his chin sat up again, as he tried forcing himself to live. Clara, Eliza knew, was Thomas' younger sister, who followed him everywhere.

"Clara will be fine," His mother soothed, rubbing gently on his hand. "She'll be *proud* of her brother, and the *hero* he was.".

"I-I want to *stay*," Thomas cried desperately, clinging to his mother's hand. "I don't want to d-die, *please.*".

"*My boy,*" The woman wept. She placed a shaking hand to Thomas' grey cheek. "Your father, he'd be so proud, Thomas. *I promise he would.*".

Thomas' head fell to the side, his dull eyes resting at Lucie's feet. His mouth croaked open to speak.

"Lucie, I know you d-don't love me…" He whispered, his eyes slowly closing over. "But I love you, from t-this life to the next, *I w-will.*".

With a final cry, Thomas froze. His chest fell limp, and slowly, his eyes dulled. When the boy's hands fell flat, after clinging to his mother with every piece of fight he had, everyone knew he was gone.

They knew that all the fight Thomas McGlynn never showed, the courage he never unveiled, was building for that moment.

Margaret's face fell to her son's chest, as she sobbed into his lifeless body. Edward knelt with a look of disbelief, struggling for air.

Eliza's heart had its first beat, after Thomas had his last. The truth took a moment to sink in, to strike her.

Thomas McGlynn had died that day, killed by the monarchy he swore to protect.

She averted her eyes to see Richard and Lucie, to see how the self-righteous king would react, to killing a boy in cold blood.

He was not there, but Lucie was. Eliza shifted her gaze, watching for Richard, who was gone from the scene. Turning fully, she saw a sight that made her blood boil.

Richard stood on the castle steps, watching. His robes were worse than Lucie's, and the crown tilted on his head. It was obvious, the so-called brave king had run away.

In that moment, as Eliza watched him, the two locked eyes.

The King, the murderer; her uncle. He stared into her soul.

The crowd were oblivious, watching the dead boy in the centre of the town, weeping and mourning.

Yet, no one noticed the gaze shared by the two.

The gaze of the murderer, and the murderous.

19

Vivat Rex

In a short-sighted blur, King Richard ran like a coward.

The sky had a peculiar darkness, laying shadows over all the lost citizens, burying them in its shade.

Eliza's eyes flickered from the people, cowering over the corpse of the knight, and the doors that The King had escaped through.

There were two options that day, and she chose in a heartbeat.

She felt her legs start to move, as she sprinted across the ground. Her hood remained óver her hair, but the people gasped and cried, watching her run through them.

'I d-don't want to die...'.

Those words rang through her head, whilst her mind ran faster than her legs did.

She was never athletic, until a surge of blood came through her, that made her feel like she could crush the world if it were not beneath her.

"*Wait!*" Edward yelled, his voice booming from behind her. His face was cold, as he shakily stood to his feet.

Her footsteps gave a snap against the stone floor, as she reached the entrance to the castle. Edward shook his head, specks of blood spotting his face.

Her legs wobbled beneath her, and there was the urge to go back, to give up the strength she was not sure she had.

Yet, the death of the knight made her realise; she needed to do what she was there for, for what she was still alive. She understood her own father's motives then.

The best outcome would be to stop Richard, or make him realise what he had done, even if it took forceful convincing.

'You know that will never happen,' Her mind intervened, *'The good can turn bad in a second, but the bad cannot retreat.'.*

Opening her eyes, Eliza darted through the doors. She stumbled into the central hall, mesmerising her eyes.

The same nostalgic gold, glimmering lining of the palace throne ran ahead of her.

The brick walls surrounding, and a red carpet leading up to where The King would be seated.

There were doors to the left, hallways to the right, crimson banners lining the brick.

She realised, since she had always entered from behind, she was unsure where each hall lead.

She flinched as the door slammed behind her, locking her into the castle. No turning back, and no road ahead.

"Argh!" A voice boomed, and her head shot up to the right. A bang followed, like the person had fallen over their own feet. There was a stone staircase, and the sound of footsteps thundered through it.

Eliza jumped, frantically looking for a hiding place. She clutched onto the door, unable to hide anywhere.

The source of noise got louder, and a banging came from the stairs. That would be it, she would be caught the minute the person saw her. A thud came from the bottom of the staircase.

'*This is it,*' She thought, '*I'm done for before I began.*'.

Nothing happened, as she awaited what she did not know. A voice, a pain, a feeling; anything.

She turned to the stairs, only to sigh heavily in relief. The footsteps she heard was the echoing of a large barrel, tumbling down the stairs and emptying at the pit.

She stared from the barrel to the stairs, wondering. The person at the top of the stairs had tripped over the bucket, which was what the yelling was.

Then, it had fallen and tumbled down the steps. Eliza pitifully laughed at the thought.

Then, her mind sharpened. The yelling, the voice; she knew who that was. Richard had run up the staircase, and obviously fallen over an unseen barrel. That meant he was near.

Eliza ran over to the stairs, gently pushing herself up them. The stone clicked beneath her, as her feet took one step at a time. A soft firelight was her only source of lighting.

As the short stairs reached their end, there was a light at the top. Eliza's feet sped up, whisking ahead to the end.

A hallway at the top revealed the same tone, with pinpoint light. An emerald carpet lined the hall, and portraits accompanied the brick.

As she took a step out, the floors creaked beneath her. Eliza swallowed a breath, her heart racing. The icy metal of the sword hit her leg.

'The sword,' She thought, *'Use that for protection.'*.

Gently, Eliza held the waistband of her skirt out, and untied the sword from its unsecure hold. The rope-tie spun through her fingers and carefully loosened.

She gripped the hold and pulled it out, raising the sharp point to her nose. Eliza recounted all the lessons her father gave. She skilfully raised the sword in the air, both hands gripping the hold.

Eliza continued walking on, satisfied that if any dangers came, she could at least move the sword. A crack came from above. The sound of concentrated footsteps came, agonisingly slow.

Her feet moved efficiently across the hall, searching for the noise. The banging above grew louder, like a person, quickly pacing the room.

She spotted a glimpse from the dead-ended hall, another daunting staircase leading upwards. Wherever she was in the castle, Eliza could tell she was getting increasingly high up.

Up the second staircase, her steps echoed like clinking coins. The child inside her wanted to run far away, into the woods, or her father's arms.

That child inside was long gone, tickling her mind as a memory.

Crackling pieces of stone pressed underneath, as the noise from above came closer. Her heart knew before she did; this was the end, or the beginning, and there were no second options.

The staircase made a turn, and only a few steps separated her and whatever lay within that room. Tightening her grip, Eliza stared up.

The new room was lit by fires, adopting the same dark atmosphere. There were ill-decorated, rough brick walls, and a glimpse of raw light shone in.

If she were not careful, her trembling hands would easily drop the sword. The smell of coarse wood and an eerie, acidic scent came from above. Staring to her feet, she noticed the spots of crimson on the stone stairs.

'Please, not another dead body.' Eliza pleaded in her head.

Forcing herself to move, she conquered the next few steps. Wooden pillars sat against the walls, scraped with sword marks and splinters.

'What if he's dead?' Eliza thought, *'Would he kill himself?',*

Her question was soon answered, as her eyes drifted upwards, spotting the figure standing there. To her disgust, he was smiling.

"*Well, well...*" Richard grinned, with a chilling, low tone. "I figured *you* would appear, sooner or later.".

Eliza's voice stuck in her throat. In that moment, it all became a reality.

She no longer had the security of being the well-respected, darling maiden that was Lucie. No longer owning that authority, she was only Elizabeth.

That was all she could be.

Richard's white robes were drenched worse than before, splattered in crimson. Strands of hair dangled over his face, and the crown has tilted.

"You *figured*?" Eliza said, taking a step into the room. "Strange, considering I was rotting in a tower.".

"Yet, you are standing here.".

Internally, she shrunk underneath his gaze. It frightened her, but she would rather die than let him see it.

"What do you *want* from me?" Eliza whispered, shaking her head. "Are you just desperate to watch me lose it all, and still continue walking?".

Richard scoffed, turning his back to her. A force urged her to run and kill him while she had the chance, but her heart denied it. She needed answers first.

"You truly are, *clueless*." Richard murmured, skimming his hand over the walls. "It is quite apparent, where you got *that* from.".

"My mother?" She raised her voice, loud and clear, "The one you stole from her own home? Your sister?".

He froze, his eyes darting to her. His eyes went wide, but his stern chin held face.

"You do not understand.".

"I would not *wish* to.".

Richard glared across the room, plummeting his hand into the wooden barrel. He pulled out a shining, intimidating sword and aligned it at his side.

Eliza's heart skipped a beat, as he swung the sword the same way she did, through his fingers and in the air.

"My understanding is that you know, then?" Richard began, suddenly averting the topic. "The truth, all of it?".

The tense atmosphere was haunting her, as her feet ached to run away.

"I know who my mother was, and who I am." Eliza began, "Yet, you knew I was your blood; what made you *target* me?".

Richard laughed, throwing his head backwards. There was a short, unsettling silence between the two.

"Think, Spinner," Richard dragged out. "Is it not obvious, the threat you put to my bloodline, *my throne?*".

She stood, narrowing her eyes on him. He let out an exaggerated, long sigh.

"Threat? You are afraid I will cast a spell, or curse you in your sleep?" Eliza scoffed, tilting her head. "That's *quite* pathetic.".

The King gave an irritated titch, spinning the sword through his fingers. She stared, blinking quickly to clear her vision.

"*Foolish girl,*" He murmured, "You are, biologically, my niece. I have no other living relatives, and countless enemies who would take boundless joy in displaying my head on a wall. Is my dilemma not clear?"

Eliza's face furrowed, backing away from him. While the thought sunk in, she began to realise things she should have long before.

"That does not make sense," Eliza whispered, shooting her eyes to him. "Is it not a priority for a ruler to *have* an heir?".

"Not one who was born and raised by a *commoner,*" Richard sighed, "You are an insufferable, whining, loud-mouthed *girl* who brings disgrace to my bloodline, and you are *his* daughter through and through.".

Her heart sunk at the memory of her father. Even if offered, she would never want to be a ruler, not after the ones before her.

"My father is a *good* man, and he's done *no wrong* in comparison to *you.*" Eliza shouted back, clenching her free fist.

"He's a disgraced *fool,* and you are *indifferent,*" Richard yelled, "It would be a curse in my bloodline to allow any spawn of *his* to the throne, I needed to execute the possibility of it.".

She always knew that there was a mutual hatred between her father and him, but she realised; it was a family disagreement.

"Upholding a bloodline means nothing for a man who has *spilled* more blood than he is worth." Eliza declared, "It will be cursed regardless.".

Richard's head darted around, as fury came out of his nose. His fists turned a sick white, and he raised the sword up to his face.

"A piece of advice, Elizabeth," Richard announced, "As long as the blood spilled is not your own, it is irrelevant. That is the key to power.".

"You're vile.".

He shook his head, unbothered by the statement. Eyes meeting the sword ahead, his face turned dark.

"Better that, than a fool." He replied, smirking to the air. "It is one thing to know you are powerful, but entirely another for people to believe it; your *old companion* is the prime example of that.".

Eliza's heart twinged. Lucie and Richard's faces had continuously filled her nightmares. Having to face him, in that daunting tower, was her literal worst nightmare.

"I'll never know why she married you," Eliza replied, "Although, she's changed from the girl I knew.".

The metallic scent revisited her nose, and scanning The King, she realised how he smelt faintly of blood.

"Then, perhaps you never truly knew her." Richard smirked, "Her marriage to me gave her the life she dreamed, and all it took was an ounce of information."

"At the expense of ruining my life," Eliza remarked, "Not exactly a fair trade, and not one I agreed to.".

Richard raised his right hand, his silver ring glistening in the air. Grinning to himself, he held it out.

"Your life did not compare to the one she would receive," Richard continued, "She was desperate for a wealthy marriage, for something greater. I needed information, and an heir that was my own. I could achieve both, by marrying her.".

The two raised their weapons simultaneously, and she took a step forward, prepared for the unknown.

"I heard this story before," Eliza said. "What kind of information did she give you? Why?".

"I wanted to know who you were, and if you knew the truth." Richard answered. "I needed to see whom would take England's throne, if not a son of mine. When I saw your outlandish, misfitting place in society, I knew the one solution was to *execute* the chances of you succeeding me.".

"You would *kill* your own niece, just because of who she was?" Eliza winced, "Or would you?".

"*What?*".

She took a step from The King. He was slowly advancing to her, preparing his sword. Then, it all made sense.

"I never understood why you kept me alive, now I see." Eliza said, staring into his eyes. "You are a *coward*.".

Richard's face turned hard. His walks toward her stopped, as he frighteningly stared her down.

"You dare call me a coward, you *foolish* little girl.".

Eliza barely listened. She was thinking over her newfound revelation, realising the easy truth.

"There is a reason you kept me in the tower, why you refused to let me die." Eliza spoke, "I'm the only piece of Ruelle that you have left, and you can't bring yourself to kill me.".

Richard's eyes clenched shut, turning from her. Eliza could see it; he knew she was right.

"*No,*" Richard snarled, "You are a filthy *witch*, and you are *nothing* like my sister. You are *nothing* to the royal lineage.".

"Do you believe that witchcraft exists, that it is not some hoax you invented, to justify what you have done?" Eliza shot back. Richard's expression was unreadable, as he stared back.

"Yes, and no. It is not what people say, not some absurd *hocus pocus.*" He said lowly. "It exists, and cursed women like yourself are the exact image. A *witch* is one who curses society, puts a dent in perfection.".

Eliza could not believe what she was hearing, and the urge to kill him grew. For her mother, for herself, for all the innocents.

"That justifies killing innocent people?" She yelled back, gritting her teeth. "Your ideologies are absurd, sickening.".

"This comes as a surprise, Elizabeth?".

Her mother, the one this man had stolen from her. He opened his mouth to continue, as Eliza interrupted.

"You killed her, didn't you?" Eliza said. "You killed my mother.".

His eyes lowered to the floor, fidgeting with his sword. In her heart, she felt she knew the answer. Yet, she needed his truth. The truth he withheld for seventeen years.

"I didn't--" He gritted his teeth, with a gravelly tone. *"Enough.".*

"No, you will answer me." Eliza spat, eyes brimming with tears. Her voice turned to a scream; *"Did you murder your own sister and take a mother from her child!?".*

"I said *ENOUGH!"* Richard roared, raising his sword to the air. Eliza let out a shriek, as his sword swung over his shoulder, slicing through the air.

She dodged it, flinching away from his aim. Richard swung his sword a second time, prepared to cut her in half.

The third time, Eliza bent to her knees, raising her own sword in a steady position.

It clashed against his, as both dug their sword against the other. The weight he put sent shocks of pain through her arms, and it took every ounce of strength to fend him off.

She threw herself up, yelling out. Richard grunted, he swung down from his right shoulder, his fists tighter.

Eliza wasted no time defending herself, and the two swords clashed.

She got a glimpse of his face, focused on his sword, determined to kill.

He was backing her into a corner, continuing to clash his sword against hers. She squirmed from his reach, as he attacked again.

The clinking and clashing of the swords echoed in the room, along with their panting breaths.

Raising her own sword, she swung down on him, only to be blocked and thrown backwards.

His sword came inches from her face, and Eliza cried out. Richard's angry breaths brushed her face, as he leant over her, pushing her down.

All her bones ached, and a trickle of blood ran down her face, after the sword lightly sliced it when it came too close. Pain burned all over, and she could barely feel at all.

Richard's swings became heavier, angrier. His sword wavered over his shoulder before whipping down, then faster than he could master, was shakily swung to his far right and swung again.

'Block him, Eliza.' She thought, *'I can't let him win.'*.

She blocked every swing he sent, until he stopped, and swung the sword overhead. Eliza flinched, clenching her muscles tense. His sword came clashing down, and she winced as it did.

The deafening clash rang in her ears, and her fingers begged to be released, as she held onto her sword with the little strength she had.

The pressure he enabled was immense, and his sword pushed her down. As she opened her eyes, she had no time to react before screaming in pain.

Richard's foot kicked forward and slammed into her stomach, knocking her flying across the room.

Eliza's lungs created a spasmed shock-pain, as she wheezed out and cried in agony.

The impact of his foot pulsed and sent waves of pain through her, as she flew backwards and collided with the windowpane. She sunk to the floor, weak.

Her back muscles slammed against the wood, sending worse pain than she could have imagined. She could not move or think.

Her vision was clouded over by the tears in her eyes, and all she wanted was to cry out for mercy, to beg him to stop.

'That is not who you are.' A voice said, overpowering her mind, *'Get up and fight, don't give him the satisfaction.'*.

Her arm reached for the wood, where she shakily stood. It was agony and worse, as her lungs wheezed, heart pounded, and muscles cried out.

'You never came this far to give up,' The voice returned, *'You are only as strong as you let yourself believe.'*.

She raised her tear-stained eyes to Richard. His smirk slowly fell, perplexed by her moving at all. She had been booted across a room and slammed into a wall, he, and she both knew she should not have been able to move.

'Fight, Elizabeth,' The voice finished, *'Fight like it is your last day alive, because it just might be.'*.

With aching, and tired skin; Eliza stood. She clenched her sword, staring right into his eyes.

"I do not fear you, I never will," Eliza whispered, voice trembling. "And you can kill me, beat me, hurt me; but I will be unafraid to the point where, you will fear not what I can do, but who I am.".

Richard did not respond, but his eyes intently watched her. She knew then, fear was what he craved. The fear from others is what he lived on, and if she did not show it, he held no greater power.

"Very good." Richard commented, "You've inherited *that* from your Raford bloodline; a fight that never dies, even if you do.".

"You're wrong about that," Eliza whimpered, pushing her trembling legs to stand. "I'm Elizabeth Spinner, and I fight because I never had the choice.".

Richard smirked, raising his sword. He propelled it down to her. In the force, she was thrown onto the windowpane, arching her back over the wood.

Eliza's head turned sidewards, in a quick realisation. Pushing his sword into hers, he was slowly pushing her back, bending her out of the open window.

Her waist on the wood was the only support from falling out, and her heart began to race. Richard leant over her, with the wickedest, cruellest smile.

One wrong move, she would fall from the tower to her death.

She saw a change in Richard's eyes. He gazed to the stone ground beneath the tower, then back at her. The change was not a good one, it never was.

Eliza cried out, defending herself with all her might. Her hips slowly began to slide, tipping further out the window. The backs of her kneecaps held her strongly against the wood, stopping her from tumbling out.

'He's going to kill me; he's going to kill me.' Eliza thought.

Eliza's eyes reflected the fear she dared not to show. Not fear of him, but of falling, of dying a gruesome death and losing it all. She had a choice, like she did at the very beginning, life, or death.

Except, her choice was a genuine one.

Her eyes turned to see Richard's gory, blood-stained face inches from hers. If he gave one more force-filled push, he could throw her from the tower.

"Pity it all ends so soon, *Elizabeth,*" Richard grinned, the pupils of his eyes swelling. "Now, you are no more than you were at the very beginning; a girl on her course to die.".

He was right, she knew, unless she did something. If she made her move, and saved her life, she could rewrite history before it was written.

Eliza was seconds from falling, as her chopped hair blew in the forceful wind. Her neck was forced backwards, as she gritted her teeth and prepared for the worst.

With the tilt of her neck, a chilling metal struck her chest. The locket, that Richard had given her, nipped into her skin. She realised; that was it.

Richard thought he gave the locket to Lucie, in that private meeting. Yet, she wore it. The silver necklace fell out of her blouse, revealing itself on her neck.

"*Careful,* Richard." Eliza taunted. "I can't risk breaking *another* locket.".

The King's eyes furrowed in her face, before slowly drifting to the locket. She watched as his eyes went wide as saucers, in slow recognition.

"How did you... " Richard's jaw fell, as his eyes fixated on hers. "*Lucie?*".

Eliza kicked her leg upwards, swinging it into his low stomach. Using every ounce of strength, she gripped him by the collar and flipped them over.

Richard flung through the air, slamming into the windowpane. The roles had reversed, now she was leaning over him.

"*Elizabeth—*" Richard gasped, gripping hold of her forearms. Tears brimmed his eyes, and she enjoyed the fear she finally brought him.

Eliza stood up, holding him down with her foot. Slowly, stepping backwards, she pulled him from the windowpane.

She saw relief wash over his face, quickly fading upon seeing hers. Her expression was cold, unforgiving. Eyes shadowed like nightly brim; teeth gritted like a blood-hungry bear.

"You are *such* a coward, it's pathetic." Eliza taunted, a devious grin meeting her bloodied mouth. "*I told you that you would fear me.*".

Watching the horror creep onto his face, as he slobbered and stumbled, begging under his breath; Eliza smiled for the first time.

Her next move would be the release of her problems, or another one added with them.

Eliza took an overdue breath, pulling herself to her feet. Richard stumbled in her grip, nervously grinning at her.

Yet, that vexing grin, from the cruellest of men. It burned in her mind, and her heart pounded in a frenzy. In an angry yell, she shoved him away.

Without realising how hard she did it.

Richard flew backwards, stumbling over numbed feet. He collided with the windowpane. Except, his knees bent backwards. The glimmering crown came flying off his head, soaring through the air.

Eliza painfully forced out her hand, but it was too late, far too late. King Richard went flying out of the window, and in seconds his upper half was gone, leaving only the shadowy sky.

311

The soles of his boots fell last, tipping over the edge with a crack. Then, there was nothing.

A raw, gut-wrenching roar came from beyond the window. The screaming grew quieter, and quieter, until there was nothing at all.

A loud bang came from the pit of the tower, silencing the screams. Eliza's mouth was fallen, covered by her shaking hand.

All she could see, through blurred vision, was the dark sky from the outdoors. No emotion ran through her, she wondered if even her blood ran, and if it did; it was ice cold.

'This isn't real, it can't be real.'.

Her eyes fell to her feet, and her knees bent, reaching her hand out. The golden crown was beneath her, and she held it through shivering hands.

The crown of the man she killed.

The crown she owned.

20

A King With No Crown

'Is this what justice is meant to feel like?' Eliza thought, standing alone in the large room.

Her vision ran wild with spots of colour and shadows. She had flinched once or twice, upon thinking that she was seeing the ghost of the man she killed. There was nothing there, each time.

Her eyes turned to the crown, dangling in her hand. It was a strange thought to think, she owned it now. The throne, the crown, everything. Unless there was someone else.

Eliza gripped onto the crown as it tore into her fingers, before launching it across the room. It rebounded off the windowpane and shot back, landing at her feet.

'It is yours now,' A voice said, that darned voice. *'Isn't that what you wanted, Elizabeth?'.*

"*No, no—*" Eliza pressed her hands to her temples, praying that it was all a terrible dream. "I never wanted t-this, not *this…*".

Tears brimmed at her eyes, as her hands shivered. The room surrounding was deprived and lonely, and she had the feeling it was mocking her.

"Please, *please…*" Eliza whispered, "Let it be a nightmare, a bad dream. *I can't have done this.*".

As her vision blurred, she could swear the blood on her hands was there. That stains of crimson were lining her palms. It was her doing. Richard's dead body lay beyond the window, and it would only be a matter of time before it was found.

Eliza reached for the brim of her hood, pulling it over her head. Taking a sorrowful, shaky breath, she decided to do the only thing she knew how.

She had to run.

Turning on her feet, Eliza ran across the room and gripped onto the doorframe. Bloodied tears ran down her face, as she refused to turn back, hurrying down the stairs.

Skipping down the steps, she spun around and ran across the hallway. No sword for protection, her hood down, and covered in blood. If anyone saw her now, she would be killed.

'That's what you deserve,' The voice returned, *'You're just as bad as him now, you both have blood on your hands.'*.

"Stop…" Eliza whispered, clenching her eyes shut.

Shooting her head from left and right, she noticed yet another staircase ahead of her, one she had not noticed before. Eliza darted for that, wiping her painted tears away. A smudge of dried blood showed on her hand, and she quickly rubbed it off against her skirt.

Stepping out, she sprinted down the stairs through aching legs. It was a painful experience, while she had bleeding skin and sprained bones.

'It's all over now,' The voice continued, *'What good have you done, Elizabeth?'*.

"It wasn't my *f-fault*," Eliza winced, gritting her teeth. "I n-never meant to kill him, I didn't—".

'*Of course, you meant to,*' The voice never ceased, '*It was destined to happen all along.*'.

"If I could take it all back, I would," Eliza cried, "It was a *mistake*, it was.".

'*Convince yourself that, if you wish,*' The voice replied, '*You're truly a witch, after all.*'.

"*I'm NOT a WITCH!*" Eliza screamed, slamming her fists into the brick. She sobbed and held herself in her arms, wishing for her mind to ease.

Her crooked feet urged her down the staircase, as she realised how long it was. There was a faint light at the bottom, as she peered inside. The room gave her a wave of déjà vu, but not a good one.

The dungeons, grim as ever, sat ahead. The grisly chains hung down from the walls, and the cells were locked shut, but no guards in sight.

"Oi!".

Two mucky, fleshy hands gripped onto a chain and rattled it, causing the sound to echo across the hall. Eliza glanced over, stumbling out into the dungeon hall. The man gave her a toothless grin.

"Aye, I've seen you…" The man growled, one she faintly remembered.

His face could be recalled from anywhere. The King's sidekick for snooping, James Willberry.

Turning to move on, Eliza took a step away. The man's chains rattled again, as she sighed before glaring back.

"*What?*" Eliza spat, narrowing her eyes.

Willberry smirked, reaching out a hand. His cheap grin was foolish, and any reasonable person would have moved on. Reviewing all she had done, Eliza felt anything but reasonable.

"Care to keep me company, witchy-witch?" Willberry chuckled, wiggling his fingers through the air. Eliza ignored his hand, sinking against the wall. She felt defeated and had no motives to continue.

Satisfied, Willberry sat in the cell, relaxing onto his knees. The two sat in silence, avoiding one another's gaze.

"Why's you covered in the sticky stuff?" Willberry drawled.

"...Sticky stuff?".

James giggled, playing with his fingers. The chains restraining him covered half of his face.

"I won't blame you if you *did* kill somebody, it'd be a *spoof* if I said I haven't done it." He laughed, a strong accent from his voice.

"I don't deserve your pity." Eliza lamented, murmuring under her breath.

"Wasn't *offering* it, witchy." Willberry laughed again, throwing his head backwards, cruelly. She glared at the reckless man, who jokingly pouted in response.

"*Hero's guilt,* is it?" Willberry sighed, "Never does be the same, after your first kill. If you are willing to do it once, it'll never be your last.".

"It was an accident.".

Willberry's eyes squinted at her, as he let out an exhausted groan. "You don't kill by accident, that's only what you *tell* yourself.".

Eliza pressed her hand to her forehead, taking long breaths. Tears were freely running down her face, as the truth hit her in slow thoughts.

"If it were the new *royal bride*, I'd congratulate ye," Willberry joked, "Pardon my mouth, but she sounded like a whiny—".

"It was The King." Eliza whispered, barely audible.

She watched as his face turned pale, his jaw drooling against the bar. Willberry's eyes sparked, as he sat up straight.

"You—" The man lowered his voice, "You truly *killed* him? He's *dead*?".

"I didn't want to, I told you it was a *mistake*.".

Eliza sobbed into her arm, burying her face. Willberry's expression turned neutral. He held one hand up to his mouth, pretending to whisper.

"Tell you the truth, kid," Willberry shrugged, "It was bound to happen, although I never would have guessed it'd be *you* to do it.".

"Neither did I.".

Willberry grunted in response, as his eyes scanned the blood on her hands and face.

"I'd wash the sticky-stuff off if I were you, witchy," He pointed out. "Get a bucket, dunk your head in, solves everything.".

Eliza scoffed, soothing her aching hands. The clinking of the man's chains was the only sound in the hall, and the rest was abandoned.

"Why are you the only one here?" She asked, her voice quieter than a mouse. Each cell was deserted, except his. He shrugged, tilting his head to the end of the corridor.

"I'm last to go, I've been preparing myself for execution," Willberry explained. "After doing nought to deserve it, mind you.".

"I know the *feeling*.".

The man sighed, sniffling to the floor. The energy drained from his face, and his hands hung from the bars.

"By killing him, you've saved me from kicking the bucket," Willberry shrugged, "I owe you, kid.".

Eliza shrugged, taking a breath against the wall. She knew she deserved no praise, or even sympathy.

'How did I get from a lavish lifestyle to this?' She thought, *'A murderer, lying in a stinking dungeon with a toothless fool.'.*

Willberry fidgeted with the bars, barely offering her a side-glance. His eyes brightened up, as he excitedly turned back.

"Might that mean you'll let me out of here, witchy-witch?" He asked, showing her a rotten grin.

Eliza crawled up to her feet, adjusting her hood over her face. She turned to walk, unsure of where she was headed.

"I *could* do that," Eliza replied, watching the hope in his eyes. Memories flashed back of the past year, how the man had stalked her and gave all information he could find. Her face turned cold, "But I'm *not*.".

His face sunk. Eliza could not help it, after all; it was tit for tat.

"Fair, I'm only testing my luck after all," Willberry sighed, "Silly old me.".

She gave a final glance, before quickly moving on.

Even she could not say why she chose to sit with him, but it was a moment of peace among the havoc.

"'Till our paths cross again, *witchy!*" Willberry called out, waving her a solemn goodbye. "If I'm still standing to tell the tale!".

Reaching the end of the corridor, Eliza crossed the exit. It began at the bottom of another stone staircase; one she knew well.

Skipping up the steps, she took a breath. Her emotion had built up, leading to her wondering if she could feel at all.

The stairs lead to the main hall, the one she had entered at the beginning. The large doors were spread open wide, and the people still gathered around the town centre.

Eliza blankly crossed the hall, taking one glance at the throne. A vision of Richard sitting there, overruling citizens flashed before her.

Then, his ghostlike body slowly morphed into a female, wearing a royal gown and the same crown he had.

It took her a moment to realise; it was herself she was imagining, but older and fairer than she was.

Stunned, she took a step back. Her eyes turned to her hands, the hallucinations of blood, more than there already was, returning through her eyes.

'Is that what I am to become?'.

The thought frightened her more than any other, as she clenched her fists together. It all seemed too real, too terrible to be true.

'Perhaps it runs in the family, it's been in my blood all along.' Eliza thought, vigorously shaking the thought away. *'Not if I can help it; I never want to be like he was.'*.

Clearing her head, Eliza shook herself awake, quickly headed for the doors. She stared out, watching the same crowds from before.

Fear, the genuine feeling, was distant. Instead, she felt nothing at all. The people who had made her life miserable, her disloyal ex-companion, all of them. Why did they deserve her pity, and for what?

"Eliza!".

She paused, spinning her head around. Edward marched across the hall, coming from the side of the castle.

"*No,*" Eliza said, pushing her hands out. "Please, don't come near me.".

Edward did not comply, walking straight up to her. She flinched away, clutching her bloodied hands. It did not take him long to notice.

"Listen, it's me." Edward whispered, taking her hand in his. "You can talk to me.".

She stumbled over words, staring at his face. He barely noticed how tightly he held her hand, instead focused on her.

"Edward, I—" Eliza paused, "*I killed him, I'm sorry.*".

Her eyes fell, landing on his chest. She could not bear looking at him after that. Slowly, Edward knelt. His eyes looked up at her.

"I know." He said. "We heard the thud, and I tried to come find you.".

He did not look surprised, in fact, his eyes were understanding. Edward lifted her other hand, warming both inside his fists.

"Why aren't you mad?" Eliza whispered. "You shouldn't *forgive* me.".

"Did you mean to kill him?".

"*No*, he was trying to push *me* from the window, and I shoved him away. He stumbled backwards and fell, there was *nothing* I could do." Eliza cried, shaking her head.

Edward nodded, with a comforting smile. He was calm, voicing gentle reassurance, while she was on the edge of a breakdown.

"That was self-defence, Eliza." Edward murmured, "It's alright.".

She struggled to breathe, burying her tears. A flush of embarrassment came over her, for letting him see her so weak.

"That's not *all*," Eliza winced, preparing herself for what she would say. "I'm his niece, Edward.".

The captain's eyes went large. He mumbled underneath his breath, nervously laughing.

"You're *what?*".

"Princess Ruelle was my mother." Eliza said softly. "She never disappeared; she ran off to marry my father.".

Edward's eyes drifted away, as he thought. He mumbled under his breath, before turning back.

"*Yes*, that makes sense." He whispered. "That is why he put you in the tower, isn't it?".

She nodded, watching as the penny dropped. Edward's eyes gave a bright spark, as he squeezed her hands.

"That means…".

"I am next to the throne." Eliza whispered, wiping the tears away.

Immediately, he pulled her hand to his chin. Edward kissed it gently, bowing his head to the floor.

"*Your Highness.*" Edward said, in disbelief.

She softly laughed, pulling her hand away. Even if he knew her, his first instinct upon knowing she was a royal, was to greet her like one.

"Please, stand." Eliza giggled, as he stood to his feet. "Edward, I don't want the throne.".

Edward's chin fell, in worse shock than before. He looked from her to the throne, gesturing toward it.

"Eliza, the castle needs an heir." Edward said, "You would make a fine ruler, better than he was.".

"I'm sorry." She replied, "I just need time away. I need to flee this town, it's not right for me to take the throne.".

He looked disheartened, staring off into the open town. No one had spotted them yet, still stuck in their own worlds.

"I understand." He mumbled, and his eyes shone in the light. She saw his hurt, the pain in his eye. It was clear, how he suffered from the night's events; the ones he had and had not seen.

Eliza, before she could help herself, placed her hand on his cheek. She brushed his tear away with her thumb.

"I want you to take it, Edward.".

His eyes shot to her. He could never truly take the throne, but he could protect it.

"Me?" Edward whispered. "I'm not an heir, I cannot.".

"You have my consent, to maintain order in town, for now." Eliza whispered. "And I know you will make a fine ruler; I trust you to be.".

He solemnly nodded, raising a hand. Sadly smiling, he saluted her. No emotion was clear, but she could sense his pride.

"As you wish, Lady Elizabeth.".

She scoffed, rubbing at her eyes. Her heart still felt strange, like a slow-sinking ship. Yet, she clung to the comfort, that it was not her fault.

"One last thing," She smiled to herself. "Lady Cynthia shall remain here, in court. She's being forced to marry a rotten man, and I want to use my title to help others, like my mother would have wanted.".

"I will do," Edward said, "And your trust will not go to waste. I swore my oath to the monarchy, and now we finally have a ruler worthy of that promise.".

She nodded, smiling up to him. The two shared a look, living in the peace of another's company, amidst the chaos.

"Thank you for everything, Edward." Eliza whispered, "You are a king without a crown.".

Eliza stood on her tiptoes. She left a light kiss on his cheek, holding onto his shoulders. The captain flushed pink, smiling.

"Eliza, there's something I---" He was cut off by a bang from the town. The people were shouting, arguing amongst themselves.

She took that as her cue, to flee while they were distracted. They scattered with the noise, and that meant it was time, for Eliza.

"Yes?" Eliza asked, turning back to him. "What was it?".

The knight gulped, rubbing the back of his neck. With a sad laugh, he shook himself straight.

"Nothing." Edward sighed, "Be safe, wherever you go.".

Eliza smiled, walking away. It felt like there should be more said, that she should have pushed him to speak. Yet, some things were better left unsaid.

"You will return, won't you?" Edward asked, staring after her. He looked tempted to run after her, to not let her go. "I will see you again?".

"You will." Eliza smiled. "I hope that then, times will be better.".

She reached the doors, stepping into the frosted air. Her hood blew back, revealing her pale face.

The people's eyes darted to her, standing tall at the entrance to the castle. Smears of blood marked her face, crumbling specks of it on her hands, torn clothing.

The image of fear itself, but not her own, no longer her own.

She could read their faces; wide-eyed and fallen jaws. A blast of frostbitten air blew across the scene, and the sky shadowed like a thousand nights combined.

Eliza stepped down from the entrance, a sharp gleam in her eyes. Not the good kind, not one that reflected joy and satisfaction.

Rather, the opposite; one that brought fear and discomfort, one that made you rethink who you were and why.

Her loose hair blew past her face, and she scanned the faces of the distraught people. A woman stood ahead of her, but bowed her head instantly, when their gaze was shared.

As she began to walk forward, the villagers parted like a scarce ocean. People pulled their families and friends out of her path, mumbling apologies. Thomas' body was gone, and tension struck the town.

She was unsure where she was headed. That did not matter, none of it did.

Watching the expressions, the fearful glimmer in the eyes of all those who wronged her; it was thrilling.

Eliza stood in the centre, surrounded by a circle of people. Their grim, blank faces gave her an uncertain look. One individual caught her eye.

Lucie Benson, the newly wed widow, stared back at her.

Her hair was a mess, sticking out at all ends. Her makeup was smudged and dirtied, and her glamourous wedding dress had been split open at the hem. Lucie locked eyes with her, as the girl opened her mouth to speak, wordlessly.

Eliza stepped out towards her, watching the young bride's eyes fill with fear. The closer she got; the more Lucie trembled. Inches away, Eliza opened her mouth to speak.

Lucie backed away, and before she got the chance to speak, the girl darted through the crowds.

The back of Lucie's dress flew in the air behind her, while the girl ran. It did not take longer than a second, for Eliza to plan her move.

Her feet carried her off, as she sprinted after the girl. Her hand reached out, determined to grab Lucie's dress.

The night loomed over the two, and the people's gasps echoed across the town.

Lucie's head shot back, and she let out a squeal, before shooting around the near brick wall and down an alleyway.

Eliza followed, pounding her tiresome legs against the floor. The darkness of the alley cowered over them, and Eliza saw red once more, stopping at nothing to catch the girl.

The surge of need for answers, revenge, closure. It all ran through her. Three paradox needs, all confined in one strange emotion.

Running at a high-paced speed, Lucie's free hair blew through the air. They were headed for the evergreen, daunting forest.

The shadow of Lucie disappeared into the forest's abyss, and she wasted no time pursuing.

A scream came from the woods, making Eliza freeze. It was from near, not too far. Taking a gulp, she pushed past the hanging branches and entered the woods.

The whimpering grew louder, and it sounded like an estranged bird, calling out for its mother.

Then, she noticed a light parting through the overshadowing trees, landing on a small figure. Eliza sucked in a sharp breath, squinting her eyes at the sight.

Lucie lay against a tree, clutching a bleeding ankle. Her leg had a slim, open slice caused by forest nettle. The girl's dress had ripped entirely, revealing her full injured leg.

As she sat on the grassy ground, Lucie spoke up.

"Are you going to kill me, Elizabeth?".

21

Rising Dawn

The two eyes met in silence, and a crestfallen feeling crept into Eliza's She opened her mouth to speak, but what was there to say?

'How can I answer that?' Eliza thought, *'Why did I follow her, at all?'.*

A gulp formed in her throat, while she averted her eyes. Lucie shuffled awkwardly on the floor, cuddling her injured leg.

"No," Eliza whispered, turning back. "Do you genuinely believe that I would? That I would hurt you, or anyone, intentionally?".

Her voice came out as a plea, desperate for an answer. Lucie shrugged; her shimmering eyes focused on Eliza's face.

"Do *you* think you would?" Lucie murmured back, grabbing Eliza's immediate attention. "That you could?".

An uneasiness sank into the pits of her stomach, as she searched for an answer. Lucie made her consider it.

"It's my worst fear," Eliza whimpered, "It frightens me, because it is not something that I would rule out.".

She flinched for a moment, unsure of why she was oversharing to anyone like that, let alone Lucie. Yet, the reality of it soon hit her.

Lucie was the only one that ever listened, wasn't she?

"What changed?" Lucie whispered, her voice preserving the delicate space between them. "You used to be so adamant for good, now you are unsure.".

Eliza winced, her breaths hitching. She felt like glass, that she could shatter and fall apart at any moment.

If that were true, what was holding her up?

Eliza could not give an answer, it was impossible. Truthfully, there was no answer.

"I changed, along with my life.".

Lucie took a long, recollective breath. She gripped at her ankle, wiping smears of blood away with the hem of her gown, leaving crimson marks across the pure white.

"What happened to us, Elizabeth?" Lucie said. "I dreamed of my happy ending, but not one without you.".

"Then, you shouldn't have done what you did.".

Lucie shakily reached for the tree's branches, wobbling to her feet. The girl brushed down her torn gown, flicking back her wild, undone hair.

"I didn't *think* it would go this far," Lucie sobbed, "I wanted to be happy, I never realised that he would take it this far. *That's why I—* ".

Lucie's voice cut off, as she buried her head away. Her face had gone a bright red.

"Why you...*what?*" Eliza prompted.

The girl rubbed at her nose. Lucie looked distraught, as her face creased.

"Why I chose to help you, in our plan to swap places," Lucie sighed, "I was buried in sleepless nights and *guilt*. When Richard first offered the agreement, it sounded harmless. Then, I found out what it really took, and it was too late to backtrack. Richard would have killed us both, so I thought if I helped you, it would ease my suffering.".

Lucie's voice was desperate, begging in sharp whines. She started crying, wiping away her own tears. Eliza realised then; it was the first time she had cried before Lucie did.

"You still trusted him and agreed to his scheme." Eliza grumbled, shuffling away.

Lucie nodded, struggling for breaths. She clutched her arms and rubbed them for comfort.

"Yes, I did," Lucie sighed, "I was naïve. When you confronted me, I was outraged and blinded by hate. I convinced myself to forget it, to focus on the future, but still I wept, unable to look at myself in the mirror.".

Eliza understood, in a strange way. Hatred blinded both, and it rebounded in two vastly separate ways.

"I understand." Eliza mumbled, unsure of what else to say.

She found it difficult to forgive Lucie, but a part of her urged her to do so. The two stood in still tension, and Eliza turned away, whilst Lucie's eyes remained solely on her.

"I don't expect you to forgive me," Lucie whispered, "Understanding is a grace, and it is enough.".

Wind brushed past her shoulders. For once, Eliza's mind silenced, and she felt more at peace than ever before. She thought back to her talk with Richard, and one question stuck in her mind.

"Did he ever mention her?".

Lucie's eyes perked up, only to be replaced by a strange look. Her eyes averted away, appearing in thought.

"Did who mention who?".

"Richard, did he ever mention his sister?".

Lucie was clearly disturbed. She shrugged.

"Yes, I suppose he did." Lucie awkwardly answered, "Why do you ask?".

Eliza froze, staring off into the sky. She wondered how, from her previous state, she had gotten so calm. There was a change of heart in her, a part that told her, it was for the best, even if she regretted it.

"No reason," Eliza softly replied, "Simply curious.".

'That's not a lie,' She thought, *'Lucie doesn't need to know, for now.'*.

Lucie did not appear convinced, but lightly shrugged it off. The girl thought for a silent second.

"Richard never spoke to me. We met to discuss our agreement, and no more," Lucie pondered, "Once, we stood beside a portrait of his mother and father, with him and the princess. I did ask then.".

After speaking, the girl forced a laugh, before turning red. Eliza could sense Lucie had the same feeling that she did, wondering why she was oversharing information so easily.

"And what did he say?".

"That she had disappeared and was *likely* left for dead." Lucie shrugged, counting her points with her fingers. Eliza sighed, frustrated that she still found no answers.

'I suppose I will never know if he did kill her' Eliza thought, *'It might forever be a mystery.'.*

The tension looming over the two was suffocating. It was an indescribable feeling within her. In ways, she wanted to hate Lucie, but in others, she wanted to speak to her and giggle like old times.

Perhaps, reminiscing on the old days were the closest they would get, to being that close again.

"There was a thud earlier, and a scream I convinced myself I didn't recognise." Lucie shook, her voice trembling. "Tell me the truth, *did you kill Richard?*"

Eliza's stopped, staring into her lost friend's eyes. Lucie's face was long and exhausted, freckled with excess tears.

The girl stood awaiting an answer, sobbing in the shadow. Eliza's heart tore at the sight of her. The girl was hoping, praying that she was wrong.

The exact same way Eliza had, when Lucie had done her wrong.

"*I'm sorry,*" Eliza whimpered. "He tried to push me from the tower, to kill me. I shoved him off, but I never realised how close the window was.".

The girl's face creased, in a flood of tears. Lucie held out her left hand, staring at the shimmering wedding ring.

"If I could have convinced him to end our fight, I'd have done it." Eliza whispered, "But it was my life or his.".

In that moment, she had no idea what Lucie would do next. If she had tried to kill her in that moment, Eliza would not have blamed her.

"How am I supposed to feel?" Lucie sobbed. "I *wanted* to love him; I really did.".

"I'm sorry, Lucie.".

Lucie's head shot up, eyes flaring in the light.

Eliza's heart skipped, amazed at the unseen side of Lucie, one she would be insane to not fear, by the look alone.

"I'm not crying because he's *dead*, Elizabeth.".

Eliza's face fell, as she stared helplessly. A confused hope fell into place.

"…You aren't?".

Lucie shook her head, turning her glistening eyes to the stars, which reflected within them.

"I wish I was, I wish I truly loved him, that I was smitten in grief, because it would have been a love *worth* living." Lucie cried, "It wasn't love, but I wanted to pretend it was. I was willing to live like that, until recently.".

Eliza had never been in love, and clearly neither had Lucie, but she tried her best to relate. The two stood sniffling in the dark, a few feet away from one another. It was a sentiment, a practice of peace.

A crowd of voices came from behind, making both girl's heads shoot up. They stared at one another with an unsure glance, before voices overpowered the scene.

"The witch is in there!".

332

"Spinner captured the lady! She'll hurt her!".

They were getting closer, advancing towards the woods. Lucie's face turned pale, and her eyes connected with Eliza's own.

Eliza did not move, she barely flinched. Instead, she smiled to the sky, laughing while the tears streamed down her face.

"This is it, isn't it?" Eliza spoke to the sky, in a soft tone. There was no running away or fighting back.

"No," Lucie said, softly. "This is a new beginning.".

It was clear the people had found The King. A few muffled voices spoke of that, and her name was mentioned in the same sentence.

Eliza turned her head, and took a breath, taking in the night.

"Our story took a tragic turn; it was never meant to end this way.".

"No, it's nothing like we dreamed.".

"We don't have to shut our storybook; we don't have to throw away the key." Eliza said. "This is a turning page for us both, it's a new beginning.".

Lucie sighed, nodding. For once, it looked like she understood.

"I need to leave, to get far from here." Eliza whispered.

The two shared a knowing glance, while their sticky faces glimmered in the moonlight. It would be a bewitching scene, if not so tragic.

Eliza strolled across the grass, getting closer to where Lucie stood. Smiling to herself, she reached into her blouse pocket, pulling out a flower.

Curling the stem, she tied it into one of Lucie's loose hairs, the pinkish flower brightening her face. With that, Lucie looked more like a bride than before.

"It's rosemary." Eliza commented, wiping her final tear away.

"Rosemary is for remembrance." Lucie quoted back, smiling to her.

In one quick movement, Eliza felt herself being tugged into the girl's arms, pulled into a tight embrace.

She awkwardly patted Lucie on the back, as the girl held onto her without release. A louder surge of noise came from beyond the woods.

The people shouted Lucie's name, then Eliza's, then some Latin saying neither could interpret.

Lucie gripped onto Eliza's shoulders and hurried her along, urging her to run.

"Elizabeth, take this." Lucie said, clutching her hand. She tugged off her silver ring, and reluctantly pressed it into Eliza's open palm.

"I can't take this.".

"I don't want it, you can sell it to a merchant, for a reasonable fortune.".

Before she could object, Lucie folded her fingers shut, enclosing the ring in her hand.

"Where will you go?".

Eliza thought about it, before staring into the distance.

"I'll find my father on his path home," She murmured, "Then, I have the world and more ahead of me.".

Lucie smiled with a nod. She pushed Eliza along, letting go of her hand. The crowds were increasing pace, like a restless swarm of birds.

For one, final time, Eliza turned back. She leant into Lucie's ear, lowering her voice to a whisper. She whispered a few words, leaving her with simply that.

A few words that changed it all.

Yet, if a few words were enough to cast a spell, to change a nation, to turn a person's life around; It was enough.

THE END

Printed in Great Britain
by Amazon

61764536R00193